ROLLOVER AND DIE

Life's a lottery...when there are £100 million
motives for murder

MATT BENDORIS

Also by Matt Bendoris

Wicked Leaks

DM for Murder

Killing with Confidence

For more information, please visit www.mattbendoris.co.uk

To my wife, Amanda, children Andrew and Brooke
My mum Annie for never giving up the fight, and my brother Sean.

This book is in memory of my beloved aunt and uncle
Sam and Ian.

Prologue

Beware the Ides of March

March 15th

Harry Hanlon's obese body fell into the water with a splash, sending waves lapping over the sides of the giant outdoor hot tub's faux wooden frame. As blood pumped from the deep knife wound in his back, it quickly began to mix with the powerful streams of bubbles coming from the spa's water jets, turning the water bright red, like a large, boiling witch's cauldron.

Harry had been easy to kill: he had not offered up any defence after finishing off his second bottle of vodka of the evening. If he'd had his wits about him, he may have seen the warning signs that his life was in imminent danger.

Harry was not a very bright man, though even he would have been aware of the significance of the date of his death, the 15th of March – the Ides of March. But what he lacked in intelligence he more than made up for with his vast wealth. For Harry had become very rich overnight after winning £100 million in a rollover lottery jackpot. From the moment he beat the incredible odds to scoop the vast fortune, his life was in danger.

And each one of his seven children who lived with him in Ruckhouse, Scotland's most deprived and crime-ridden housing scheme, had a hundred million reasons to kill.

Ten weeks previously
JANUARY 2ND

April Lavender woke at 7 am, when her alarm would normally go off to get ready for work as a senior investigative journalist at the *Daily Chronicle*. Strange, since at weekends she would regularly sleep in until noon. Why, after a lifetime of complaining about the dreaded alarm, would she still find herself awake and alert at 7 am now she was retired? The truth was, she hadn't been ready for retirement; instead, she was forced to take it early after being made redundant the previous year.

Her cat, Cheeka, gave April a lazy look with one eye, hoping not to be forced from the comfy spot on the duvet, wedged between April's feet.

'Sorry to disappoint you, Cheeks, but time to move.'

The cat let out a disgruntled meow as April struggled to lift her feet. 'I think you've put on weight since my retirement. Come on, move,' she said, nudging the cat-shaped lump that was pinning her to the spot. She eventually freed herself and made her way to the bathroom, where she caught sight of herself in the mirror and didn't like what she saw. 'I think we've both piled on the pounds.'

April dug out the bathroom scales from under the cistern and wiped away the months of accumulated stour. They were a talking set her daughter Jayne had bought for her at Christmas, which had led to a very frosty atmosphere over the turkey.

'How do you switch this damn thing on again?' April mumbled while searching for the scales' one and only button. She finally located it and the device's electronic voice wished her 'Good morning', before promising it would only take 'a few moments' to auto-calibrate. When the device announced it was ready, April crossed her fingers and stepped onto the scales. Because of her stomach, she couldn't actually see the display, but she knew it would keep a record of her weight.

She stepped off again and was scared to look. The display seemed to be in some state of distress, flashing up various figures before it announced that April was 16 stones and 13 pounds.

She was now just one pound off the 17-stone mark.

'Oh my,' she whispered, feeling quite faint. 'I've really overdone it this Christmas.'

April put the kettle on to make a cup of tea. She began adding her usual four heaped teaspoonfuls of sugar to her mug but stopped herself after the first one and tried the brew for taste.

'Yuck.' She spat, before adding another spoonful, going through the same rigmarole, then adding another. 'Well, three spoonfuls has to be healthier than four,' she said, pleased with her final act of willpower.

She sat at the kitchen table and decided to phone her former colleague, Connor 'Elvis' Presley. They rarely met these days as he was so busy trying to run the *Daily Chronicle*'s special investigations desk single-handedly. He hardly ever went into their favourite haunt, the Peccadillo, either, claiming it was because he didn't like to eat alone, although April secretly knew it was really because he feared the waitress – his ex-lover, Martel – would spit in his food.

'Guess what my speaking scales said this morning?' she said with no preamble whatsoever when Connor answered.

'Just one at a time, please?'

'No, you cheeky wee bastard. It said I had gained 35 pounds.'

'Really? And you with the appetite of a sparrow, too.'

'I know. I'm one pound off a very embarrassing weight. I can't believe I've let myself go like this. I'm a fat pig.'

'There, there, little piggy. You just need to do something to burn off the calories and shift the timber. Have you thought of walking?'

'Can't walk. Bunions.'

'What happened to those swimming classes?'

'I was so hungry afterwards I started gaining weight.'

'Sex?'

'Too much effort.'

'Eat less?'

'Tried that, too. I just spent the whole day miserable, thinking about the food I can't have.'

'So you won't exercise and you point-blank refuse to eat less, but you don't want to reach this humiliating half metric ton mark, or whatever it is.'

'That's the long and short of it.'

'Okay. Then you need your old routine back.'

'What?'

'Well, you've always been a glutton, so it must've been work that was keeping the beef off. You need your old routine back.'

'And just how will I do that? I'm retired.'

'But not dead yet. Meet me in the Peccadillo tomorrow at 9 am.'

Connor hung up and April stared at her phone in disbelief. Was it really that simple? Did her body require the routine of working life to keep the weight off? She looked down at her stomach, which seemed to spill out in every direction from under her nightgown.

'I'm like a sack of spuds. Oh well, Cheeka, from tomorrow morning you're on your own again.'

The cat eyed her up suspiciously, its tail flicking back and forth in agitation as if ready to pounce on unsuspecting prey.

'Because if I keel over from a heart attack, you're going to eat me, aren't you?' April said, ruffling the cat's fur and provoking an annoyed swipe of a paw – confirmation, if any was needed, that April would indeed end up as a feline feast.

2

Independence
MAY 1ST

Scotland's new chief constable, Eric McNeil, arrived at the Parliament buildings at the foot of Arthur's Seat in Edinburgh. Unusually, the sun was blazing, with forecasters predicting today could be Scotland's highest recorded temperature for the month of May. McNeil was feeling the heat, especially in his ceremonial police uniform, but it wasn't just the weather making him uncomfortable: he was on his way to meet Scotland's First Minister, a woman with a fearsome reputation.

McNeil wasn't normally the anxious type, but today he felt strangely nervous. He tried to take his mind off things by pausing for a moment to study the Parliament building. He had been used to assessing crime scenes during his years as a homicide detective, but he couldn't make head nor tail of what the architect had in mind with this place, from the crazy angles and sloping roofs to what looked like bamboo cladding. What that had to do with Scotland was anyone's guess.

He turned and faced in the opposite direction to study the old-fashioned splendour of Holyrood Palace and wondered what Her Majesty the Queen must make of this modern monstrosity as she gazed from the windows of her official Scottish residence.

McNeil dispensed with the sightseeing and got his game-face on as he marched briskly to the entrance. He had little patience for politicians at the best of times, but he would certainly make sure his personal feelings were well hidden – he'd heard that First Minister Angela Stewart was a real ball-buster.

She was waiting for McNeil in her office. Plump, with that cast-iron hairdo almost completely unique to female politicians, and the flushed complexion of someone who liked a drink, Stewart also had a vice-like handshake.

'What height are you?' she said, looking up at McNeil.

'Six foot six inches, ma'am,' he replied.

'The taller they are…' she muttered ominously. 'And don't call me "ma'am", I'm not the Queen, God bless her cotton socks.' She opened the drinks cabinet in the corner of her office and poured the new chief constable a single malt whisky. 'Water?'

'Neat, please,' McNeil replied. He wasn't a whisky drinker, but had once heard that true connoisseurs of the grain took theirs unpolluted.

'Have some water. Just a dash to release the flavour,' she urged, pouring them both generous measures – although her own was slightly more generous than her visitor's – before placing the bottle on the table between them. The politician took a sip that seemed to satisfy: 'Now that's what I call a whisky. Prometheus. Twenty-seven-year-old from the Glasgow Distillery. I know the owners well.' She took another sip. 'I do what I can to promote Scottish produce. Of course, it helps when the produce is so damn good.'

'Indeed, First Minister,' McNeil said, nodding dutifully.

'And don't call me First Minister, either. On official duty, I'm First Minister. Over Prometheus, I'm Angie.'

'Yes, Fir … Angie.'

'It was no surprise to anyone when your predecessor died, you know. Cruickshank liked his whisky even more than I do. Not fine drams like this, mind you,' the First Minister said, holding her glass up to the light to inspect the contents, 'but cheap shite. The real gut-rot crap.'

McNeil had been warned the First Minister had a foul mouth. He had also heard the rumours of how the late chief constable was often to be found comatose in his office. He died from a massive cardiac arrest that everyone had seen coming. Many blamed the added pressure heaped upon Cruickshank's shoulders by the person sitting directly opposite him now.

'His death was a blessing in disguise. Sorry if that sounds disrespectful, but I tend to see every negative situation as an opportunity. It's in my nature. The glass half-full type, so to speak.' She raised her whisky to demonstrate the point.

McNeil gave a cursory nod. He had always been taught never to speak ill of the dead, but it was clear the First Minister didn't abide by the same rules of decency.

'He got nowhere with that lottery murder from the very start. He should have thrown everything he had at it. Everything.' The First Minister snarled, sending a spray of saliva over her trouser suit. She wiped herself uncouthly with the back of her hand, before undoing the button at her waistband as she poured herself another large measure. McNeil had barely touched his.

'This murder has been used to sum up the entire state of our country. Have you heard what those Sassenach bastards have been saying down south?' Stewart asked rhetorically. 'How can we be a fucking independent country when we can't even solve the murder of one of the country's richest men?'

McNeil noticed a clear correlation between how much the politician drank and the increase in her profanities. She was the type McNeil would end up slamming in the cells for the night when he was a beat cop. He thought of all those young staff members of the First Minister's 'communication team' he had passed on the way into the office and imagined working for her would be a nightmare.

'The thing is, Eric,' Stewart said, leaning forward as she spoke in a conspiratorial tone, 'I hope you won't have the same … misgivings. You may find that being chief constable without the full support of myself and my cabinet can make life very difficult indeed.' She eyeballed Scotland's top policeman. 'This case is to be your number one priority. Absolutely top of your pile. It's not just your future that's at stake, but the entire country's.'

No pressure then, McNeil thought to himself.

'If we can show them we can solve this damn murder, our citizens will start to have faith in our ability to govern ourselves once more,' Stewart droned on. 'It is absolutely imperative you crack this. Think outside of the box. Take extreme action. Just do whatever you have to. And I mean WHATEVER you have to. But get it done.' She took another glug of whisky. 'Catch Harry Hanlon's killer and the country will rediscover its independent spirit once again.'

The First Minister finished her monologue and sat staring into space. Eric McNeil thought this would be as good a time as any to leave. He got up slowly and bade farewell to Scotland's premier politician, who failed to acknowledge his departure, as she sat in her trance-like state, lost in another world. A world that featured an independent country, McNeil hazarded a guess.

Several moments later Angela Stewart realised she was all alone. She glanced over at her visitor's whisky glass, which was still nearly full, before emptying its contents into her own.

'It's lonely at the top, McNeil,' Stewart said to the empty room. 'I just hope you've got the balls for this job, for both our sakes.'

3

The biography
JANUARY 3RD

April could not have been happier as she tucked into her full fry-up in her usual seat in her usual café. It was their first day of opening since the festive break and the waitress Martel seemed genuinely pleased to see April, giving her a peck on each cheek before placing the *Daily Chronicle* next to her cutlery.

'Oh my, I feel like royalty this morning.' April beamed, flashing her gold incisor.

'I hope you haven't been snubbing us for some other inferior café?' Martel asked, sizing up April's increased girth.

'No, no, dear, this is all my own work,' she said, playfully patting her wide hips. 'I've been bulking up because I hear the snow's on the way. They reckon it could be as bad as the winter of '78.'

Martel stared blankly.

'Of course, you weren't even born then, but they had to dig the sheep out of the fields. It was a winter that just never seemed to end,' April explained.

Their conversation was broken up by Connor's arrival. Martel shot him a dirty look then disappeared into the back kitchen. He frowned at her hasty departure then hugged his former colleague.

'My, how you've grown,' he said, struggling to contain his laughter.

'Shut up,' April said. She slapped his shoulder but was secretly delighted to see him again, even though he was being as insulting as ever. 'But you're right. I'm a right little butterball, aren't I?'

'So what have you been up to? Apart from the obvious.'

'Nothing, really. I got the garden sorted out and the fountain installed as I'd always wanted.'

'Doesn't the sound of running water make you want to pee all the time?'

'How did you know? I can't sit in my chair beside it without constantly needing the loo.'

'And sometimes you don't make it that far?' Connor smiled knowingly.

April blushed ever so slightly. 'You can read me like a book.'

'Talking of which, did you ever start writing "the book"?' As long as Connor had known April, she had always threatened to make an impact on the publishing world, but somehow never got round to committing a single word to paper.

'I haven't found the time,' April mumbled, refusing to make eye contact.

'Been too busy eating and pishing yourself?'

'I've been looking for inspiration.'

'But haven't found it?'

'Exactly.'

Connor had embarked on a joint book project with April two years previously, detailing the inside story of the Scottish-born television host Bryce Horrigan, who was brutally murdered in the US, but April had quickly pulled out of the joint venture, once again claiming she didn't have the time.

'Your writer's block is all in the mind, you know. You never had this problem at work. You could batter out copy quicker than any journalist I've ever known. You almost typed in real-time. It's because you keep telling yourself it's a book that the shutters come down. You need to relax. It's just like writing a feature. A really, really long feature.'

'I think you're right. I've just been approaching it all wrong. Like I've got to write some literary masterpiece.'

'Very few accomplish that. You should just do what you're good at and write stories about people you've met and interviewed. No one got real-life stories out of folk better than you. Go back through your archives. There must be someone with a book in them. What about that lotto winner?'

'Harry Hanlon? That man can hardly string two words together. He also has wandering hands.'

'Ha, what did he call you again?'

'Can't remember.'

'Yes, you can. What was it?'

'A "cracking big bit of stuff",' April replied, her face reddening again.

'That was it. So you've got an in there.'

'Who wants to read a book about a thick millionaire?'

'Everybody – it was one of the biggest UK lottery wins of all time. How has it changed him? Changed his family? Didn't his wife divorce him just before he won? You could speak to her, too.'

'I could,' April said, her eyes lighting up.

'They've no doubt spent money on a load of tat. Interview them all. Find out if their lives are better, or worse. Call it *Diary Of Scotland's Biggest Lottery Winners*. Spend half a year interviewing them, detailing their lives. Charting what they do,' Connor said.

'You think I could do it?' April asked hopefully.

'Of course you could. Just treat it like a job. Meet here for breakfast every morning then head up to interview the Hanlons at home. You'll enjoy that as you're a nosy cow. No one else has the time to do it, but you do. I can put you in touch with some publishing contacts.'

April beamed from ear to ear. She hadn't missed her colleague's constant barbs, but she had missed his endless enthusiasm: Connor was a great motivator. And he had just given April's stale life a new purpose.

4

Three wise monkeys
MAY 2ND

'Explain it to me again,' Chief Constable McNeil said while drumming his fingers angrily on his desk.

'Three wise monkeys. See no evil, hear...' But McNeil's deputy, Mike Bruce, was cut off mid-flow.

'Yes, I am aware of the Chinese proverb.'

'The residents of the Ruckhouse live by it.'

'And they pride themselves on this, do they?' McNeil spat.

'They do, especially where the police are involved.'

McNeil sat reading over a background report on the area, annually listed as Scotland's most deprived community for a record-breaking thirteen years in a row. Various governments and council leaders had launched countless initiatives to improve the prospects of the residents of the sprawling housing estate on the outskirts of Glasgow, which had some of the highest illiteracy, teenage pregnancy, crime and drug abuse statistics to be found anywhere in the UK. But no matter what they tried, it did little to improve the lot of the people from Ruckhouse, where the average life expectancy was appallingly low – just half of the people on the estate lived to see their sixty-second birthday. Several developing world countries had better survival rates.

Ruckhouse had also been a dumping ground for 'anti-social families' for generations. It was only the worst of the worst that were transferred into 'the Ruck', as it was known by almost everyone – The Hanlons had been one such family.

McNeil scanned the lengthy background report compiled on the Hanlons themselves. He had read it several times already.

Harry Hanlon had been a homicide victim waiting to happen long before his lottery win. His previous offences included regular bar bust-ups and convictions for assault, domestic abuse and breach of the peace stretching back to his teens – so it was no real surprise that his wife, Kristine, divorced him after years of what must have been misery. After scooping his fortune, Harry vowed to buy a place in Spain. He never did. Instead, he chose to spend considerable sums converting his ex-council house into a Spanish-style villa.

Robert 'Shifty' Hanlon had taken his father's place as the head of the family. He had been a low-level street thug that matched his low-level IQ. He was the drug supplier to the many junkies of Ruckhouse. At forty-one, he now had designs on bigger things.

Kendal was the glamorous member of the Hanlon family. She was thirty-nine, still single, but had no shortage of suitors. She had worked at the local chemist, until her father's windfall. The report's author had noted she was 'physically attractive', but with the caveat not to let her looks fool you, as she had two convictions for serious assaults. One was an attempted murder charge, reduced to reckless endangerment of life, when she stabbed a man in the neck with her stiletto heel. Her defence was that he had sexually assaulted her. The truth was, he had only accidentally spilled her drink on the dance floor.

There wasn't much to write about the triplets Mo, Jo and Flo – Maureen, Joanne and Florence Hanlon – except to say that, at twenty-five years old, they appeared to do most things together. They were all in relationships, but never stayed at their boyfriends', choosing always to spend the night together in their family home.

Billy Hanlon had been named after Harry's favourite singer, Billy Joel. He was a nineteen-year-old, wheelchair-bound, learning-disabled adult. His main carer appeared to be his brother Michael, who was named after Harry's second favourite singer, Michael Bublé. Just seventeen, Michael was the brains of the family and had recently been accepted to study medicine at the University of Glasgow.

The family was represented by Paul McFadden, one of Scotland's most high-profile barristers, and all had been interviewed as 'witnesses' to the murder of their father. On the instruction of McFadden, they had given 'no comment' answers to every police question. Investigating officers concluded they were protecting each other and that one of the 'witnesses' was undoubtedly the murderer.

'If we really want to solve this case, there is always the nuclear option,' Bruce said.

'After reading this report I think a bomb going off would actually improve the Ruck,' McNeil said.

'We need to bring in someone with local knowledge,' Bruce replied. 'Someone who knows these people, who knows the Hanlons.'

'And you're going to tell me Police Scotland has a detective that ticks all these boxes, who is currently on the force and just raring to go?' McNeil replied sarcastically. 'If that was the case, why weren't they assigned sooner?'

'There are certain "issues".'

'Issues?'

'He's currently suspended on full pay. In fact, he is in the final phase of disciplinary, before dismissal.'

'And should he be dismissed?' McNeil asked.

'Most definitely.'

'But you believe we should now bring him back into the fold?'

'I believe if we're to get anywhere with this investigation, he will be our only option.'

McNeil sat in total silence, thinking for what seemed an eternity. His instincts told him to stay clear of a troubled detective. But then the First Minister's warnings about the consequences of failing to bring the case to a conclusion began to swirl around his head.

'Okay, let me meet this man with "issues". See if he still

has the fight for the job,' McNeil said, bringing their meeting to a close.

As Bruce left, he wondered if it would have been more humane to the people of Ruckhouse to hit the actual nuclear button than drop the ticking time bomb on them that was Detective Chief Inspector David 'Bing' Crosbie.

5

When Harry met April
JANUARY 5TH

April pulled up outside Harry Hanlon's home in Ruckhouse and took a moment to marvel at its utter vulgarity. All the other mid-terrace houses looked drab and grey compared to the bright Mediterranean colours of the lottery winner's house. Replicas of Ancient Greek sandstone columns had been added to an elaborate porch entrance. Red terracotta roof tiles sat atop the white-washed walls, which were stained by the near-constant rain, while all the rectangular window frames had been replaced with sandstone-coloured arches to match the columns. The small front garden space was landscaped with stepping stones, which forked through the white chippings to the entrance and veered off to the elaborate water fountain feature, with a naked statue of Venus.

Above the entrance was a marble mosaic that spelled out the word *Macarena*, in a variety of colours. The name had April humming a tune and tapping her foot in her car. She couldn't remember any of the words to the song, mumbling the first verse before she suddenly let out a hearty 'Hey Macarena!'

'Who sang that?' she said to herself as she asked Google the same question, only to be told it was sung by the Andalusian duo Los del Rio, whose flamenco pop song became a surprise worldwide hit in 1993. It had obviously been a favourite track of Harry Hanlon, whose whole house now looked as if it had been transferred brick by brick from sunnier climes into the middle of Ruckhouse.

'Oh Harry, why didn't you move out?' April said aloud. She had been desperate to leave her own family council home from the moment she realised there was more to life than six cramped apartments living on top of each other. She began clawing her way out with any work she could get, from serving behind bars to cleaning toilets – anything to build a better life for herself and her young daughter. But it was so hard. Thank the Lord her parents had still been fit and able to help out with childcare when she needed it the most. Then came the lucky break, a job at her local newspaper as a secretary to the editor.

She had always wanted to be a writer, but at that time the unions had the monopoly on who could and couldn't do what in the print industry. Fortunately, her editor was stronger willed than the paper's father of the chapel and April got a foot in the door writing human interest stories, at which she excelled. Five years later she became the editor herself before being poached for the *Daily Chronicle*. Her love life may have been a disaster zone, but by sheer chance her finances blossomed. By the time she was forcibly retired last year, she had a healthy property portfolio and pension.

Her home was now a large Victorian house in Glasgow's Southside. But she knew someone like Harry could never leave the Ruck, despite his immense wealth: money had not given him the self-confidence to mix with anybody other than his 'own folk'. He would have been out of place in the leafy suburbs with professionals for neighbours, who would look down their noses at him regardless of his millions. Instead, he chose to stay put where he felt like a king, lording it over his own community.

April got out of her car and shivered; it was getting cold enough to snow. Perhaps the forecasters would be right about a long winter. She began to make her way to the Hanlon house when someone shouted out from across the street: 'You won't get Harry at this time, hen.'

April looked across the road and saw a bald man leaning

out of a window on the first floor of a derelict-looking block of flats opposite the Hanlons'.

'He gets a taxi every morning at five to eleven, for opening time.'

'Opening time?' April asked.

'At the Woodchopper, up the road.'

'Thank you,' April replied, genuinely grateful.

'Best to catch him early. He's always shit-faced by mid-afternoon,' another woman added, returning from the local shop with a blue carrier bag and dressed in her nightwear. April had heard there were whole schemes where people thought nothing of walking their children to school in their slippers and fleecy pyjamas. But as a teacher had once told her, at least these kids were still being taken to school. It's the ones who weren't you really had to worry about.

April thanked the nightwear woman for her sage advice and drove in the direction of the pub. She knew what the Woodchopper would be like before she even saw it – she had once worked in places just like it, with their deadbeat regulars and their war stories that always grew arms and legs with every retelling. April liked her drink, but in private, sitting in her comfy chair with the cat on her lap while browsing on her iPad. She didn't do pubs, except on the odd occasion Connor had dragged her into one after work, but even then they had been nice bars and she only ever stayed for one or two.

April parked her new Peugeot convertible in the large and empty car park, under a sign proclaiming, *Woodchopper patrons only*. She looked around to see only a couple of works vans. She didn't imagine this was the type of establishment many 'patrons' would drive to.

The building itself was a low-level affair, with slim rectangle slits for windows, designed to keep the daylight out, and covered in a rusty web of metal mesh. The main entrance had a lighted sign above it but most of the bulbs had blown, so it read *THE _OOD_HOP___*, instead of *THE WOOD-CHOPPER*, which made April chuckle.

She locked up her car and headed for the heavy black wooden doors. Metal ashtrays, bolted to the walls either side of the doors, were overflowing with cigarette butts, which had scattered on the ground beneath them. It did not make a great first impression, but April felt that first impressions were not high on the owner's priority list. She took a deep breath and was about to enter when the unmistakably rotund figure of Harry Hanlon came barging out, a cigarette pack and lighter in hand.

'Hello, darling,' he said to April as he lit up. 'Fancy a ciggie?' He thrust the open packet in her direction.

She knew she shouldn't, as each and every time she reached for a cigarette the disapproving face of her daughter would pop into her mind. But she could never resist, especially given such a perfect opportunity to speak to her target privately.

'Don't mind if I do,' April said, popping the cigarette into her mouth and leaning closer to the flame of Hanlon's lighter, which was just a plastic disposable affair. It was a bit cheap for a multi-millionaire, she thought. Then again, so was the pub.

'Harry, isn't it?' April asked.

'Aye, do I know you?' he replied, suddenly suspicious.

'Kind of,' she said, enjoying the first hit from the smoke. 'I interviewed you for the *Daily Chronicle* when you won.'

'That's right, a "cracking big bit of stuff",' Harry said, smiling at the memory. 'I knew I recognised your face.'

'You certainly know how to charm the ladies.'

'So what are you wanting now? I'm not up for doing more newspaper stories. You journalists always twist my words, printing a lot of crap about me. Saying how I spend my days getting steaming in here. So what if I do? It's my money.'

'I want to do a book about you.'

Harry smoked in silence for a moment as he considered what April had said.

'What's in it for me?'

'You'd get to set the record straight. It would all be in your own words. You'd see everything before going to print. You would be a hope and inspiration to everyone who buys a lottery ticket.' It was a line April had rehearsed earlier.

But what Harry asked next definitely had not been in the script: 'Financially. What's in it for me, financially?'

'Oh.' April was wrong-footed for a moment. 'A straight 50/50 split of the royalties?'

'What about the advance?' he continued while crushing his cigarette butt under his shoe.

'I've been offered two thousand pounds,' April replied. 'Although that's only from the first publisher I tried. I could see if I could get more.'

Harry lit up another cigarette, failing to offer April one this time. 'I want half the advance and you've to pick me up from my house every morning at exactly 10.55 am and drive me here. That'll save me a taxi fare as well.'

The man with £100 million in the bank shook hands with April, looking very pleased with himself for negotiating a fifty per cent cut of the royalties, a £1000 advance and saving £3.50 each morning on a taxi fare.

'I think it's time for a celebratory drink,' Harry said by way of inviting April into the bar. She just knew she would be paying.

Hot shave

MAY 3RD

'Bing? It's Joan. The chief constable would like to meet you.'

DCI Crosbie had known Joan Nicol since he was a raw recruit and she had been part of the secretarial pool before becoming personal assistant to the last three chief constables. They had always got on well – at one boozy office Christmas party, in particular.

'Can I run through some mutually convenient dates with you?'

'They're all mutually convenient for me, Joan. I'm on gardening leave.'

'I have Thursday, the...'

'This afternoon, Joan,' Crosbie interrupted. 'I've just remembered that the only convenient day for me is today.' He rolled over to check his bedside clock; it was only just after 9 am.

'Err, I don't know if that will give the chief constable time to prepare.'

'Joan, honey, if he's asking you to call me then he's already prepared. Let's get whatever it is over and done with.'

'Please give me a moment,' she said as she placed Crosbie on hold. Seconds later she was back on: 'This afternoon at 3 pm, Bing, and try not to swear too much.'

'I'll try, Joan doll. I'll fucking try,' he replied, his mind already working out a thousand possibilities.

Crosbie hung up the phone. 'I better get shaved then,' he said and turned over to face his neighbour's wife, who was still lying naked under the sheets. 'What about you?' he asked.

'Not again. You shaved "it" last night. My husband's going to get a shock when he's back from his business trip. What is it with you and shaving?' she asked.

'I'm a very sick individual. But I'm also a great lover,' and he disappeared below the covers to inspect his handiwork.

Paying with interest
JANUARY 6TH

'Wait a minute. You agreed to hand over £1,000 to one of Scotland's richest men?' Connor said incredulously.

'I know, ridiculous isn't it?' April replied through her customary mouthful of food, as she tucked into her hearty breakfast at the Peccadillo. 'He wasn't even interested in what I was going to write, just the money.'

'Bloody hell,' Connor said in genuine amazement.

'He actually looked as if he'd won the lottery all over again.'

Connor got out his iPhone to use its calculator function. 'Okay, if the old miser has hardly spent anything and his £100 million pot remains largely untouched, even after tax he would rake in thousands of pounds a day from the interest alone. Yet he's still happy to take a thousand notes off you and begrudges paying a fucking taxi fare?'

'I'm not all that sure it has sunk in for him.'

'But, he won it months ago.'

'He's a pretty "basic" human being.'

'Are you being diplomatic?'

'I have to write his book, so I'm trying to stay as positive as possible,' April explained.

'Do you know of Sir Rob McIntosh? Captain of industry, blah, blah, blah.'

'Of course,' April said, shovelling another heaped forkful into her mouth.

'You'll know he was raised on a housing estate, too. Clawed his way up, through education and his God-given talent to make money. Anyway, I once asked him if he ever worries about being poor again. He paused for a moment and said, "Every morning I wake up and, for just one moment, I think I've lost it all. It's the most horrible feeling in the world." Now, Sir Rob is one intelligent fella, worth ten times what Harry Hanlon won, yet even he still has pangs of panic about being poor. I think if you've always been rich you would never know any better. But to have had money then lost it must be dreadful. So maybe Harry thinks someone will take it all away again?'

'His own family, no doubt,' April said, not looking up from her plate.

'Why do you say that?'

'I haven't met them yet, but I told Harry I would need to interview them, too, and he seemed very suspicious of them. Although he seems suspicious of everyone.'

'Something to hide?'

'I think so. It's hard to tell. He's not the brightest. He starts stories and then wanders off at a tangent; I have to fill in the blanks.'

'You're one to talk. At least it'll keep you off the streets.'

'Especially in this weather,' she replied, looking out of the café window. It had snowed heavily last night and Glasgow city centre had turned completely white. 'But I think being a street walker would be an easier option – and they don't have to pay their clients upfront, either.'

Talking Italian
MAY 3RD

'Detective Inspector Crosbie to see you, sir,' Joan Nicol announced through her phone's intercom system.

'Send him in,' McNeil replied curtly.

Crosbie always likened a visit to the chief constable's office to being summoned by a school headmaster. He gave Joan a bouquet of flowers before striding into his boss's office. He was in his full police uniform, which was normally reserved for ceremonial and official occasions – or perhaps for the day you're fired, he would soon find out. Deputy Chief Constable Mike Bruce was also waiting to greet him.

'You're looking fit and healthy, Crosbie,' Bruce remarked. 'Nice tan, too. Been away?'

'No need, sir, with all the sunshine we're having. Police Scotland couldn't have picked a better summer to send me on gardening leave,' he said jovially. 'I have actually become quite green-fingered, trimming lots of bushes. In fact, I've even been trimming the neighbour's bush, too.'

'Well, we're glad we could haul you away from your bushes. Please meet your new chief constable, Eric McNeil.'

Crosbie and McNeil shook each other's hands firmly, studying each other momentarily.

'Nice to meet you, sir,' Crosbie said.

'And you. How are you feeling?' McNeil enquired.

'Tickety ... boo,' Crosbie replied with a slight pause – he had considered inserting one of his favourite expletives.

'Fit enough to resume active service?' Bruce asked.

'What about my disciplinary?'

'It's having a period of probation,' Bruce continued.

Crosbie noticed how McNeil was scrutinising his entire body language while Bruce did the talking.

'For as long as the case takes.' It was McNeil who now took the lead.

'The lottery inquiry, sir?' Crosbie replied.

'Yes, how did you guess?'

'I could say detective's hunch. But it was just logic, sir. No arrests have been made, which I take it means you are getting zero compliance from the Hanlon family and the good folks of Ruckhouse. And, you'll no doubt have been told, I'm from the Ruck.'

'I was also told you had been a damn fine detective, before all the ... nonsense.' Even the chief constable was being diplomatic. It was more than 'nonsense'. Crosbie was up on a gross misconduct charge after he ended up in hysterics when a member of the public with the name I. M. Cumming called to report his neighbour's house being burgled. By the time Crosbie had composed himself to take down the details, the burglar had fled the scene of the crime, leaving Mr Cumming's elderly neighbour almost beaten to death. So the chief constable must be really desperate to need him back after that, Crosbie thought to himself.

'How would you handle this case?' McNeil enquired.

'First, I need a new recruit, sir.'

'Why? You could have a whole team.' McNeil was perplexed.

'No, sir. I need a clean slate. Someone who hasn't already formed an opinion about me.'

'Sounds a bit paranoid,' McNeil replied.

'It's not, sir. I just want to get on with the case without having to negotiate all the internal politics as well. I have a very firm game plan. I need a new wingman to help execute it. Two, tops.'

The senior policemen shot glances between each other, before Crosbie detected a slight nod of the head from Bruce.

'You can have one full-time, a second on a need-by-need basis,' McNeil said.

'Thank you.' Crosbie beamed.

'So, are you ready to come back firing on all cylinders?' McNeil asked, his eyebrows arched in anticipation.

'Yes, sir. I am. And I appreciate the second chance.'

'We all deserve that,' McNeil said. Crosbie could see the look of relief on the faces of Scotland's two top policemen. He had never imagined he would have been welcomed back into the fold like this. It really was a second chance.

'So what else have you been up to during all your gardening leave?' Bruce asked.

'Learning Italian, sir.'

'Oh, how wonderful,' McNeil interjected. 'I know a bit of French but not a word of Italian. My son's fluent in it, mind you. Worked in Rome for a while.'

'It's easy if you have the time, sir. I could teach you some phrases, if you like.'

'Go for it.' McNeil laughed.

'Try *figlio di puttana* for starters, sir.'

'*Figlio di puttana*,' McNeil said, rolling the phrase around his mouth a couple of times. 'I rather like the sound of that. I'll call my son tonight, see if I can impress him with my Italian.'

'You do that, sir,' Crosbie replied as he headed for the exit, leaving the chief constable repeating the phrase *figlio di puttana* over and over again.

Crosbie wondered how impressed the boss's son would be when his father announced he was the 'son of a whore'.

9

Mocking bird
JANUARY 7TH

'Where do I put the password?'

Connor had long since stopped correcting April on her lack of telephone etiquette. He had learned to accept that she would bring him in midway through a conversation fully expecting him to know exactly what she was talking about. He also knew that the fact it was Saturday had no bearing on April Lavender when she had a tech issue.

'Usually in the password box.'

'Yes, yes, I know that, but I can't see any place to put it.' April had no time for Connor's flippancy when tackling technology.

'Is there a "next" option on the screen?'

'Yes,' she said, so loudly Connor had to momentarily pull his iPhone away from his ear. 'Ah, now I've got the password box. C-H-E-E-K-A.'

'Are all your passwords the cat's name? You're a hacker's wet dream.'

'Well, I can't remember any others,' April snapped back.

'What the hell are you signing up for, anyway? A dating site? NotTooFussy.com?'

'Netflix.'

'Netflix? You're shitting me. Welcome to the twenty-first century. And what's brought this revolution on?'

'I have my granddaughter Lucy staying over and she says the stuff I watch on TV is boring. She has a point – it bores me, too. Jayne said I should get Netflix but didn't tell me how. I had to look that up for myself. So now I'm signing up for a month-long trial of Netflix.'

'Will wonders never cease?'

'Right, that's me in. I'm cooking with gas. Oh, it's got *To Kill A Mockingbird*. I haven't seen that since...'

'The premiere?'

'Cheeky bastard.'

'They do have other stuff that's not in black and white, you know. There's *Breaking Bad* or *Orange Is the New Black*.'

'*Orange Is the New Black*,' April repeated while typing. 'Found it.'

'I thought this was for your granddaughter? They've got Netflix Kids, too.'

'So they have. I love this technology malarkey. Dead easy.'

'Isn't it just? And all you needed was your own IT man on call,' Connor replied sarcastically. 'How's the book coming along?'

'Fine. It really is like writing a long feature, just as you said. I feel as if I'm back at work.'

'And has it helped with the you-know-what?'

'It has, actually. I've lost quarter of a pound already.'

'Did you drop your hamburger or something?'

'Must've.'

'And are you still eating like a pig?'

'Yup, my snout remains firmly in the trough,' April replied proudly.

'Well, isn't that amazing? It was your job that kept you so svelte and good looking all these years.'

'I know. The many benefits of work. Anyway, must dash. The Netflix is on for Lucy and this book won't write itself, you know. Bye.'

'The Netflix.' Connor chuckled to himself; April always made him smile. 'I've missed the crazy old bat.'

10

Recruitment drive
MAY 4TH

Crosbie stuck to the 70 mph speed limit on the M876 using his Nissan SUV's cruise control. It was most unlike him. He normally liked to tear along this stretch of road towards the oil refinery at Grangemouth doing over a ton.

'You have changed,' he told himself proudly.

He took the turn-off for the Kincardine Bridge, which spanned the Firth of Forth, as he headed for his final destination, the police training college at Tulliallan Castle. Crosbie had already phoned ahead to arrange a meeting with the chief training officer, only to be told DI Andrew Hunt 'was busy'. Crosbie had ominously warned the operator to make sure Hunt was 'unbusy' by the time he arrived.

The sun was beating down as he crossed the eighty-year-old iron bridge, arriving at Tulliallan shortly afterwards. He was immediately directed to a meeting room where DI Hunt stood waiting impatiently. He was around 6 ft, with the well-built physique of a personal trainer, bald and red-faced, but that was most likely from the anger he felt after being dragged away mid-class.

'This better be important, Bing,' Hunt growled.

'Good to see you, too, Andy.'

'Cut the pish, Bing, I'm busy.'

'Alright, Andy. Tell me: who's this year's class swat?'

'I don't have swats. I produced well-rounded trainee detective constables.'

'Come on. Just tell me who the little brainbox is?'

'They all are,' Hunt replied, folding his arms.

'Oh, for fu … Who won this year's book prize?'

Hunt stared at Crosbie.

'Your endeavour award, then?'

Again Hunt just stared at Crosbie.

'Andy, stop screwing around.'

'Why do you want to know?'

'Because I'm going to commandeer them.'

'On whose authorisation?'

'Chiefie's.'

Hunt remained silent for what seemed an age. He knew Crosbie would only have the authority to hire a new recruit with the express permission of the chief constable. His dilemma was, he did not want to have all his hard work undone by handing over his star pupil to someone he considered unhinged.

'Cough up, Andy. Any longer and your hair might grow back. Who's your teacher's pet?'

'James Dugdale,' Hunt replied.

'Did he win the book prize or endeavour?'

'Both.'

'Good. Think he'll make a good detective?'

'I did, until now.'

'Look, Andy, there's been a lot of water under Kincardine Bridge since we did our training.'

'I wish you'd jumped off it.'

'Now, now, no need to get so personal.'

'You bring out the worst in me. Look, Bing, I've spent all these years teaching new recruits to be nothing like you. Why didn't they just pay you off? They got rid of all the other dinosaurs.'

'They were going to. Well, not paid off exactly, but they were certainly going to get rid of me. Then they must've decided they need a dinosaur for the job, after all. Where's Dugdale?'

'Having coffee upstairs with his family. It was his passing out ceremony today.'

'Family?'

'Mum and dad.'

'Good. Let's go meet him.'

'Let's go ask him first, Bing. He has the right to say no.'

'He has the right to remain silent, but that's about all. In my day, when a superior told you to jump, you asked how high.'

As Crosbie went to leave, Hunt grabbed him firmly by the arm. 'Don't go ruining my boy, Bing. Got it? He could make a great detective one day … if he's tutored the right way.'

The DCI looked down at the hand holding him tightly. Hunt relented and relaxed his grip.

'Don't worry, Andy, he'll still make a great detective.' Although Crosbie had absolutely no intentions of tutoring him in the 'right way'.

Bear necessities
JANUARY 9TH

'The usual?' Martel asked April as she joined Connor at the Peccadillo.

'Yes, please, but with a side order of white toast and marmalade. I have this hankering for marmalade this morning, for some reason. I feel like Paddington.'

'I'd love to hibernate like a bear,' Connor said, 'and wake up when all this bloody snow is gone. It's getting to be a real pain in the arse.'

Martel took April's order, completely ignoring Connor as she disappeared off to the kitchen.

'Just a cup of black tea this morning thanks, Martel,' he shouted as she retreated.

'Black tea?' April asked in amazement. 'I thought you always took it with loads of milk?'

'I do. But black tea makes it harder for Martel to spit in it.'

'She wouldn't do that, would she?'

'Have you seen the way she looks at me?'

'Right enough. Better stick to black for a while.'

'Although I don't know if that'll stop her pissing in my cup.'

'Please, it's too early for spit and piss talk. Did I tell you I've started taking a hula-hoop class? Did my first one last night with Lucy.'

'"Nana, Nana, your hula-hoop has got stuck again".' Connor sniggered.

'You can laugh, but they did actually have to find me a bigger one. There wasn't enough room for it to spin round.'

'A bit too much hula and not enough hoop?'

'Yes, something like that. But it's actually great fun.'

'Bet your face was bright red.'

'It's still a bit scarlet. You should've seen it last night; I looked like a giant strawberry with hair.'

'You paint pictures with words. I thought Netflix would have kept you busy?'

'So did I, but Jayne had a date so I had to take Lucy to her class. That's when she suggested I try it. And get this, after telling me to sign up for Netflix, Jayne then ticks me off for letting Lucy watch it all day. Said I needed to actually do something with my granddaughter, not just let her binge on "crap". It was good enough for her when I used to plonk her in front of the video player for hours on end, so I don't see why it isn't good enough for Lucy.'

'But hula-hoop worked, didn't it? It got you exercising.'

'It did, but my face really turns so crimson it's embarrassing.'

'Have you thought about getting your blood pressure checked out?'

'Don't go killing my buzz.' April frowned. 'I honestly had no idea exercise could be so enjoyable.'

'And it only took you till sixty to find out.'

'Fifty-nine,' April snapped.

'Alright, keep your hat on, Paddington.'

'I used to break into a cold sweat at the mere thought of exercise. I was always deliberately forgetting my gym kit at school to get out of PE. I would rather take the belt from the teacher than run about. But last night I felt right at home. Not just because Lucy was having fun, but because there were other women there just like me. The same size as me ... well, almost. I didn't feel out of place. We all had a hoot.'

'Bet you slept well, too.'

'I was out like a light. Marvellous sleep. Although I'm bloody ravenous now.' April actually rubbed her hands together in anticipation as Martel placed her fry-up in front of her, with the side order of white toast, butter and a small jar of thick-cut marmalade. April picked up the jar and examined it. 'I used to love the band Marmalade.' She then started singing 'Ob-La-Di, Ob-La-Da' a little too loudly for Connor's liking.

'Jeez, pipe down, Junior bloody Campbell. You're an embarrassment.'

'Ha, you sound just like Jayne. Great band. Scottish, too.'

'Yeah, but that song was Lennon and McCartney, although actually written entirely by McCartney.'

'Are you sure? Can't imagine Paul McCartney writing something like that.'

'He wrote the "Frog Chorus", didn't he?'

Martel practically flung Connor's cup and saucer at him, making a loud rattling noise, then thumped a small silver teapot in front of him before leaving in a marked manner.

'A teapot?' April said quizzically. 'That's unusual. I wonder if Martel had a few of McCartney's frogs in her throat this morning?'

Connor poured his pot of black tea, sniffing the contents of his cup suspiciously before taking the tiniest of sips. 'It's not even hot,' he moaned.

'You know what they say?' April beamed. 'Revenge is a pish best served cold.'

12

The bald facts
MAY 4TH

Trainee detective Dugdale was standing poker straight when Crosbie was led into Andy Hunt's private office to meet him. He was around five feet nine inches and his immaculate passing-out uniform perfectly hugged the muscular triangular frame of his torso.

Crosbie shook his potential recruit firmly by the hand, receiving a strong, confident grip in return. Dugdale was good-looking, with a youthful but serious face and a thick head of chestnut-coloured hair, but it was his rockabilly quiff that caught Crosbie's eye.

'James Dugdale, this is Detective Chief Inspector Crosbie,' Hunt said, with no discernible enthusiasm. 'He has a proposal that you are free to accept or not, whichever you see fit.'

'Although you may find I'll make you an offer you can't refuse,' Crosbie interjected, causing Dugdale to momentarily smile, before returning to his poker face. 'I have been given a task personally by the chief constable to head up a high-profile murder inquiry. I can't tell you what that is right at this moment, but it promises to be complicated. I understand you're single?'

The change in tack seemed to throw Dugdale, who stuttered, 'Er, yes, sir,' while shooting a sideways look towards his trainer.

'So, no wee girlie waiting to be taken to the movies?'

'No, sir.'

'Or wee boyfriend?'

'You can't ask that,' Andy Hunt interrupted angrily.

'No, sir,' Dugdale answered, seemingly unfazed.

'Doesn't bother me which way you swing – could be both ways, for all I care – but this case will have long, anti-social hours, so it's best for all concerned if you're unattached.'

'I am, sir,' Dugdale said, while staring straight ahead at some fixed spot on the wall, allowing Crosbie to steal a glance at the trainee's hair. Something wasn't right. Whenever Dugdale's facial expressions changed, the quiff remained steadfastly unmoving, as if it was floating on top of his head like a wig, even though Crosbie was pretty sure it wasn't.

'In the interest of transparency I feel I must tell you that if we fail then my career will most certainly be over, and you will have a black mark against your name. But failure ain't a motherfucking option as far as I'm concerned. So, are you up for the cup? Or do you need time to think?'

'When do we start, sir?' Dugdale replied.

'Attaboy. I'll see you first thing tomorrow morning.'

Andy Hunt stomped out of the room with Dugdale in tow, but as his new recruit walked past Crosbie towards the door, the DCI was able to inspect his hairstyle even more closely. Halfway down the back of Dugdale's head his hair had been parted and combed upwards and over the top of his cranium.

Crosbie waited until he was alone before he let rip: 'That's the worst fucking comb-over I've ever seen. He's bald as a coot.'

The DCI made his way back to his car, chuckling all the way at his follicly challenged new mentee and the elaborate lengths he had gone to disguise his premature hair loss. 'You hid it well, Dugdale, but not well enough from Detective Chief Inspector Crosbie.'

13

Cryptic clues
JANUARY 9TH

'What is that you're always doing?' April said to Harry as she joined him in his booth in the Woodchopper. She shed her faux fur coat and matching hat and gave her neck an ample application of Elizabeth Arden Red Door perfume that anyone within a ten-foot radius would be able to smell – April never believed in the minimalist mantra of less is more.

'Cryptic crossword,' Harry replied, not looking up from the newspaper's puzzle page he was filling in with a 'borrowed' bookies pen. He had the paper tucked under his arm when April had picked him up at the Macarena, and hadn't said a word on the short journey, staring at the puzzle page instead.

'I thought all crosswords were cryptic?'

'Nah. They're just straight clues. Cryptic crossword clues all have double meanings. They're harder.'

'I see,' April said, although she didn't. 'How long have you been doing them?'

'Dunno. Years. They're good brain training. Supposed to help with dementia. My folks died of that so I thought I'd try to do something about it.'

April thought that if Harry was so concerned about his longevity he could do with losing some weight, and adopting a healthier lifestyle, although she was one to talk. 'My mum and dad had dementia, too,' April replied. Harry had never talked about his parents and she wanted him to open up some more. But the opportunity seemed to pass as he was only interested in discussing puzzles.

'You should start doing the crosswords. They're good for the old grey matter,' Harry said, tapping his head with his fist as if knocking a door. 'Here, have a shot.' He spun the newspaper to face her.

The *Daily Chronicle* was folded open at the puzzle page. She had often heard that readers only bought the paper for certain sections, perhaps the sports pages or the horoscopes. But Harry bought his for the cryptic crossword. During all her years working at the *Chronicle*, April had never taken the time to read any part of Harry's favourite page. Just like the sports section, it meant nothing to her at all. Now she was being asked to look at it for the first time. It was full of gobbledygook: brain-tease this, number generator that and something called a quick quiz. April hated anything with a double meaning; she preferred something to simply state what it is.

'Try that one.' Harry pointed to one of the clues.

April readjusted her glasses to the tip of her nose to focus on the fine print. '*Judge passing notice grabbed by one royal supporter?*' She said it again and then she tried mumbling it. Finally, out of sheer frustration, she exploded. 'That's impossible. And stupid. It's stupidly impossible. I don't understand the question, never mind being able to answer it.'

'And that's an easy one, too.' Harry laughed. 'Jacobite.'

'How on earth did you figure that out?' April said, her mouth hanging open in genuine amazement.

'Firstly "royal supporter" is the straight "definition" part of the clue which will confirm the answer's meaning. That leaves "Judge passing notice grabbed by one". Judge normally just refers to the letter "J" in cryptic crossword clues and "passing notice" is an obituary, or obit, right?'

'Right,' April said, trying to look as if she knew what he was talking about.

'But "grabbed by one" means that the "obit" part is surrounded, or grabbed by the letters of, a word meaning "one". In this case that's "ace", as in an ace in a deck of cards.

'So if you start with the "J" then wrap "ace" around "obit", you get "J-ac-obit-e".

'And that's how cryptic clues work. Want to try another? Here' – he didn't wait for her answer – 'try this one: *Shed first tear in court over writing.*'

April repeated the words slowly before snapping once again. 'That doesn't make sense. I don't get this.'

'You don't have to. They're designed to throw you off the scent. So you just take it bit by bit, so here "Shed first" means the first letter of "Shed", which gives you "S", and "tear" in this case means "rip".

'Follow me so far?' Harry asked, gently prompting April.

'Yes,' April replied truthfully.

'And in cryptic crosswords "court" is usually abbreviated to "CT". So "tear *in* court" gives you C-RIP-T.'

'Script?' April asked tentatively.

'Spot on.'

'I got it. I actually got it. That actually feels good,' April said, feeling strangely pleased with herself.

'Now this one: *Bush having tip of spine inside to pierce.* As you can see, it's a five-letter word beginning with "G".'

'Gorse,' April replied instantly.

'Now you're getting the hang of it.' Harry leaned back on the booth's curved couch, causing it to creak as he drained his whisky glass. 'I write my own, too. There's a crossword forum where we exchange ideas for clues.'

April thought that there must be a forum for everything because somewhere in the world there would always be a like-minded individual.

'You should start with some easier puzzles then work your way up. You'll be surprised. Once your brain trains itself to know what it's looking for, it soon catches on.'

April had seriously doubted her brain would ever catch on, but it had. And talking about cryptic cross-words had produced the most meaningful conversation she'd had so far with Harry Hanlon. She hadn't figured that this 'basic' human being would even have the intelligence to read such difficult questions, let alone answer them. Maybe if she kept practising cryptic crosswords, it would finally give them some common ground to talk about.

'I'd like you to put some of my own crosswords into the book – people will like my crosswords,' he said grandly.

April imagined the dreariness of writing a chapter about crosswords, but she readily agreed, telling herself that every great album also has the odd filler track.

Marina

MAY 5TH

DCI Crosbie threw his car keys towards Dugdale, whose quick reflexes saw him catch them firmly mid-air. They were at Police Scotland's West of Scotland Glasgow HQ in Dalmarnock, where Dugdale had been going through his formal introduction with the human resources team.

'You drive. I'll observe,' Crosbie informed the new recruit as he took the back seat, to allow him to study Dugdale's hair unimpeded.

'Where are we going, sir?' Dugdale started the engine.

'The Ruck, Dugdale. We're going to be spending a lot of time in the Ruck. Have you ever been?'

'No, sir.'

'Ah, then you're in for a treat, what with the beautiful promenades and vistas to die for. And their new marina along the waterfront is spectacular.'

Dugdale gave Crosbie a quizzical glance in the rear-view mirror.

'Sadly, it has none of those things. It's a shit-hole. The biggest shit-hole in Scotland and, believe me, that's quite an achievement given the stiff competition.'

'My mum always said you can't judge people by where they live, sir.'

'Your mum's talking bollocks, Dugdale, no offence.'

'None taken, sir.'

'All the smart ones left, myself included. To replace us, they shipped in every troubled family they could find, filling each crumbling tower block with hopeless junkies who maim and murder each other over £10 bags of crap. There are parts of it which are almost completely lawless. Where police patrol cars are stoned and the fire brigade leave fires to burn themselves out. Then, lo and behold, right in the middle of this melting pot of garbage, Harry Hanlon wins £100 million. It wasn't a question of if he would be murdered, but when. It took less than six months for someone to plunge a twelve-inch blade into his back, slicing his heart in two. The knife would have come out his chest if he hadn't been so fat. The blade also broke two of his ribs. Do you know how much force it takes to break rib bones, Dugdale?'

'No, sir.'

'Me neither, but the pathologist says it takes a lot.'

'Was it one of the locals or his family, sir?'

'Oh, everyone's pretty certain it was one of the Hanlons. But this is where it gets complicated. There are only two men in the house with that sort of power. One is Robert "Shifty" Hanlon, a low-grade thug and street-corner drug dealer with delusions of grandeur, and the other is a learning-disabled adult: Billy, who has the mental capacity of a six-year-old. Oh, and Billy's also wheelchair-bound, completely unable to walk.'

'So it was Robert, sir?'

'Congratulations, you've solved the case. Let's arrest him right now and go home.'

Dugdale thought it best he remained silent while his new boss was in sarcastic mode.

'The problem is, Dugdale, the Hanlons have circled the wagons,' Crosbie said, grabbing a sneak peek at the back of Dugdale's head again. His comb-over almost defied the laws of physics. He wondered how on earth his quiff didn't fall apart and come flapping down around his ears. Maybe it would one day. Crosbie hoped he would be around to see it. 'They're saying nothing. We can suspect Shifty all we want but we've no eyewitnesses linking him to the crime. We have DNA from a blood sample taken from the handle of the blade that doesn't match Harry Hanlon's and is certainly from a close family member, but all the Hanlons have refused to be tested.'

'So what do we do now, sir?'

'We announce our presence. Make sure word gets around that there's a new sheriff in town.'

Dugdale refrained from asking any more questions – he was certain that he would soon find out what his new mentor had in store.

Pulling power
JANUARY 10TH

April picked up Harry Hanlon at precisely 10.55 am from the Macarena, and drove to the Woodchopper for opening time. She had got used to negotiating the icy roads, but with more snow on the way, she was seriously considering winter tyres, but had baulked at the £600 price she had been quoted.

The Woodchopper was always fairly quiet at that time, giving April the chance of an hour's solid interview time before Harry got distracted by the arrival of the lunchtime crew. Driving also meant she didn't have to become her subject's drinking partner, and she was often able to slip away when he was too drunk to speak or found other company to keep, usually in the shape of various women, including sixty-year-olds still dressing and acting like they were eighteen. They all wanted to meet Harry, for obvious reasons. From the sidelines, April would watch all their flirtations and interactions; but if they thought they were going to get their hands on Harry's millions they were in for a shock, as he was undoubtedly the meanest human being she had ever met.

Penny-pinching didn't begin to describe Harry's miserly ways. He regularly commented on the taxi fare April saved him by picking him up each morning. She was now keeping a discreet note of her subject's thriftiness in case she could use it for any articles she might be asked to write to promote the book. Harry was always happy enough to play the Big I Am at the bar, with people eager to be his friend, but he only ever put his hand in his pocket for himself.

If one of the flirty grannies was going to get lucky, he would buy her a drink before taking her back to his place. April knew the women around here were willing to fight over a man on long-term disability allowance – considered a golden ticket, which came complete with a subsidised car and VIP parking, otherwise known as the blue badge to use the disabled bays.

But that was nothing compared to Harry Hanlon, who had taken on local hero status, a standing April knew he didn't deserve. Harry was an unreconstructed human being, except when it came to his crosswords, which made him a bit of an enigma in her eyes. But, the more time April spent with Harry, the less she liked him. If she was ever going to get her book done then she was going to have to just grin and bear it.

16

'Cuffs
MAY 5TH

'Now, some coppers swear by the truncheon,' DCI Crosbie explained to Dugdale as they stepped out of the SUV. 'But the problem with a baton is, it's hard to get out and swing about when some little bastard is trying to punch your lights out. That's why, for me, cuffs will always be the master. Now I don't want you to do a thing, no matter what happens, understand? Allow me to demonstrate.'

DCI Crosbie led his young protégé towards a tenement close to where five young hard-looking men, and a girl of indeterminate age, were loitering. They eyed Crosbie and Dugdale suspiciously, knowing cops when they saw them, before someone cracked an inaudible joke, and they all sniggered accordingly. They had been talking to the occupants of a dark blue car that had been modified so much with additional spoilers and extra lights that it was hard to tell the make and model, while the windows were darkened beyond legal limits, which made identification of anyone inside impossible.

Crosbie had been used to seeing these cars growing up in Ruckhouse, with their silencers removed, revving and screeching around the streets at all hours with complete impunity from the law. The police had once tried curbing this menace to the community, but high-speed car chases and attempted road blocks caused more hassle than they were worth as it got to the stage that the boy racers would goad the law enforcement to pursue them, endangering all involved. So the cops just left them to create havoc however they felt best.

As the DCI and his trainee approached, the souped-up car sped off, with the driver and the passengers flicking them both the V-sign.

'I trust you got the number plate,' Crosbie demanded more than asked.

'Yes, sir.'

'Then I'll deal with those pricks later.' He made straight for the wise guy who was clearly the leader of the pack. 'Got something funny to say, dickhead?'

Wise Guy's demeanour changed from cocky to aggro. 'Who're you calling a dickhead?'

'You,' Crosbie said, jabbing a finger into his chest while going eyeball to eyeball with his target. The DCI was able to dodge the head-butt just in time, and he grabbed Wise Guy's wrist, turning his back on the blows that followed.

The rest of the gang scarpered, knowing full well the consequences of attacking a cop. Dugdale took a step forward to intervene, only for Crosbie to bark, 'Back off.'

Crosbie pushed Wise Guy into the stairwell past the broken door entry system, where they wouldn't be seen by prying eyes or videoed by anyone's mobile phone, which would then undoubtedly be posted on social media for all to see. Wise Guy resisted as much as he could, his fists striking Crosbie's shoulders, neck and the back of his head as the DCI crouched protectively at his assailant's waist level.

Dugdale couldn't believe what he heard next: his commanding officer began speaking as if he was delivering a training drill.

'What this suspect will quickly discover is, it's actually far more difficult to punch downwards than it is at shoulder level. You also can't get anywhere near the same amount of power. Also, by the feel of things, this rather unfit individual is quickly running out of steam.'

Crosbie's taunt upped his attacker's work rate, who rained down jabs on the detective with renewed vigour.

'In a situation like this, it's imperative that you get hold of just one of your suspect's hands, like so…' Crosbie waggled Wise Guy's trapped hand in Dugdale's direction. 'Then you just snap on one of the cuffs and bend, like this.'

The blows stopped instantly as Wise Guy's knees buckled beneath him. He crumpled to the concrete steps and the DCI resumed a standing position, now towering over his attacker.

'Rigid cuffs are, by far, the best piece of kit the police force ever introduced. The metal plate between them gives you incredible leverage,' he said, pushing them closer to Wise Guy's face, who was now on his knees, clutching his right wrist in agony. 'As you can see, when you're able to do that, then your suspect is quickly neutralised and rendered useless. Although, this one was pretty useless to start with. Now, a word to the wise, Dugdale: if you get the cuffs on between the wrist and thumb, you can pretty much apply as much pressure as you want without doing too much lasting damage. However, if it slips past the wrist towards the elbow, like this' – Crosbie repositioned the cuffs further up Wise Guy's forearm – 'you are in danger of breaking bones, which involves a lot of paperwork. Well, most of the time.'

The DCI now turned his attention back to Wise Guy, his voice changing from instructor to street. 'You knew I was a cop as soon as you saw me, didn't you?'

'Aye,' Wise Guy replied, grimacing in pain.

'Yet you still tried to head-butt me?'

'Aye, I'm fucking sorry, alright?' Wise Guy replied, still on his knees and holding his cuffed wrist with his free hand.

'"Sorry" doesn't cut it with me, you little prick.'

Crosbie suddenly yanked Wise Guy's arm skywards – the sound of his wrist snapping was so loud it reverberated around the closed stairwell. Dugdale was shocked, but not as shocked as Wise Guy, whose face was frozen in a silent scream, before he finally caught his breath and emitted a piercing roar of agony.

Crosbie unlocked the cuff from his wrist, which now hung limply at an awkward angle.

'You broke my fucking wrist,' Wise Guy screamed, tears streaming down his red face.

'Okay, I'm glad you've accepted a verbal caution as it

means I won't have to take you in for questioning. But, in future, you should be careful in these stairwells: they're very slippy and you can easily break a bone or two, as you've discovered. In fact, I would probably seek medical attention for that wrist. Now, off you trot,' Crosbie said cheerfully.

Wise Guy clasped his ruined wrist, pain and rage filling his eyes as he staggered from the close as quickly as shock would allow him.

'There was no need for that, sir,' Dugdale said, his face ashen.

'There was every need, Dudgale. Now all the little fuckers in the Ruck know Bing is back. And I mean business. Let's see if word of my return reaches the Hanlons before we do.'

17

Rocket Man

JANUARY 11TH

April was already eating when Connor arrived at the Peccadillo. Curiously, her head wasn't buried in the *Daily Chronicle* as usual; instead, she was busy reading her Samsung smartphone while shovelling in mouthfuls of greasy food.

'Just got a "breaking news" tweet,' she said by way of introduction, spraying some contents from her mouth in her former colleague's direction. 'The Met Office are predicting tonight could beat the coldest temperature ever recorded in Scotland, beating minus 27.2°C from Braemar in 1982. I remember that winter well. There wasn't as much snow as '78, but it was colder and all the pipes in the street froze. The army even had to bring out their ancient Green Goddess fire engines to set up water stations.'

'Since when did you start subscribing to Twitter alerts?' Connor asked, unable to hide his amazement.

'Ages ago. Old news now, sonny. I also have Google Alerts, TMZ, Mail Online, Sky News, BuzzFeed and the BBC, although they're probably the slowest.'

'How the hell do you know about TMZ?' Connor genuinely stunned. He liked to think he was social media and tech-savvy, but even he hadn't subscribed to the celebrity showbiz site.

'Back when they broke the news of that wee fella. You know, the singing midget. Wore high heels and flares.'

'Prince?' Connor asked, secretly pleased April's powers of recall hadn't matched her technological advances.

'That's him. Never understood the attraction. I found him creepy. Don't think I could date a man who wore more make-up than me. He looked too girlish. Did I tell you the first time Husband Number One saw me without make-up?'

'He shat himself or something?' Connor was sure April had told him the story before, and he was quickly losing interest.

'No, he said I looked like Elton John.'

Connor spluttered his tea. He had not heard that one before. 'From his "Rocket Man" days? Or his wig-wearing era?' Connor asked, suddenly interested again. He loved how April dropped random information from her three doomed marriages so casually into conversations.

'I didn't ask. The point was, he said I looked like a bloke. I belted him.'

'You could get done for domestic abuse for that.'

'What judge would convict me?'

Connor was now studying April's face from different angles. 'Your ex had a point, you know. There is a touch of Elton about you.'

'That's what made it worse. Every time I looked in the mirror after that I saw Elton bloody John staring back.'

'Did Husband Number One apologise? Or did "Sorry Seem To Be The Hardest Word"?' Connor sniggered.

'It was the beginning of the end, let me tell you. What sort of man tells his wife she looks like a bloke? Idiot.'

'Ooh, "The Bitch Is Back",' Connor said, enjoying himself just a little too much.

'Fortunately, I met Husband Number Two shortly afterwards.'

'"Were You Ready For Love?"'

'Yes, I was actually,' April replied, completely oblivious to Connor's corny Elton references. 'And let me tell you, he never saw me without my slap on. I wasn't going to take that chance again.'

'And Husband Number Three?'

'Nope. In fact, I don't think he ever saw me naked.'

'Yuck.'

'What do you mean, "yuck"? You cheeky pig. Anyway, he's dead now. In fact, Number One is gone as well now.'

'But Number Two's "Still Standing"?'

'Far as I know,' April continued blithely. 'Weird, isn't it, though? How people you know are here one minute, then gone the next?'

'Ah, "the Circle of Life".' Connor snorted.

'What the hell are you giggling about?'

'"Circle of Life"? "I'm Still Standing"? They're Elton John songs.'

'Are they?'

'Oh for fu ... I thought someone of your vintage would have known that.'

'Never really cared for his songs. He's yesterday's man now. Technology is the future.' She took a slurp of coffee and returned to her small screen.

'April Lavender, the social media junkie. Who'd have thunk it?' Connor said quietly to himself, as he read a new WhatsApp instant message. Someone else was also riding that technological wave after years of deliberately remaining offline.

Connor replied to the message: *Didn't have you down for a WhatsApp user, Colin.*

Elvis, long time no hear. Have you been ignoring me?

Not ignoring you, Colin. Just been busy, he typed back.

Yeah, we're both busy but that doesn't mean friends shouldn't keep in touch.

Connor bristled at the word 'friends'. They were anything but. Colin Harris was always referred to in newspapers as a 'Glasgow businessman', which was code for 'ruthless gangster'. Connor also knew he was a cold-blooded killer who would stop at nothing to control the entire city's drug trade.

Connor wrote back, *So what's with the WhatsApp? Unlike you to leave an electronic footprint.*

Ah, but I'm not Elvis. It's encrypted. All encoded and untraceable. The messages are only stored on the server until they're delivered, then deleted. Perfect for people like me who prefer to keep themselves private. Or for contacting friends…

With that last, hanging sentence it was almost as if Harris could sense Connor's discomfort. The journalist's relationship with Harris – such as it was – stretched back several years to when the serial killer Osiris Vance had murdered Colin's prostitute sister. Vance had also nearly beaten April Lavender to death. Harris would never admit it, especially in a court of law, but it was believed that him and his goons had found Osiris first. The killer's body was discovered weeks later with clear evidence of torture while his genitals were stated as 'missing' in the post-mortem report.

Harris only ever called Connor when he needed something, and here he was again: *We should meet. Soon.* It was more of an instruction than an invite.

Sure. I'm free today after work. Usual place?
The usual place and the usual drink.

18

DVR
MAY 6TH

DCI Crosbie sat in the car outside the Macarena, staring at the architectural eyesore. 'Money really can't buy taste,' he said to Dugdale as he stepped out of his car.

The garden gate still had the remnants of police tape attached to it and flapping lazily in the wind. The tape had cordoned off the house as a crime scene but had snapped long ago after the family returned to live in the place where their father had died.

It was raining for the first time in ages, but the drops felt warm on their faces – even the rain hadn't broken the heat-wave – and Crosbie tilted his face to the heavens in order to savour the temporary relief. As he did so, he spotted two CCTV cameras attached to each of the Acropolis-style columns by the entrance. He frowned. He hadn't seen any CCTV images in the extensive police reports: maybe someone had switched them off or destroyed the footage long before the police got there?

He passed the ornamental fountain with the figure of Venus that greeted visitors. Crosbie seemed to remember from one of the crime scene reports that the fountain had fish in it. But he had no idea whether they were dead or alive, as the water was now almost black and impenetrable to the eye.

Crosbie had to ring the doorbell twice before it was

answered by a stoned-looking youth, who didn't match the descriptions of any of the family members.

'Police, can we come in?' Crosbie asked. The youth just shrugged before disappearing back down the hall and out of sight. 'I'll take that as a "yes",' Crosbie said, closing the door behind them.

The floors and every available surface were littered with butts from cigarettes and joints, while empty beer cans were strewn everywhere. The kitchen was even worse, with discarded syringes, needles and cigarette burns on the expensive oak surfaces.

'Party central,' Crosbie remarked.

'You'd think they would put some of it in a bin bag, sir,' Dugdale said. He had never seen anything like it.

'Too wasted,' Crosbie replied.

They moved from the kitchen towards the French doors that led to the back garden, and the hot tub where Harry Hanlon's body was discovered. The sixteen-person spa was the size of a small swimming pool. It had been drained after the murder by forensics and no one had bothered to refill it. Now it was just a giant garbage receptacle.

'Imagine living next to this lot,' Crosbie said as he scanned the row of houses on either side of the Hanlon's home.

'They appear to be empty, sir,' Dugdale observed.

'The council probably had to move them away from Animal House.' Crosbie pointed to another CCTV camera high up the back wall of the Hanlon property. 'Harry obviously feared for his safety. I wonder why there's no footage.'

They disappeared back inside to the modest-sized sitting room dominated by a large, white-leather corner sofa scattered with gold brocade cushions. There was barely enough room between the couch and the wall for the wrought-iron coffee table with its smoked-glass top. The obligatory huge flat-screen TV took up almost one entire wall. It was so large and so close to the couch that viewers would have to turn their heads to see what was going on at either side of the LCD display, a bit like watching a tennis match. A pale marble fireplace looked to be a recent addition, with matching green jade and gold fringe table lamps at either side, while an ornate gold mirror completed the look. The final pièce de résistance was a white-leather, horseshoe-shaped cocktail bar with a glass shelf gantry illuminated with ever-changing multicoloured lights to display the array of whisky, gin and Malibu bottles. All of which were empty.

'Malibu. The height of sophistication in the '80s.' Crosbie snorted.

On the surface of the bar was an ice bucket, tongs, cocktail sticks and umbrellas. Dugdale picked up a pewter frame containing a photo of a family with perfect hair and even more perfect teeth.

'Who are they, sir? I haven't seen them in any of the reports.'

'The classic council house clan, Duggie,' Crosbie said.

'They don't look like they're from around these parts. They look American.'

'They probably are. People buy the frame and end up keeping the photo that comes with it. They'd rather look at the perfect American family than their own brood, and who could blame them?'

The roar of a BMW X6 came to a halt outside. Dugdale watched a well-built male get out of the Typhoon model, with its 750 horsepower. The trainee immediately recognised the shaven-headed individual as the eldest of the family, Robert 'Shifty' Hanlon and main suspect for the murder of their father. He was followed by a short blonde in high heels and figure-hugging dress.

'We have company, sir.'

'Shifty, no doubt?'

'Yes, sir, and a female.'

Crosbie stepped towards the window and watched Shifty playfully slap his companion on the backside, guessing they planned to head straight to his bedroom. He hated to be anyone's buzzkill, but police business was police business.

Shifty Hanlon opened the front door only to be greeted by DCI Crosbie.

'What the fuck are you doing in my house?'

'Nice to see you too, Robert.'

'Who gave you permission to enter?'

'Some eccie-jawed youth. I haven't seen him since.'

'Did you break his wrist, too?' Shifty asked. Crosbie was inwardly pleased that word had already got out about his encounter with Wise Guy. 'Only I can give you permission to come into my house. Got it? Now fuck off.'

'Sure, I only wanted to ask some questions about your dad,' Crosbie said.

'All questions go through my lawyer.'

'Who's your lawyer?'

'McFadden.' Shifty smirked.

Crosbie had crossed swords before with defence advocate Paul McFadden, both in and out of the witness box.

'Aye, not so cocky now, are you, Bing?' Shifty laughed.

'Is that Bing Crosbie?' Shifty's female companion piped up.

'It is indeed.' Crosbie grinned.

'It's Angie? Angie Wyper.'

Crosbie recognised his former classmate now under the layers of make-up. He recalled her cruel nickname at school had been 'Bum Wyper'. It wasn't a sophisticated moniker but ironically appropriate as her first job on leaving school was as a care assistant in an old folks' nursing home.

'Angie Wyper, it's been a long time.'

'This isn't a high-school reunion. Now piss off,' Shifty growled.

Crosbie headed towards the front door with Dugdale, before he paused to say his farewells to Shifty's girlfriend. 'Really nice to see you again, Angie. You're looking great.'

'Thanks,' she replied, beaming at the compliment. Crosbie enjoyed witnessing Shifty's obvious displeasure. As he closed the door he heard him berate Angie: 'What the fuck you flirting with that pig for?'

He dreaded what the unpredictable oldest Hanlon sibling would do next, but it felt good to get under his skin all the same.

Back outside, Crosbie looked across at the council flats opposite. 'Your first solo task will be to gain entry to one of those apartments and set up a 24/7 surveillance on the Hanlon house,' he told Dugdale. 'I want to see who is coming and going from these all-night raves. That might give us some new leads. But do it yourself, not through work – I don't want anyone to know, got that?'

'Yes, sir,' Dugdale replied, the cogs already whirring as he started to figure out what cover story he would tell the council. After a few moments, he said, 'Sir, the original report indicated that the DVR may have been removed before officers arrived at the scene. If the murder was premeditated then it would have been easier just to switch it off.'

'DVR?' Crosbie enquired.

'The digital video recorder, sir. It looks a bit like a normal Sky box. It was noted missing by the first investigating officers. They asked the family about its whereabouts but got stonewalled.'

'There's a fucking surprise.'

'But that suggests the crime was recorded, sir. Otherwise, why remove it?'

'A very good point, Dugdale. Andy Hunt said you were good.'

'Not really, sir, it's only logical.'

'As Doctor Spock would say.'

'Yes, sir. Although it's actually Mr Spock.'

'Trekkie twat.'

'I am indeed a Trekker, sir. But if the DVR has been removed in haste, it may be hidden rather than disposed of.'

'Why?'

'Because the DVR will have a hard drive inside, and they are notoriously difficult to destroy. So whoever removed it wouldn't want to just throw it away, in case it was ever discovered.'

'Yes,' Crosbie said enthusiastically, 'hidden until the coast was clear, then destroy the DVR and get rid of the evidence.'

'If we can find it, we can probably recover the images, even if someone has tried to wipe them. A friend of mine works for a crisis IT company.'

'Emergency services for computers?' Crosbie smiled.

'Basically, sir. He says he was once able to recover ninety-seven per cent of the data from a hard drive someone had burned and stuck a screwdriver through. Apparently the data is pretty much always there, no matter what you do to them. The DVR might even still be on the property, sir.'

'I doubt it, none of them are that stupid.'

'Or close by? I could speak to the original investigating officers about their search for the DVR?' Dugdale suggested.

'No point, they'll just cover their arses. We'll do everything for ourselves, Duggie. Everything.' Crosbie's mind was now in overdrive.

19

Just A Minute

JANUARY 11TH

The usual meeting place for Connor and Colin Harris was the Portman Bar in Glasgow's rundown Kinning Park district. Colin's usual drink was Chablis Les Preuses Grand Cru, which cost around £160 a bottle. The journalist was happy that he wasn't buying.

Unlike a fine wine, the Portman had not improved with age. It was still a dump. Outside, Connor clocked the black customised Audi R8, which sat across the road from the bar containing two hulks of meat otherwise known as Colin Harris's minders. They stared menacingly at the reporter, but looked mildly comical in their trapper winter hats, with the furry flaps over their ears. Their boss had obviously ordered them not to draw attention to themselves by keeping the engine idling, so the ridiculous-looking hats were an attempt to keep warm in the plummeting temperatures.

Inside the bar, Connor recognised some of the dead-eyed regulars, who barely glanced in his direction or even acknowledged his existence. Connor scanned the room, taking in the scuffed bare floorboards – which were badly in need of a wash, never mind varnish – and the booths, with their burst, torn or suspiciously sliced maroon vinyl upholstery. The barmaid was a squat lady with layers of make-up that made her look as dated as the interior. She had to turn sideways to squeeze through the narrow hatch on the bar, bustling past Connor with two wine glasses and a chilled bottle of Chablis in her hands.

'This way, son,' she said, indicating the reporter was to follow her to the furthest away booth. He figured she didn't get too many people in suits visiting her establishment unless they were attending a funeral. Or were the accused.

Connor could see a pair of brown hush puppy shoes under a table but no more than that as the barmaid's sheer girth obscured the rest of his vision. When she moved, there were two glasses of wine on the tacky hammered brass table-top. A small figure in owlish glasses took to his feet to shake Connor's hand warmly.

'Bloody hell, mate, you're looking great. Must be all that boring running you do,' Harris said, beaming at Connor as if he was an old lost friend.

'Thanks, you're looking ... well,' Connor replied, his eyes being inadvertently drawn to Harris's hair, which had clearly had some cosmetic tinkering, leaving perfect rows of hair follicles that reminded Connor of a Lego brick.

'It's a mess, isn't it?' Harris said, his eyes lifting skywards.

Connor took it as an invitation to have a closer look. His head certainly was a mess, with a mix of freshly healed scabs and thinning patches of hair that gave a Brillo pad effect.

'Botched hair job. The charlatans at the clinic who did this will regret ever dealing with me.'

'I bet. Do they have any kneecaps left?' Connor asked.

'Jeez, Elvis, what do you think I am? I've got my lawyers on to them. I'm not a Neanderthal!'

'No, they're in the Audi outside.'

Harris let out a hearty, genuine laugh. 'Yeah, I doubt Bill and Bob have a full set of brain cells between them. But they're ... useful.'

'Ah, slight hesitation there, Colin. Define "useful".'

'What is this? *Just A Minute*?'

Connor raised his eyebrows, taken aback that a feared gangster even knew of the long-running Radio 4 panel game.

Harris sensed his surprise. 'I never miss an episode, Elvis. Goes back to my time "inside". Nicholas Parsons. Paul

Merton, hesitation, repetition and deviation. It's brilliant for improving your vocabulary. I would learn a new word every show. Sometimes two. Occasionally three. I wish I'd met old Nicholas before he died. His trick was, he always played it straight, which allowed everyone else to get the laughs.'

Harris certainly wasn't your archetypal gangster. *Just A Minute* aside, he also didn't conform to the image of the cold-blooded killer that Connor knew him to be. For starters, he was short, around 5 ft 6 in, and his once-lean frame was now podgy in places, with man-boobs protruding from under his beige pullover, while a cardigan lay folded on the vinyl-covered seat beside him. And that was another thing: Harris didn't dress like a gangster. More like a middle manager at an insurance company. His unassuming look had served him well, right back to his youthful days as a two-bit street assassin – no one would suspect the scrawny, speccy kid of being a threat until it was too late. Connor suspected many had lived to regret judging a book by its cover, if they had lived at all. Harris had little need to demonstrate his ruthless nature anymore as his reputation was menacing enough. But Connor knew that danger always lurked just below the surface.

The two men took a sip of their wine. 'Delicious,' Connor said, 'but don't you ever get sick of drinking the same thing all the time?'

Harris smiled as he held his glass aloft to a half-broken ceiling light, studying its contents. 'Elvis, I have paid small fortunes for wine. I once spent £12,000 on a 1962 Burgundy and it was totally tasteless. I've had better £5 Riojas from the supermarket. But when I first tasted this Chablis, I knew this was the one. You always know when you meet the right one, don't you? By the way, how is that Russian girl of yours? Not married yet?'

Connor was stung by Harris's question. He had never told him of his relationship with Anya.

'Been keeping tabs on me, Colin?'

'Hahaha, don't flatter yourself, Elvis. I had lunch in her restaurant the other week and she had a newspaper clipping framed on the wall with your byline. I asked her about it and she said you two are dating. She seemed very proud of you.'

Elvis relaxed at the entirely feasible explanation.

'God, you're a bit jumpy, Elvis. Everything all right at the paper? Still working alongside mad April?'

Harris clearly had not been keeping tabs on Connor that closely if he didn't know that April had been made redundant the previous year.

'Nah, she was forcibly retired.'

'Oh, I must send her a card. She was lucky to make it to retirement after all that Osiris business. I've always had a soft spot for old April. What's her tipple, Elvis? I'll send her a bottle of something.'

'Anything.'

'What do you mean?'

'I mean she will drink anything you send. She's partial to the odd whisky, wine, red, white, rosé or sparkling. She also likes sherry, vodka, gin – botanical or supermarket specials, she cares not a jot – and enjoys the odd beer in hot weather. As I said, send her anything.'

'It really is a surprise she reached retirement with that lot. So who are you working with now?' Harris asked as he refilled their glasses.

'No one at all. I'm a one-man band.'

'That can't be much fun.'

'It isn't. There's so few staff left, sometimes I can go almost a whole shift without talking to anyone. I'm convinced I'm going to forget how to speak one day.'

'Jeez, papers today, Elvis. I'm not surprised: I haven't bought one in years. Get it all off the net now.'

'For free.'

'Of course.'

'Bit of a crap business model for us though, isn't it? Spend a fortune putting content together then give it all away for nothing.'

'I thought advertising would pay for it?' Harris asked.

'Nope. They're not stupid. They'll know exactly how many hits they're getting for what and from whom. They adjust their rates accordingly. They tell us what they are going to pay now. Changed days.'

'That's mental,' Harris said, shaking his head. 'Wouldn't work in my line of business.'

'Doesn't work in any line of business,' Elvis replied, deliberately not asking Harris to describe exactly what line of business he was in.

Harris sipped his wine and then put his hands on the table. 'You heard about the Gallacher brothers?' he asked, studying Connor's reaction as he spoke.

Connor knew that Harris had now switched to the true purpose of their meeting. He just didn't know where the rock group Oasis fitted into all of it. 'Of course. Oasis. Noel and Liam.'

'I'll give you one point for that,' Harris said in the style of Nicholas Parsons. 'Oasis were the Gallagher brothers. These are the Galla-cher brothers. But they do come from Manchester and they are named after Oasis. Mum and dad were a couple of mega fans. The oldest is Noel Gallacher and the youngest Liam. Just like the group.'

'They're nothing more than a Beatles tribute band in my book,' Connor said dismissively.

'Agreed. Was never much of a fan myself. All the songs sounded the same, like Status Quo, although I preferred Noel's voice to Liam's, funnily enough.'

'They totally bombed in America. Even their heroes Lennon and McCartney said they didn't feel like they'd truly made it until they cracked the States.'

'Yes, our American cousins seemed to see through all the hype. Didn't help that they kept falling out on tour, mind you. Anyway, unlike their feuding namesakes, the Noel and Liam I'm talking about are young and a tight-knit unit. Pick a fight with one Gallacher brother, and you've started a feud with them both. They're pretty hardcore. Then again, I'm sure people said that about me once.'

'They still do,' Connor blurted out, the wine loosening his tongue just a little too much.

'Ha, you are funny, Elvis. That's why I like you. News is, the Gallachers are in town.'

This fact alone would be enough to give Connor an exclusive page lead – *OASIS GANGSTERS ROCK SCOTLAND* –

especially as it was clear they had established players like Harris already rattled.

'I'd like to know why they're here,' Harris continued.

'Sure, I'll keep my feelers out,' Connor replied.

'And so shall I.'

Connor had a feeling that Harris would have more success than he would, with his vast resources and network of informants.

'To make this work I will really need a picture of them together,' Connor said, all business.

'I'll find out where they meet and give you a shout.'

'You're not worried about the Gallachers, are you, Colin?'

The gangster gave a short, loud laugh. '"Worried" is not the word. "Curious" is more accurate.'

'Just thought you might be worried they're muscling in on your patch,' Connor pressed further.

'Must penalise you for repetition of the word "worried" there, Elvis' – although Connor was now finding this game of *Just a Minute* every bit as tedious as the radio version – 'but it is true, I'm worried they might upset the applecart. I have business plans in place, and the last thing I need is an unknown quantity turning up. There's too much at stake, especially as I am moving operations into different territories.'

'Care to elaborate?' Connor asked, knowing fine well Harris wouldn't.

'Not really. But in layman's terms I don't want the Gallachers fucking up all my good work.'

'Mind if I quote you?' Connor said. 'As an unnamed source, of course.'

'If you must, but if I were you, I'd wait until you find out what they're actually up to, instead of some wishy-washy story about the Gallachers "muscling in on my patch", don't you think?'

Connor knew Harris was right, but it was still an easy page lead. And news editors liked easy stories, especially if they were readily available for their insatiable daily news list to be presented before the editor at midday conference, when all the heads of departments tried to flog their wares for the next day's paper.

'Okay, I'll let you know what I hear, Colin, and I would appreciate it if you'd do the same for me.'

'Deal,' Harris said, proffering his hand to shake.

'Think things could get messy between you and the Gallachers?' Connor asked bluntly.

Harris laughed for a final time. 'I'm a businessman, Elvis. I prefer business solutions.' He poured the last of the wine into their two glasses, before adding ominously, 'Of course, if that fails then there's always the messy option.'

—

CONNOR CALLED April after leaving the Portman on his way to catch the subway to his West End flat.

'Don't be surprised if you get a bottle of something through the post from Harris.'

'Oh, I like Harris Gin,' she said.

Connor could hear her still typing on her laptop. 'Not the Isle of Harris, from Colin Harris.'

'You didn't give him my address, did you?'

'He didn't ask. I presume he's got it. He seems to know where everyone lives.'

April's concern didn't last long. 'What's he sending me?'

'Don't know. I said you'd drink anything.'

'Cheeky bugger,' April replied as Connor hung up. Her eyes settled on the beautiful flute-edged, blue-bottomed bottle of Harris Gin in her drinks cabinet. She checked her wall clock; it had just gone 7 pm and she had been working on her Harry Hanlon book all afternoon. It was definitely G&T time.

20

Surveillance
MAY 7TH

Dugdale had welcomed the chance to start up the surveillance operation of the Macarena on his own, even if it had meant working on a gloriously hot Saturday night, when he could have been having a barbecue at his folks' instead. But he needed time to think, away from the highly unpredictable DCI Crosbie. He was still considering calling DI Hunt to ask his advice, but he had a feeling his old instructor would talk him into turning whistle-blower and report Crosbie's vicious attack on Wise Guy. It was a serious-enough assault to see anyone rightly jailed, but if Dugdale flagged it up he would not only be ending Crosbie's career but most likely his own, as no one ever wanted to work with a whistle-blower. It would also likely sound the death knell on the entire Harry Hanlon investigation before it had even properly got started. So, instead, he bit his tongue and kept quiet.

But it was hard. His conscience barely let him sleep. He could still hear the wrist snapping loudly in his head. However, it was the look of pain, anguish and confusion all over the young man's face that troubled him the most. The victim had been minding his own business when Crosbie had goaded him to strike first. He had looked to Dugdale for help and got none. *Semper Vigilo* – Always Vigilant – was Police Scotland's motto and Dugdale had failed to uphold the basic principles of keeping citizens safe at the first time of asking.

He tried to put his thoughts to one side and concentrate on the comings and goings from the Macarena. A council worker had given the trainee detective access to an empty flat directly across from the Hanlon's home.

Dugdale already knew from his limited experience that a surveillance van, however innocuous, would attract attention from a community suspicious of any strange vehicle. In this part of the world, they were either TV licence detector vans, covert teams from the Department for Work and Pensions, or the cops. All were as welcome as an outbreak of Ebola in the Ruck.

The council worker happily informed Dugdale that the flat was a 'piss palace' when he had let him into the abandoned apartment. The smell of stale urine and who-knows-what-else had been an assault on all his senses.

'Last person who lived here was a junkie,' the council worker told him. 'Died when he tried to strip out the wiring to sell the copper. Daft bastard forgot to switch the mains off first. Now we've got to go round every council property putting up notices saying you're in "danger of electrocution if you tamper with the wiring".'

Dugdale thanked him for his help before adding the warning, 'Not a word I'm in here to anyone. Okay? If the Hanlons find out, I'll know who told them.'

The old council worker eyed the young cop up and down. 'No need to threaten me, son. I've lived here all my life and learned a long time ago it's best to avoid the Hanlons at all costs. They're bad news. They also have eyes and ears everywhere. So here's my advice to you, son. Watch yourself. The Hanlons don't care who gets hurt, even a young cop like yourself.'

Dugdale had been well and truly put in his place by the older man. He berated himself for his clumsy attempt at acting the bad cop. It was the sort of thing DCI Crosbie would have pulled off successfully. He feared he was already picking up worrying habits from his mentor and he didn't like it.

Half an hour later, the first of the Saturday night party guests began to arrive at the Macarena, keeping Dudgale's camera shutter busy. It may have only been 8 p.m. but the rave was already in full swing. He noticed that none of the revellers had 'carry-outs', that uniquely Scottish phrase for a bag of clinking bottles of alcohol. There was a time when no self-respecting Scot would arrive at any social occasion without a 'carry-out', so these people either knew that all the drinks were on the house or it was the sort of party where powder was preferred to Pernod. The detective suspected he was probably right on both counts.

The noise was loud enough to make the windows of the commandeered apartment vibrate, especially the 'thump, thump, thump' from whatever god-awful music they were playing through their powerful sound system. Dugdale was a young man – he'd just turned twenty-eight – but the sort of sounds emanating from across the road were lowest common denominator stuff, as far as he was concerned. Bass-heavy brain rot pumped out to kids off their heads on drugs. It had been little wonder many residents had been forced to leave the street, with the anti-social Hanlons virtually unstoppable now they could afford the very best Queen's Counsel – in the shape of Paul McFadden – to fight their legal battles for them.

By half four in the morning most of the revellers were leaving. With the spring dawn light, Dugdale was able to snap them all again as they left the Macarena.

'It's like *The Walking Dead*,' he whispered to himself. It had just gone 5 am when he captured the last stragglers departing before texting Crosbie: *Got over forty faces, sir.*

The three dots instantly appeared on his iPhone, meaning Crosbie was already up, or hadn't been to sleep in the first place.

Brilliant. Meet me at 8 am. Sunday breakfast is on me.

Dudgale checked his watch again. If he was lucky, he could grab three hours' sleep before he had to meet his boss.

———

CROSBIE, on the other hand, turned over in bed to embrace his neighbour's wife: '*é, stato una bella scopata.*'

'I love it when you speak Italian. It's so damn sexy. What did you say?' she asked.

'You're a good shag.'

'It's probably best I don't ask for the translation, kind of ruins the moment,' she said, but pulled Crosbie closer anyway.

'I only speak-a da truth,' he replied in a terrible Italian accent as he disappeared beneath the duvet again.

21

Manners maketh man
JANUARY 13TH

Harry had agreed that April could interview his disabled son, Billy, but she still had to get past his younger brother and carer, Michael, who insisted sitting in on the conversation. It was a fraught situation, with Michael intervening from the start over the most basic line of questioning, before April finally snapped.

'Michael, it is virtually impossible to conduct an interview if you interrupt like an American courtroom lawyer every few moments. The whole art of any interview is to build up rapport, which I cannot do with you chirping in all the time. It's also the height of bad manners.'

Her stinging rebuke seemed to hit home, especially the accusation about a lack of manners. Michael believed manners maketh man and prided himself on instilling them in Billy. He apologised sheepishly.

'So, Billy, let's start again,' April said. 'You seem a very happy man. Do you feel happy all the time?'

'Aye.'

'"Yes", Billy.' Michael gently reprimanded his brother before apologising for interrupting again.

'Yes, I am happy. Most of the time.'

'When are you at your happiest, Billy?' April pressed.

'With Michael. And going to day centre. I have friends at the centre.'

April noted that Billy's sentences were no longer than five words, common with many learning-disabled people. But he spoke coherently, obviously under constant coaching from his younger brother.

'And when are you not happy, Billy?'

'I don't like parties. Too loud. I can't sleep. They go on all night. Then all day. Then all night.'

April shuddered at the thought. 'Do you join in, Billy?'

'No really...'

'"Not" really, Billy,' Michael corrected him again.

April asked, 'What do you mean by "not really"?'

'I want to be left alone. But sometimes they'll come get me.'

'Come and get you?'

'Yes. If Michael's not here. They'll come and get me. They make me do things.'

April dreaded where this was going. 'Like what, Billy?'

'They push me in the hot tub. And other things...'

'They make him fight, Ms Lavender,' Michael explained. 'I came home once to find Billy taking part in a bare-knuckle fight. Apparently, the joke is you can punch my brother repeatedly in the face without eliciting a response. But when he does eventually react, the results are spectacular. It's like poking the bear. Even in his wheelchair he can still pack quite a punch.'

'They'll punch Billy in his wheelchair?' April said, aghast. 'That's horrendous.'

'Oh, it gets a lot worse than that,' Michael said, looking at his brother with a sense of hopelessness. 'They get him drunk and stoned, too.'

'Who does these things?' April demanded. 'His other brothers and sisters? Your father?'

'No, just the dregs that come along for a free booze-up. My dad is usually too out of his face to notice.'

April changed tack; she could see the memories of the parties were leaving the young man agitated. 'Billy, do you know your father is a very rich man?'

'Rich man,' Billy repeated.

'Does his money mean anything to you?'

'Rich man,' Billy said again, laughing this time.

'What's so funny about that, Billy?' April asked gently.

'Sorry to interrupt again, Ms Lavender, but my brother has no concept of money whatsoever. Whether my father has £100 or £100 million makes no difference to him. I've tried teaching him the basics but sadly it is one thing which simply does not register. A blessing in many ways, not knowing you're living on the breadline when your father is so wealthy.'

'The breadline?'

'Yes, my father believes that we should all earn our own way in life, like he did. He's most intransigent when it comes to Billy, as he says the state should pay for him.'

'And what about your studies?' April asked. 'When do you start university?'

'September,' Michael replied, glumly.

'You don't exactly look thrilled.'

'I have a lot on my mind,' Michael said, glancing in his brother's direction.

April had expected her book to look like a shopping catalogue, with a list of price tags from all the cars and holidays bought by the Hanlons. Instead, she had a story of a family being given this once-in-a-lifetime opportunity, only for it to hit their home like a lightning strike, briefly illuminating their existence before destroying all in its path.

April looked at the brothers sitting together, happy in one another's company. United. She suddenly felt a crushing sadness. Michael was trying to hold it all together – to keep his vulnerable brother safe. But it was a losing battle and he was failing because looking after Billy was a full-time job that someone with a place in medical school could never manage alone. It had always been survival of the fittest in the Ruck, and April feared for them both.

22

Results

MAY 8TH

DCI Crosbie was already sitting at the back of the trendy coffee shop across from his flat in Glasgow's West End, eating a bacon baguette with a skinny latte while flicking through the Sunday newspapers, when a bleary-eyed Dugdale joined him.

'You look like shit,' Crosbie said.

'Matches how I feel, sir. Not much sleep.'

'Sleep is for losers, Duggie. Right, what've you got?' Crosbie stuffed the last chunk of his bread roll into his mouth.

Dugdale checked over both shoulders before sliding an iPad across the table.

'Christ, you look like you're doing a drug deal.' Crosbie chuckled.

'Just don't want anyone seeing, sir.'

Crosbie started swiping his greasy finger across the screen as he scanned the pictures, giving a running commentary. 'Waster, junkie, twat, prick, village idiot, slut, mega slut, wanker…'

On and on he went, leaving Dugdale both amazed at how easily the profanities flowed and embarrassed at how his boss seemed oblivious to the fact he was attracting looks from other customers.

'Ah,' Crosbie said, jabbing at one particular photo, 'Hammy the Hamster. Haven't seen him in a long time.' The

DCI seemed lost in thought when a sullen waitress appeared to take Dugdale's order. The new recruit cleared his throat to warn his superior they had company.

'Ah, it's joyous Jackie.' Crosbie smiled, switching off the iPad screen. 'My rather sleepy young colleague here could probably do with a coffee and a bacon roll.'

Dugdale nodded his approval, and Jackie scribbled on her notepad before heading back to the kitchen without saying a word.

Crosbie watched her go and commented, 'I come here for the ambience, of course.'

'I think you should be careful with that iPad, sir,' Dugdale warned. 'Don't want word getting out about the surveillance.'

Crosbie was about to reprimand Dugdale over his mild rebuke, but thought better of it. 'You're probably right, Duggie. Okay, I think we'll start with this character. The Hamster. A nasty piece of work.'

'The Hamster, sir?'

'Yes, because he burrows weapons all over the place. Drink that coffee. You'll need to be on your toes for this character.'

'I was going to get some shut-eye, sir,' Dugdale complained.

'You'll get all the sleep you need when you're dead, which may be sooner rather than later working for me. I'm taking you to see the Hamster. He knows everything that goes on in the Ruck. He probably even knows who killed Harry Hanlon. If I ask politely, he may even tell me.'

'That sounds easy, sir.'

'Ah, but you haven't met the Hamster,' Crosbie added, winking at his trainee.

Dugdale was already dreading another repeat of the wrist-snapping incident.

23

Gratuity
JANUARY 14TH

The guests arguing inside one of the Marsden's leather-clad booths had earned furtive glances from the restaurant staff. Eventually, they had got rowdy enough for the maître d' to intervene.

'Would you like another drink, gentlemen?' It was said loudly and firmly enough to gain their attention.

'Nah, just the bill,' a strong Mancunian accent demanded. The maître d' was glad they would be leaving without a fuss. It was a Saturday night and the restaurant was jam-packed. As he left their table he lingered just long enough to overhear the Mancunian saying to his dinner guest, 'You promised us big numbers and we're getting shit here. Where I come from, a promise is written in stone.'

The maître d' had fine-tuned his listening abilities over the many years working in the trade to sift out the normal restaurant din to home in on what people were saying. He had heard many things of great interest – from the salacious, which would grace a newspaper gossip column, to crown prosecutors discussing the strengths and weaknesses of their cases. The maître d' had discovered long ago that much of what he saw and overheard had monetary value, if you knew the right people. And being head waiter at Glasgow's premier restaurants, he knew all the right people and all the players. The

Mancunians were new faces but their threat had very much been directed at one Robert 'Shifty' Hanlon.

Shifty begrudgingly settled the bill, using cash, which was highly unusual for most of the Marsden's clientele but did help separate the business and legal profession regulars from the drug dealers. All the criminals settled their bills in cash. The maître d' knew their names and faces well.

Shortly after Shifty and his English guests left, the maître d' informed his deputy he was taking a cigarette break. Even though it was dry outside, he pulled on a rain jacket over his uniform, to make sure it wouldn't smell of smoke. He exited through the kitchens to the alleyway behind the restaurant where the bins were kept and there was no chance of being spotted by any patrons or, just as importantly, the proprietor. He lit up and leaned his back against the brick wall and called someone he knew would be interested in what he had just heard.

After just a few rings, his call was answered.

'And that's exactly what you heard them say? "You promised us big numbers and we're getting shit here. Where I come from, a promise is written in stone".'

'That's exactly what I heard,' the maître d' assured his contact.

'Let me write this down,' the person down the line said, as he made the maître d' slowly repeat the phrase again.

'They also booked a table for the night after tomorrow. Same time.'

'Most interesting,' Colin Harris said. 'Most interesting, indeed.'

The maître d' didn't know it then, but Harris wrote '£500' beside the initials MD in his ledger, in his flowing handwriting style that had been self-taught during his last lengthy stint inside. That was the tip the maître d' would receive the next time Harris dined at the Marsden, making everything legal and above board. Just the way Harris now liked business to be done.

24

Hammy
MAY 8TH

DCI Crosbie led Dugdale past the main entrance door, where a half brick kept it permanently wedged open, not that the apartment block would have been very secure anyway as the intercom entry system was hanging from the wall. Like many of the door entry systems in Ruckhouse, it was only being held up by its mass of multicoloured wires.

'Damn shame what they've done to this place,' Crosbie said. 'The council spend a fortune doing up the flats, only for their scumbag residents to wreck them.'

Dugdale gave a non-committal shrug. He didn't tend to go in for mass generalisations.

'And this chap we're visiting really is the lowest of the low. Hamish Hutchinson. Almost two dozen convictions for fighting, and that's just with the police. It's made him some sort of cult hero around these parts. They've even got a song for him.'

Crosbie started to hum an indecipherable tune, as he tried to recall the lyrics. Suddenly he remembered them:

> *'Don't fight with Hammy,*
> *Don't fight him, son,*
> *Don't fight with Hammy,*
> *He'll rip you another one.'*

'It's rather a catchy little ditty, isn't it?' he remarked while knocking on an apartment door that looked like it had been kicked in as many times as the Hamster had been arrested. There was no answer. Crosbie tried again, before adding, 'Rise and shine, Hammy. It's a lovely Sunday morning and your friendly Detective Chief Inspector Bing Crosbie is paying you a visit.'

They heard movement behind the door and Crosbie said, 'Come on, Hammy, I can hear you scuttling about like the little rodent that you are. Open up.'

'What the fuck do you want?' a nasally voice said from within.

'A wee chat, is all. About the Hanlons. I heard you were at the Macarena last night.'

'Aye, so what if I was.' And with that, the door flew open to reveal a small, wiry, sickly-looking man brandishing a huge crossbow. Crosbie hit the weapon upwards as the Hamster discharged the arrow, which rebounded off the hallway's concrete ceiling before narrowly missing Dugdale's head. The arrow had been so close that the trainee had actually felt the air being displaced at the back of his neck.

Crosbie flew at their attacker, propelling him down the hallway, causing Hammy to land heavily on his head. The detective followed it up by kicking him as hard as he could in the ribs.

'Jeez, Hammy, that was like booting a bag of spanners. I think you've broken my foot,' Crosbie complained.

'Go fuck yourself, Bing,' Hammy spat back.

'You're not a great host, are you, sunshine? Still hungover?' Crosbie then told Dugdale to close Hammy's front door, which he did reluctantly. He knew what the DCI got up to when out of sight. Crosbie delivered another hefty boot, this time to Hammy's guts, causing the man to let out whatever air had been in his lungs. He lay crumpled and winded, unable to even spit out a curse in the detective's direction. Dugdale dreaded to think what his boss would do next. He debated whether he should intervene, although he was pretty sure Crosbie had just saved him from being shot by a crossbow bolt.

'What the fuck do you want?' Hammy managed to finally grunt through gasps for breaths.

'How about a cup of tea?' Crosbie replied breezily as he hauled Hammy to his feet and propelled him towards the kitchen. Crosbie filled the kettle and managed to locate the last of three teabags from a box on the empty shelves. After finding some cups, he went hunting for a teaspoon. 'Have you got any spoons left, Hammy, or have you used them all for cooking up your smack?'

'Fuck you,' Hammy replied, more confidently this time, having regained his breath and his composure. Dugdale hoped Hammy would be more cooperative as he had witnessed enough violence as it was.

'There aren't any differences in the world that can't be settled by a cup of tea,' Crosbie said, stirring the bags around the cups of hot water with the end of a fork. 'I'm afraid we'll have to have it without milk, fellas, as I dread to think what state Hammy's fridge is in. I'm scared to look.'

'Fuck you,' Hammy responded again, his black, sunken eyes now burning fiercely in his skull-like face.

'Hammy, I'm only after one piece of information then I'll gladly leave you alone. Heck, I'll even overlook your attempted murder of two police officers with an illegal weapon.'

Hammy put one finger to his cheek and looked at the ceiling as if in a deep train of thought, before replying, 'Well, since you've put it like that, Bing. Fuck. You.' Hammy wasn't quick enough to shield his genitals before Crosbie's right foot made full contact, which left him crumpled on the floor yet again, moaning like a wounded animal. The DCI then put his foot on the side of Hammy's neck and started pushing his full weight downwards. Dugdale made to say something but Crosbie placed his index finger to his mouth as if to say, 'Sshh.' Hammy moaned louder and louder the more Crosbie pressed down, but he eventually managed to ask, 'What do you fucking want?'

'Who killed Harry Hanlon?' Crosbie asked.

'How the fuck should I know?' Hammy spat back.

'You know everything, Hammy. Come on, you were

partying into the wee small hours at the Macarena last night. You must've heard a name?'

'I've heard nothing. And even if I had, I wouldn't tell a prick like you.'

'Come on, Hammy. Just tell me what you've heard. Even a theory. What have you got?'

'Nothing.'

Crosbie now raised himself fully upright so the full weight of his body was bearing down on the Hamster's neck, bringing it to breaking point.

'You're going to snap my fucking neck.' Hammy screamed in agony.

'Sir, I really don't think…' Dugdale said, but was once again told to be quiet by his superior.

'Come on, Hammy, before I start jumping up and down. Who do you think killed Harry?'

'Shifty. Alright? I've heard Shifty did it.'

Crosbie stepped off the Hamster's neck. 'Elaborate.'

'What?' the Hamster said, rubbing his reddened neck.

'Tell me more.'

'There's nothing to tell. All I know is, Shifty was asked by just about everyone last night if he did in his old man and he didn't say no.'

'So he's happy to let people think he's man enough to kill his father, is that what you're saying?'

'Yeah. That's all I know, but I'll fucking deny it in court, okay? It's not evidence. It could be a load of crap. Shifty is probably lying. Who gives a shit?'

'You're probably right,' Crosbie agreed.

'Now get to fuck out my flat.'

'Gladly,' Crosbie said, turning to leave. Just then the Hamster picked up a large knife from a kitchen block and lunged for the DCI's back. But not quickly enough. Crosbie turned and threw his mug of piping hot black tea directly in his assailant's face. The stainless steel knife clattered to the floor and the Hamster let out a piercing scream, his hands clasped over both eyes as he fell to his knees before rolling into the foetal position. Dugdale considered helping Hammy, but thought better of it. Instead, the detectives left him in that position. Dugdale didn't feel as bad as when Crosbie had broken an innocent man's wrist. He was worried he was becoming numb to the violence; that DCI Crosbie's blasé attitude to inflicting pain was beginning to rub off on him. His boss closed the front door behind him and began humming the Hammy tune:

> *'Don't fight with Hammy,*
> *Don't fight him, son,*
> *Don't fight with Hammy,*
> *He'll rip you another one.'*

Dugdale was beginning to wonder what he had let himself in for. Nothing he'd learned at police college had prepared him for this. Then again, he knew nothing could prepare anyone for the likes of DCI Crosbie.

25

Tip-off

JANUARY 16TH

Are you free right now?

Connor read the WhatsApp message from Colin Harris and sighed. He had been watching *Hollyoaks* with Natasha, the eight-year-old daughter of his Russian girlfriend, Anya. It was quite possibly the worst soap opera in the history of the genre, yet weirdly compelling. It was also on at the perfect time to eat, meaning they could both watch in silence while having dinner. Every family expert would tell you watching the television at meal times was ill-advised, as this was supposed to be a time to converse, but Connor reckoned that these experts hadn't been exposed to the addictive qualities of *Hollyoaks*.

Not really, I'm baby-sitting, Connor typed back, hiding behind his parental duties.

Got a good one for you... Harris replied, deliberately teasing.

Connor was now intrigued. He knew Harris was boastful and a show-off, but he also knew he rarely bothered him out of hours unless it was juicy.

This better be worth missing Hollyoaks for, Connor wrote.

This will open up a whole new soap opera for you, Elvis. Get your backside down to the Marsden with a snapper. Check out who Shifty Hanlon is dining with. And if you order the soup, make sure you get a 'Roll With It'.

Connor looked at the message and swore. He did not

fancy going out tonight as the snow had come on heavy again, but Harris had found the Gallacher brothers first, hence his cheesy reference to the Oasis song. He was now going to have to trudge with Natasha through the blizzard to take her to her mother's restaurant.

He texted the photographer, Jack Barr, asking if he was available and got an almost instant response: *I am but can it wait till the end of Hollyoaks? There's a hostage situation.*

Connor laughed and typed his reply: *There's a hostage situation every fecking week – meet me down at the Marsden.*

Ok, as long as I don't get lost in this whiteout, Jack messaged back. He was just as reluctant to leave the warmth of his home as Connor was.

———

THE MARSDEN WAS PACKED when Connor arrived. He was shown to a single seat at the bar by the maître d'. That suited Connor perfectly: he was able to use the giant mirrors behind the vast array of spirits and whiskies to observe discreetly what was going on. He also didn't mind being sand-wiched in between two overweight businessmen; he always liked visiting this place. It had an old-world feel, with the dark mahogany woods and waiters in starched white cotton aprons wrapped around their immaculate black suits. This was an establishment that took pride in its appearance, although Connor always wished they took more pride in their cooking, which he always felt was distinctly average.

He scanned the menu for the cheapest option, knowing full well that any amount was difficult to claim on expenses these days. When Connor first started his newspaper career, virtually straight from school, some of the older hacks had told him how to 'fiddle his eccies'. They would buy packets of restaurant receipts by giving waiters a bung, submitting claims for fictitious meals with contacts they never met or who might never have existed. Journalists would also swap the blank receipts between their peers on rival newspapers so as not to arouse suspicion in their respective accounting departments. It was a dyed-in-the-wool scam that had been going on since the birth of newspapers. Connor even remembered one sports reporter boasting how he would pay his monthly mortgage on the 'profit' earned from his expenses alone.

Or when a squad of journalists would take taxis to Perth races for the day, a return trip of hundreds of miles, all paid for on the fabled taxi 'chit', very much like a blank cheque, which made drivers fortunes and earned journalists friends for life, or at least until the chits began to dry up. As technology advanced, so did their scams, with an ex-colleague able to print off a variety of restaurant receipts, complete with genuine VAT numbers, on a new laser printer he'd bought himself, and which paid for itself in bogus claims within the first month.

All these old hacks had either been paid off like April, or died like Connor's mentor, Graeme Blackwood, a hard-living newspaper man who drank himself to death by fifty-five.

Connor didn't go in for nostalgia much. That was from a long-forgotten era which was never coming back. Sure, he had experienced the tail end of the newspaper excesses and they had been fun while they lasted. But in the here and now, Connor was trying to keep tabs on the ambitions of Shifty Hanlon and a notorious crime clan from Manchester, without earning a missive from his managing editor. He ordered the crab cakes, which at £9.50 he would just about get away with claiming on expenses. Although he would pay for his beer separately as alcohol was always questioned, and he didn't want to look suspicious as the only person not drinking at the bar.

Connor stared into the smoked-glass mirrors to observe the meeting taking place over his shoulder. He could hear the thick Mancunian accents in between bouts of laughter as the table guests tucked into several bottles of wine.

From a distance, Connor couldn't help thinking how much the eldest Hanlon looked like his trio of associates. He was wearing the same smart casual designer clothes and also must have been working out, with his bulked muscular frame easy to observe under his tight-fighting pullover. Connor then realised Shifty Hanlon was desperately trying to emulate the Manchester crew. To look like and be accepted by them. They must seem exotic to someone who had spent his life in the Ruck. Colin Harris, with his sagging middle-age spread, was strictly old school compared with this lot. He could see why Shifty would favour them rather than dealing with Harris. Connor suspected Harris would treat Shifty like the street-corner, drug-dealing thug that he was, and not as an equal. But here he was in an upmarket restaurant, virtually getting slaps on the back from some of the biggest players in the north of England. He must feel like a big man. It was just a pity that this Manchester mob would inevitably be using poor, dim-witted Shifty Hanlon as their pawn. The Gallachers were no doubt keen for Shifty to open up the lucrative Ruckhouse market to them, spreading even more despair and misery, while keeping an eye on his father's fortune at the same time. Connor knew this would end badly. This lot would take Shifty to the cleaners.

The journalist paid for his beer out of his own pocket then asked for a receipt for his food, which he paid by credit card. The split bill earned him a look of rebuke from the waiter, who obviously thought such trifling matters were beneath him. One thing Connor cared little for was anyone's opinions about themselves. He didn't care who he upset or annoyed, a fact reflected in the 50p tip he left behind to deliberately get up the snooty waiter's nose.

Outside, he could see Jack Barr sitting outside a coffee shop on the pedestrian precinct. He huddled for warmth under a patio heater, with a large backpack on the opposite seat no doubt covering his long-lens camera. Connor took his place beside him and ordered a coffee. He was relieved to see the blizzard had stopped so Jack would be able to snatch the Gallachers and Shifty Hanlon when they eventually left. He just hoped they wouldn't be spotted, although Jack usually moved so quickly that the pictures were taken and the camera hidden again with his targets none the wiser.

Back inside the Marsden, the atmosphere between the Gallachers and Shifty had turned decidedly frosty – just like on the previous occasion – as negotiations now moved on to concluding the deal, something the English brothers had vastly more experience of than the eldest Hanlon.

'Are you sure you can get hold of the readies?' Noel Gallacher asked directly.

'Of course,' Shifty replied confidently.

'One million is a lot of dough,' Liam said.

'It's a drop in the ocean when you've got access to a hundred million.' Shifty was now feeling cocksure. He liked being flash and talking numbers; it made him feel like a player.

'We don't like being mucked about,' Noel warned. 'If you want class A goods then you have to pay class A prices. Upfront.'

'Look, my dad has already said he'll lend me the money so we're good to go.' Shifty smiled, showing off his rows of wonky, tobacco-stained teeth. His attempt to emulate the Gallachers hadn't extended to any dental work.

'If we take the risk of bringing the goods up from Manchester then there will be no backing out.'

'There won't be any backing out,' Shifty promised.

'You'll find we have a very short fuse if you do,' Liam added.

Shifty Hanlon knew all about the Gallacher brothers' modus operandi of using hand grenades to settle disputes. 'Here's to making millions together,' he said, raising his glass, desperately trying to change the subject.

'To millions,' the Gallachers said simultaneously.

Now Shifty just had to work out a way of making his dad part with the money, which he knew would be easier said than done.

26

Disobeying orders
MAY 8TH

Dugdale had decided to ignore Crosbie's advice and approached the previous senior investigating officer who had been in charge of the Hanlon inquiry. DCI Stuart Urquhart was the type who played everything by the book – the complete antithesis to Crosbie. He also had little time for the lower ranks, and trainee detective was about as low as it got in Urquhart's eyes, but he seemed to take pity on the newbie when he discovered who his mentor was.

'So you're the poor bastard recruited by Crosbie? Word of warning, sonny, be careful with that loose cannon. He can go off at any time.'

Dugdale was getting used to being warned about Crosbie, and he changed the subject: 'Sir, it says in your report you searched for the DVR?'

'Too right we did. We knew one of those scumbag Hanlons had hidden it. And if they'd gone to all the bother of doing that then it also meant it had recorded incriminating evidence. We turned their home inside out but couldn't find it. We then had all the Hanlons watched and tailed, but none of them left the house with anything that looked remotely like a DVR. They're quite bulky boxes so it would have been diffi-cult to conceal.'

'Can you remember where your team tailed them to, sir?'

'Off the top of my head, Robert Hanlon went to the Woodchopper and staggered home pished – his father would have been so proud. Kendal returned to her house. She carried nothing bigger than her handbag. The triplets didn't leave the Macarena at all.'

'And Michael and Billy, sir?'

'To their day centre, where they always went. But they carried nothing with them. That DVR disappeared into thin air. I can assure you, young man, if it had been in that god-awful house of theirs we would have found it.'

'Thank you, sir,' Dugdale replied.

Urquhart studied the trainee detective for a moment then said, 'Once Crosbie fucks up this case, there could be a position available on my team ... That's if you haven't picked up too many bad habits.'

'Thank you, sir,' Dugdale replied again. But career advancement was the furthest thing from his mind. Right now, he was determined to find that DVR.

WHILE HIS MENTEE was disobeying his direct order, Crosbie poured over the forensics report for the umpteenth time. He flicked through the graphic crime scene photos again before he came to the section about unidentified DNA found from a blood sample taken from the base of the knife handle. There was a high probability it was left by whoever had been holding the weapon at the moment it had entered Harry Hanlon's back.

DNA profiling of all the Hanlons had been denied by the family's lawyer, Paul McFadden, until certain assurances were given that Police Scotland were not prepared to make. Crosbie decided to summon McFadden to a meeting. He knew he would have to meet Scotland's self-proclaimed top barrister at some point and now was the ideal time.

27

Runners and riders
JANUARY 18TH

'Here, what do you make of Jilly Cooper? Another number one bestseller,' April said as she took her seat at the Peccadillo café.

'You are so random. I honestly never know what you'll say next.' Connor sat down across from April and placed a copy of that day's *Daily Chronicle* on the table.

'I know, but she's in her seventies. It means there's hope for us all. I could become a bestseller. You know, once I've got this lottery book done, I could move into romantic fiction. People being swept off their feet. Oh, did I tell you Carol had the baby?'

'Who the fuck is Carol?'

'My neighbour. Do try and keep up. I've told you before. She's forty-nine. Already had three grown-up kids of her own and bam, a little miracle came out of the blue.'

Connor shuddered at the thought of becoming a parent at that age. 'We haven't even ordered yet and you've switched from bonkbusters to babies in almost the same breath. Is it any wonder I'm confused?'

'That's how Jayne came along.'

'What are you talking about now?'

'I had been reading that Jilly Cooper novel *Riders* and one thing lead to another with Husband Number One. I was even going to call her Jilly.'

'That'd have been better than calling her Riders.'

'Riders Lavender has a certain grandeur to it, don't you think?'

'No, it doesn't. It sounds like a porn name.'

'How is it you come up with your porn name again?'

'What your first pet was called, followed by your mother's maiden name.'

April thought for a second before she burst out laughing. 'Naomi Tickles,' she managed to say before dissolving in another fit of laughter interspersed with a raspy, hacking smokers' cough.

'Your mum was a Tickles?'

'Yip. Couldn't wait to get married.'

'No wonder.'

'And yours?'

'Boring. Fred Evans. Doesn't work,' Connor replied.

The waitress, Martel, approached their table to take April's order, while purposely avoiding all eye contact with Connor.

'We were just swapping our porn names. What's yours, Martel?' Connor said, crowbarring himself into their conversation. The waitress stared at him expressionlessly for a moment, before silently mouthing 'Fuck you', and heading for the kitchen.

'You know it's just a hunch, but I don't think she likes you very much,' April said, trying to contain her mirth.

'You reckon, Miss Tickles?' he said and swivelled the newspaper around on the tabletop so April could read it.

'*LOTTO WINNER'S SON GANGSTER CONNECTIONS*,' she read aloud. 'Oh, and you wrote it.'

Jack Barr had perfectly captured Robert 'Shifty' Hanlon looking decidedly like his nickname as he left the Marsden with the Gallacher brothers. The snapshot sat under the splash headline, screaming out from the front page.

'They sound like a right bunch of heavies,' April said as she read on. Connor had forgotten her irritating quirk of reading the newspaper with a stream of commentary.

Although, now he spent most of his days sitting all alone in his broom cupboard office, he rather missed it.

His article had introduced the Gallachers' long list of crimes and convictions to the readers, including their penchant for using hand grenades in disputes, which had also earned them the title of the 'Boom Boom Brothers' by the media down south. There were plenty of insider quotes, courtesy of Colin Harris, explaining how Shifty was using his father's money to bankroll a rapid expansion of operations with Noel and Liam Gallacher. It was the perfect tabloid fodder of lottery, crime and even a hint of showbiz, with the Oasis connection. The editor had also used a photograph of the real Noel and Liam just in case readers had forgotten what they looked like, even though it breached editorial guidelines by linking someone to a story that they had absolutely nothing to do with. But Connor's editor knew full well that the last thing the Gallaghers' representatives would want to do was complain and add more unwanted publicity. And anyway, being associated with real-life gangsters would do little to damage their bad boy, rock and roll image.

At the end of the article there was the obligatory 'no comment' issued on behalf of Robert Hanlon by the family lawyer, Paul McFadden.

'So what was McFadden like when you called him up? Furious?' April asked, having been on the receiving end of the lawyer's stinging rebukes in the past.

'Not really,' Connor replied, 'but he did tell me I was way off.'

'So your story's wrong?' April asked.

'No, because I had actually witnessed Shifty meeting the Gallachers in the Marsden. But when I told McFadden that Shifty has been telling everyone his dad is bankrolling his whole business operation, he said, "Whatever that idiot gets up to, his father has nothing to do with it."'

'Yeah, I'd have to go along with McFadden on that one,' April said. 'Harry's the meanest man I know. Can't see him bankrolling anything.'

'That's almost exactly what he said,' Connor replied.

'I think Harry wants to be buried with all his money,' April said as she finished her breakfast.

Shifty being bankrolled by his dad was the narrative sold to Connor by Harris. But now he was pretty sure that was untrue, which meant Harris had another motive for putting that story out there – as if he wanted the focus to be completely on Shifty, and away from elsewhere.

The reporter inside Connor was now deeply curious. He wanted to know what was really going on.

28

Concessions
MAY 9TH

A bright yellow Ford Mustang revved its engine as it parked up outside Police Scotland's West of Scotland Glasgow HQ in Dalmarnock. A short man in Cuban heels got out, his advocate's robes flapping in the wind to reveal an immaculate suit underneath. In tow was a handsome but harassed young man carrying bundles of folders stuffed with papers. Paul McFadden wasn't the type to lug his own files around.

Crosbie watched McFadden's arrival from his office, which overlooked the entrance of the building. There were many police officers, prosecutors and even judges who feared McFadden, with his sharp legal mind and even sharper tongue, which he used to cut witnesses down to size. Crosbie was about the only person who seemed to relish his jousts – or 'bantz', as he called it – with McFadden.

'Ah, Detective Chief Inspector Crosbie, always a pleasure,' McFadden said as he was shown in. 'I hear you've been busy roughing up the neighbourhood again. Snapping wrists and stamping on "Hamsters". I thought old school police brutality was a thing of the past.'

'Your hearing must be getting worse in your old age,' Crosbie retorted.

McFadden gave a loud, false laugh. The detective had

touched a nerve – the lawyer was as sensitive about his advancing years as he was about his lack of height. He desperately tried to conceal his age by dying his hair blond and using Botox fillers to give his face that Hollywood smooth look. But he couldn't hide his scrawny neck, which had earned him the unkind nickname of Touché Turtle amongst his fellow legal eagles.

'I think you need a different moniker, Bing. I shall call you Rice Krispies from now on.'

'Catchy.' Crosbie yawned.

'Because when you're around it's always snap, crackle and pop.'

'You shouldn't rehearse your quips, McFadden. It makes them sound stilted,' Crosbie said.

'Anyway enough tittle-tattle. I trust you have been busy trying to catch whoever murdered my clients' father?'

'I was hoping they would tell me who did it.'

'Hilarious, DCI Crosbie, your talents are truly wasted with Police Scotland. With your rapier wit, the comedy circuit beckons. Leave now. Quit. Give Billy Connolly a run for his money before it's too late.'

'That your pimp-mobile?' Crosbie said, changing the topic and gazing from his window at the bright yellow eyesore that passed for McFadden's car.

'Do you like it, DCI Crosbie? Customised and specially imported from the States. No change from £50,000. I could have gone for the eco-engine option, of course, but why bother when I could have the full five-litre V8? Fuck the environment, eh?'

'I hear that's not all you fuck,' Crosbie said, casting a glance at McFadden's young assistant.

'Gossip and slander, DCI Crosbie. Spread by those who are jealous of my good looks, success and immense wealth. Believe me, it's a long list. But the only thing I fuck with young Warren here is his pay packet. I barely have him on minimum wage, isn't that right, youngster?'

Browbeaten and demoralised, Warren gave a meek shrug of his shoulders in response.

'He should really be paying me for my brilliance. There

are hundreds – nay, thousands – of young men who would give their eye teeth to be in young Warren's position.'

'It's the position that's got them worried.' Crosbie sniggered.

'Very droll, DCI Crosbie. Warren, make a note for me to see my chiropractor later today. I need to have my ribs reset after laughing so heartily. But if this comedy genius has finished his routine, I would like to discuss the purpose of this meeting. How may I help you?'

'I would like to take DNA swabs from all the Hanlons.'

'On what grounds?' McFadden barked.

'To help with our inquiries,' Crosbie said.

'May I remind you that my clients are grieving relatives, traumatised by losing their father and patriarchal figure in such brutal circumstances?'

'And may I remind you that every one of them was present when Harry was killed but have offered nothing to this investigation?'

'Do not blame Police Scotland's many shortcomings and shoddy investigation on my clients, DCI Crosbie.'

'I am not. But forensics has found a DNA sample on the murder weapon and now I would like to eliminate the grieving relatives from this inquiry. Of course, if they refuse, it might look rather strange to the general public. Joe Bloggs might feel that if you've nothing to hide then there's nothing to worry about.' Crosbie was hinting that he might leak any refusal to the media.

'And I will counter that by telling the gentleman of the press that after Police Scotland's extreme incompetence they have now begun a campaign of harassment against the Hanlons, instead of trying to catch the real killer.'

'We can easily obtain a court order, but I wouldn't want to put the family through any more unnecessary grief,' Crosbie said sarcastically. 'If you force us to go down that path then it will be you who is putting them through the extra trauma.' Crosbie lowered the tone of his voice: 'Paul, let's cut the shit. Get them to take the test then we can get on with clearing their names.'

McFadden gave Crosbie a long, hard stare, no doubt

running a dozen legal permutations through his head at the same time, before capitulating. 'Very well. DNA samples as soon as I've spoken to my clients. But I have a few provisos.'

'I thought you might.' Crosbie sighed.

'Their samples are not to be kept on the police database and they're not to be cross-matched with anything on that database, either. I don't want to suddenly find my clients up for half a dozen other unsolved crimes. Their samples are then to be immediately destroyed and the data deleted, do you understand?'

Crosbie nodded.

'You can only compare my clients' DNA to the unknown sample taken from the base of the murder weapon's handle, and that's it. Once you've agreed to all of that in writing then, yes, you can swab the Hanlons until the cows come home.'

Crosbie nodded again, knowing McFadden had earned the concession points he had probably been after all along.

29

Contact

JANUARY 18TH

The hotel concierge waited until he was out of sight in a back office before he used WhatsApp on his smartphone: *The Gallachers appear to be our guests again.*

The concierge had never heard of the Gallacher brothers until he had received a message from an occasional paymaster to be on the lookout for them. The front-page story from that morning's *Daily Chronicle* then let him know exactly who he was looking for. The brothers had been staying at the plush five-star hotel on the banks of Loch Lomond under an alias, but now their cover was blown and senior management had decided to cut short their stay.

The concierge typed, *They've been told to leave. Anything you want me to pass on?*

My mobile number, came the curt reply.

The concierge wrote it down on the back of his business card and waited until he was showing the brothers to their cars, when he handed it over to the older of the two. 'This gentleman may be able to help with your accommodation needs. And other things.'

Noel Gallacher studied the handwritten name on the card and placed it in his inside pocket. They left, spinning the wheels of their car on the snow-covered gravel, sending a spray of ice and chips showering across the hotel's entrance, a protest at their shortened stay.

Minutes later, Colin Harris received the call he was waiting for.

'What do you want?' Noel asked. He was still pissed off.

'I thought I could help,' Harris replied coolly.

'How?'

'By keeping you off the front page of the papers. I tend to do my business in the shadows, not in the limelight like lottery winners.'

The Gallachers knew they would now be on Police Scotland's radar and they didn't like it.

'Want to meet?' Noel asked.

'Sure,' Harris replied. 'I know a little watering hole where you'll never attract any headlines.'

⎯⎯⎯

JUST LIKE THE rock star brothers they were named after, it was Noel Gallacher who did most of the talking while his younger brother stared almost unblinking at Colin Harris. They had agreed to meet in the gangster's pub, the Portman, although it was the barmaid Mary who was the actual licensee, as Harris's suitability to run a licensed premises would not have stood up to scrutiny under the council's strict 'right and proper' owner laws.

Both Harris and the Gallacher brothers had two minders each who had agreed to wait outside the bar in an uneasy stand-off, to allow the 'businessmen' to talk in private. The dead-eyed regulars paid the English visitors no attention whatsoever.

'So that's what I'm proposing, gentlemen,' Harris said as he refilled their glasses with his favourite Chablis, Les Preuses Grand Cru.

'Why should we ditch Shifty?' Noel asked before he took a sip from his glass then grimaced at the taste.

Harris could barely contain his amazement. He'd never seen anyone turn their nose up at his favourite tipple before.

He sniffed his own glass to make sure the wine wasn't corked. It wasn't.

'Because he's thick as a brick. He got the shallow end of the Hanlon gene pool. He's an amateur. If he was a footballer player, he'd be in the junior leagues and you two gentlemen are strictly Premiership material, from what I can tell.' Harris was laying on the flattery, even though he was still smarting about the wine.

Both Gallachers appeared unmoved by the compliment and stared at Harris in silence. They were quiet for so long he thought they may be trying to communicate telepathically.

'His dad's got £100 million,' Liam said, speaking for the first time during their meeting.

'That's the point. His DAD has got £100 million. Shifty doesn't,' Harris replied.

'We could make him give us it,' Liam continued, leading Harris to conclude that the younger Gallacher was the more volatile of the pair.

'You'll find Harry Hanlon is impervious to any threats, even those against his children.'

Liam raised one of his bushy eyebrows a fraction, which Harris took to mean he didn't understand the word 'impervious'. 'He will be unaffected by any threats to Shifty,' he added, by way of explanation.

'We could always kidnap Shifty,' Liam said.

Harris now knew Noel was the brains, while Liam was a moron. A dangerous moron, but still a moron.

'Look, Liam, you don't want to end up in a situation like John Paul Getty III.' Harris looked at Liam for any sign of recognition of one of the world's most famous kidnap cases, but found none. 'It's messy. Very messy. You will have police and the press crawling all over it. If you are going to kidnap anyone then it has to be someone who is low profile and won't be missed. Perhaps even someone who people think would be better off dead anyway. At least that's what I've found,' Harris said, making an oblique reference to the kidnap and murder of the serial killer Osiris Vance.

The Gallacher brothers had heard Harris tortured someone to death, removing his victim's genitals as a final humiliation. They decided to demonstrate some credentials of their own.

'We could always just blow his old man up,' Liam said, placing a hand grenade on the table.

Over the years Harris had handled many handguns, none of them legal, but he had never actually seen a real hand grenade. He was relieved to see the pin was still in.

'That's how we do business,' Liam added.

How Liam thought blowing up Harry Hanlon would lead to accessing his winnings was beyond him, so he turned his attentions to Noel. 'I am more than aware of you and your brother's reputations, but I believe you get more business done building bridges than blowing them up. Together I believe we can form a prosperous professional partnership. Shifty Hanlon will bring you nothing but problems and excuses.'

The Gallachers shot each other a sideways look. Harris had clearly struck a chord. Liam returned the hand grenade to the pocket of his donkey jacket, for he even dressed like the singer he was named after.

'Shake on it?' Noel asked, offering his hand.

'Sure,' Harris replied, shaking the older brother's hand before doing the same with Liam.

'Now how about a proper drink?' Noel suggested. 'I fucking hate wine.'

Harris had already figured that out. 'Mary, lager for the lads,' he shouted to the barmaid. He was prepared to let the slight against his precious Chablis slide. He knew the Gallachers would never be gentrified like himself, but they would come in handy for his expansion plans.

30

Drug deaths
JANUARY 22ND

Connor lay in bed with Anya on Sunday morning. She was still asleep from the exertions of running a busy restaurant on a Saturday night. This always allowed Connor to read the newspapers online. He still could not understand the logic of giving away all that content for absolutely nothing to the casual browser, whereas loyal customers, who trudged to the shops in all weathers, were charged for the printed version. But he was now guilty of it himself – Connor's breakfast table used to be festooned with the thick weekend newspapers and their accompanying magazines. These days, he read it all on his smartphone, entirely for free.

A small story in the 'Late news' section of the *Chronicle*'s website caught his eye. It most likely wouldn't have made the printed edition as almost all Sunday newspapers were 'off stone' early on a Saturday night. The age-old printing term meant the moment in which an edition of the newspaper was ready for print, and no further changes could be made, unless there was a breaking news event – but it would have to be of some magnitude, as any delays in printing would mean the paper arriving in the shops late and affecting the precious, ever-dwindling, sales. This was something websites never had to worry about. They didn't have the same sort of deadlines. Or loyalty from customers, for that matter.

The report stated that there had been six 'drug-related deaths' on Friday and Saturday in the city. Whenever there had been a cluster of such deaths in the past it was usually due to a batch of contaminated drugs hitting the streets, or sometimes it was heroin that was just too pure, but the police had released a statement saying they did not suspect foul play. Connor noticed four of them were from Ruckhouse and the other two were in neighbouring districts.

Connor texted April, though he didn't expect her to be up yet.

Four junkies OD'd this weekend in the Ruck – hope none of them are Hanlons, or your book will be knackered lol.

To his utter surprise the three dots immediately appeared.

I meant to say to you, Ken told me there've been loads of junkies dying in Glasgow recently.

Ken? Connor typed back.

My neighbour. Retired pharmacist. Lovely garden. Anyway, he reckons there may be a story in all the recent drug deaths. Interested?

Maybe, Connor texted back. He got out of bed and headed downstairs to make a cup of tea and phone April instead.

'Why are you up so early?' he asked.

'I'm in the dog house.'

'How?'

'Got caught smoking.'

'Like a teenager?'

'Yeah, ridiculous isn't it? Anyway, I offered to babysit last night as Jayne was really on my case. Doing the whole guilt-trip thing: "How will Lucy feel when her nana is dying from lung cancer?" So I offered to take Lucy for the night.'

'To shut Jayne up?'

'Exactly. We're going to the hula hoop class again then swimming afterwards.'

'To prove you're fit and healthy and not a knackered old has-been?'

'Yeah, something like that.'

'Listen, what exactly did your neighbour say about the junkie deaths?'

'He asked if I knew any investigative journalists, and I mentioned you, as I'm supposed to be retired. He then said that the junkies' deaths should be looked into. Something about an unusually high amount from Ruckhouse.'

'Was he suggesting it was a contaminated batch of drugs?'

'I don't think so. He said the government's methadone programme was failing. To be honest, it sounded a bit boring to me. I mean, who wants to read about dead junkies? I told him I'd mention that to you. Sorry, I forgot until you texted and jolted my memory.'

'I could use a cattle prod next time, if you wish?' Connor replied.

'No, thanks. Here, let me check. I've got Ken's number somewhere,' April said as she flicked through her ancient Filofax, which at one point had had a black leather cover but was now more of a scuffed, well-worn grey. The writing inside was every colour of ink, from green biro to pink felt-tip. But, amazingly, April could almost find a contact as quickly, and sometimes quicker, than Connor could retrieve them from his iPhone.

'Here it is. Ken Stirling. Nice man. Tell him I passed on his number and if this bloody winter ever ends, I'll come round to check his petunias in the spring.'

'Is that a euphemism for old-person sex?'

'No, silly. When we're arranging that we say, "Geraniums."'

'I thought it would be Geronimo!'

'Sometimes it is. Anyway I'll text you his number,' April said.

'Get you, Bill Gates, you're quite the tech wizard now.'

'Yes, must dash, hula hoop classes beckon.'

A few moments later Connor received a text from April with a mobile number for a contact called Ken Geronimo. *You know I'm going to call him that when I speak to him now*, he texted back.

It had just gone 11 am so now was probably as good a time as any to phone. And Connor got his first laugh when he told Ken he had his deepest sympathy for having April as a neighbour. Then they moved on to the reason for the call.

'The government's methadone programme is an unregulated, out-of-control mess,' Ken explained. 'I've said for years I've been amazed this hasn't been exposed.'

'Where do I start?' Connor asked.

'I'd put a Freedom of Information request in to the NHS. Ask them for a breakdown of how much they pay individual pharmacies, then do the old-fashioned journalist trick of following the money. You'll soon find that where there's cash, there's corruption,' Ken explained.

'So you'd obviously expect big numbers flowing into chemists in places like Ruckhouse?'

'Ruckhouse? Are you kidding? That's like Silicon Valley for the methadone programme. And a fat lot of good it's done, what with all the junkies overdosing this weekend.'

'I reckon that'd be a good place to start then,' Connor pondered.

'I think so. Anything else I can do along the way, please feel free to ask. And thanks for looking into this – it's been a long time coming as far as I'm concerned.'

Connor's journalistic instincts were tingling, but he knew April was right and he would struggle to sell this as a story to his news editor. They were hardly interested in the city's drug addicts, never mind the government's methadone programme. But Connor saw it as his job to make them interested. It was worth firing off an FOI request on Monday morning. After all, you have to cast a line to catch a fish.

31

Houston
MAY 16TH

'Fuck,' Susan Purdie said, her profanity filling the confined spaces of the Scottish Police Authority's Forensic Services laboratory, shocking her colleagues, who were not used to their senior DNA analyst swearing.

'Fuck,' she said again. It had been Susan who'd originally obtained the blood sample from the handle of the knife that had been rammed almost to the hilt in Harry Hanlon's back. It wasn't the first time she had found the culprit's blood at the base of a knife. It had also been Susan who had swabbed the entire Hanlon family after DCI Crosbie had obtained their consent through their advocate Paul McFadden.

And it was she who now held those results in her hand.

'Fuck,' Susan said once more, for good measure.

With her surgically gloved hand, Susan tapped the glass partition, which separated the DNA and fingerprint labs, to gain the attention of her line manager George Houston, who indicated he would be through in a minute. She resisted greeting her boss with 'Houston, we have a problem,' which she was pretty sure he was tired of hearing from his staff. And anyway, Susan wasn't in the mood to joke. She also happened to know that the actual quote was, 'Houston, we've had a problem', but she had got bored correcting people.

'What's up, Suze?' George asked.

That was another thing she couldn't stand, being called Suze. She had asked her boss to address her as Susan long ago, but he kept reverting to Suze, and too much time had now passed to remind him again, lest she embarrass them both.

'As you know, I retrieved a single blood sample from the base of the Hanlon knife that doesn't match the deceased.'

'Indeed,' George said with his usual breezy manner.

'Well, I've now found a match for it from the recent DNA samples I took from the Hanlon family.'

'Fantastic. Then you've probably taken a step closer to putting a killer behind bars.'

'Killers,' Susan replied.

'Killers? I thought you said you only had the one sample?'

'I did say that. But it's a perfect match for the Hanlon triplets.'

'Fuck,' George said, his cheery demeanour immediately vanishing. 'Monozygotic triplets,' he added, rubbing his temples. 'This is going to be a hard one to explain to Bing.'

'I'll do it if you like,' Susan said.

'No, I should do it. He tends to fly off the handle when the evidence screws up his case.'

'Well, I did the tests, so this is my case. I will tell DCI Crosbie he now has three suspects instead of one.'

'He won't like it. He won't like it one bit,' George said, clearly worried.

Susan Purdie had dealt with DCI Crosbie in the past and had always found him to be a chauvinist bastard. She almost looked forward to explaining monozygotic to the misogynistic arsehole.

32

The triplets
JANUARY 24TH

'I can't figure out how the triplets make their money,' April wailed down the phone to Connor.

'Their dad?'

'No, it's never their dad. They were taking regular trips to America before he won.'

April had foregone breakfast at the Peccadillo to catch up on her writing, although she still made sure she had a full fry-up at home before she retreated to her study. Her half-moon reading specs were now balanced on the end of her nose, a mug of coffee was by her side and an illicit cigarette smouldered away in the ashtray beside her laptop, despite yet again promising her daughter Jayne that she had quit for good. If it had been a typewriter instead of a computer, it would have been just like a newsroom of old. April was in the zone.

She had interviewed the Hanlon triplets at the Macarena the day before, when they were still in their pyjamas – matching, of course – and jet-lagged from a trip to Los Angeles. April had diligently asked if they had been on holiday together courtesy of their father, but they had only giggled, before Mo, Jo or Flo had said they were 'always in America', and that was the only detail they were prepared to part with.

April had also quickly concluded that any man thinking of proposing to one of the triplets would be turned down without a thought – these girls loved each other first and foremost and nothing would come between them. She had wondered if there was anything incestuous at play, but she did not have the courage to ask, even though she had tried to broach the subject. April had attempted everything she could think of, including asking if they had any plans to marry, but they would just giggle amongst themselves before giving a 'no', in perfect unison. She concluded the girls inhabited a world of their own and were quite happy living there, with or without their father's new-found fortune.

Slowly but surely, she had been piecing together the Hanlons' life stories. They were a dysfunctional family unit, to say the least, but the triplets were a total enigma.

'How on earth can three girls from the Ruck afford to travel back and forth to America?' April asked Connor. 'I mean, I couldn't afford to do it.'

'I've no idea,' he replied, only half listening as he typed away on his computer at work.

'They go three or four times a year, apparently.'

'Do you know where they fly to?' he asked.

'One of them said Lax, wherever that is.'

'Los Angeles International Airport. Its airport code is LAX.'

'Oh, like Glasgow's is GLA?'

'Exactly. Are they educated? Skilled? Worked as anything before?'

'No, they left school on the same day at sixteen. No qualifications.'

'Good looking, I take it? Nice bodies.'

'Yes, not that I really noticed.'

'Bullshit, women can spot a hot female quicker than men.'

'I suppose. They're attractive and petite, and quite busty young maidens, too.'

'Yeah, leave it with me. I don't think this will take long,' Connor said, hanging up.

He was true to his word. April was just finishing her second cigarette when he called back.

'You owe me a month's subscription,' he said casually.

'For what?'

'I'll send you the link along with my username and password. Once you're logged on give me a buzz.' And with that, he hung up.

April clicked the link that took her to a log-in page. She entered the username and password and was immediately greeted with a video freeze-frame of the naked triplets all brandishing vibrators. She clicked the 'play' button, to see them cavorting together on a couch. She paused the action and called Connor back.

'That's incest.'

'That's big business,' Connor replied nonchalantly.

'And to think we were just discussing porn names,' April said.

'I prefer your Naomi Tickles to theirs – Slutty Teen Triplets.'

'That's not very subtle, is it? And they're not teenagers.'

'Yeah, but they look like teenagers, which is the main thing.'

'And people pay for this?'

'They must do. It just cost me $20 to sign up for a trial month. $40 thereafter.'

'I thought porn was all free on the internet?'

'All the old, amateur, crap stuff is. But specialist porn like the triplets comes at a premium. You can see it's all shot in a studio. I was admiring their high production values.'

'I bet you were. There's a whole other world out there I know nothing about.' She sighed.

'I know. I thought the industry had peaked in the '70s, but apparently not.' April could hear Connor typing before he said, 'Check this out. The global porn industry is estimated to be worth $97 billion, around $12 billion is generated in the States. Jeez, $3 billion of that is child porn.'

April gasped. 'That's terrible.'

'I know. The stats are unbelievable. According to the Huff-Post, porn sites receive more regular traffic that Netflix, Amazon and Twitter combined. So now you can understand why the triplets are back and forth to the States.'

'I can and I can't. They fly all that way to be filmed having sex with men?'

'I don't think so. It's just themselves, as far as I can see.'

'So it is incest. What is the world coming to? I wonder who set up this little seedy business. They don't strike me as the brightest girls. They're being easily exploited by men for the benefit of other perverts.'

'Well, it obviously pays well. What did you say they drive, again?'

'They've a Mini each. Three of them, like *The Italian Job*. I actually feel sorry for the Hanlons. I thought I was going to be writing the feel-good story of the year and instead I've found a family in total disarray.'

'Everyone wants the fairy tale, but reality is never like that,' Connor replied.

'More's the pity,' April said ruefully.

33

Monozygotic
MAY 16TH

'What the actual fuck?' DCI Crosbie said after hearing the news from Susan Purdie. 'Has George Houston confirmed all this?'

'Yes, I had a man confirm my work.' Susan managed to refrain from adding 'you pig'.

Crosbie ignored the rebuke, if it had registered at all. 'And it's definitely come from one of the triplets?'

'I'm afraid so. Monozygotic or identical triplets means they are from the same zygote – "egg", in layman's terms. The egg then divided into three embryos creating identical triplets who share the exact same DNA as one another. Monozygotic triplets are always the same sex and blood type.'

Crosbie sighed heavily. 'This whole case is a cluster-fuck. Have you heard of anything like this before?'

'Not with triplets. I looked for other legal precedents and found a case of monozygotic twins accused of manslaughter in Spain. They were both acquitted as the prosecution could not prove which one had committed the crime.'

'This just gets better and better. It's almost as if the Hanlons knew they had us over a barrel.' Crosbie was thinking out loud. 'We'll never get a conviction. We won't even get to trial, at this rate. Their fucking father is murdered by one of his own and still they stick together.'

'Well, they do say that blood is thicker than water, and it doesn't get much thicker than Hanlon blood,' Susan said.

'What?'

'The killer's sample also had antiphospholipid antibody. It's possible the whole family has Hughes Syndrome. That basically means they have sticky blood and are prone to clotting. They could all be living under a death sentence.'

'When you've got nothing to lose … Thanks, Suze.'

'It's Susan,' she replied, but DCI Crosbie had already hung up. He was done with the science and was already trying to work out his next step. He knew that none of the petite triplets had the strength to carry out the attack. Even the three of them combined would have struggled to muster the combined force required for the blade to slice through skin and sinew and break two of their father's ribs in the process.

That could only mean their DNA sample had been added to the murder weapon to cover up for the real killer.

34

Freedom of information
JANUARY 25TH

Connor knew from bitter experience that Freedom of Information requests can be struck out on the smallest technicality. If the scope of your request was too big, the response would be that they simply did not possess the resources to supply the data. It was all bullshit, as Connor well knew, because the data for all government departments was already collated. The gatekeepers were just fiercely protective of releasing it into the public domain.

The trick to unlocking the information was to keep the requests as succinct as possible. So Connor had written the following to the Scottish Government's Health and Social Care Department:

In the last fiscal year how much did the Scottish Government spend on the methadone programme? And what was the breakdown of that payment to each individual pharmacy that administered methadone prescriptions?

Connor knew that the Health and Social Care Department had little wiggle room with this request as the retired pharmacist Ken Stirling had already told him all payments to every pharmacy were recorded and accounted for. If they did reject it on any flimsy grounds of confidentiality, he knew that an appeal to the Scottish Information Commissioner would no doubt succeed because the methadone programme was wholly funded by taxpayers' money.

Under the Scottish Freedom of Information Act, 2002, the health department had twenty working days to respond. Knowing how government departments worked, they would take that time limit up to the last day, then most likely post the results on their official website, making sure Connor's potential scoop was available to everyone.

But Connor had no intentions of sitting on his thumbs whilst waiting for the slow-moving machinery of government to churn out his results. He decided he was going to find the busiest chemist in Ruckhouse and see what was happening for himself.

35

No comment
MAY 19TH

The triplets arrived in their red, white and blue Minis and parked them in a row outside Ruckhouse police station. Their lawyer, Paul McFadden, followed closely behind, stepping out of his ghastly yellow Ford Mustang, wearing his ridiculous Cuban heels. He straightened his designer suit over his short frame before following the girls inside.

They were there by prior arrangement, but still had to be taken into custody officially, before being shown into individual interview rooms. McFadden had made sure his clients would be seen in succession so he could be present for each of them, even though he was not allowed to interrupt or speak while they were being questioned.

As the custody sergeant was going through the formalities of telling the girls everything from their rights to the nearest fire exits, the lawyer stepped into the corridor to use his mobile, only to spot DCI Crosbie striding towards the first interview room, with a pile of files under his arm.

'You know the girls didn't murder their father,' McFadden said coolly.

'Forensics says otherwise.'

'Look at them, they're like sparrows,' he said, indicating over his shoulder.

'Then they tell me who the hawk is?'

'This will be a "no comment" interview.'

'Fair enough. But I am going to find out who murdered Harry Hanlon, McFadden. And I know it was one of your clients.'

36

Keep the change

JANUARY 31ST

Harry Hanlon entered Saltire Pharmacy, which was just a short walk from the Woodchopper pub. The sales assistant looked awestruck to see him. Everyone in Ruckhouse knew of Harry and his millions.

'How can I help you, sir?' Mags Cheyne said, smiling from ear to ear. Harry was the only remotely famous person she had met during her nineteen years on the planet. The pharmacist, Elizabeth Smart, gave Harry a look of disgust from behind her dispensary.

'How you doing, doll?' Harry slurred slightly from an afternoon of drinking, and he struggled to focus on the assistant's name badge. 'Mags, is it?'

'Yes, Mr Hanlon,' Mags replied eagerly.

'Wonder if you can help me. I need a DNA kit. Got one of those?' he asked, his eyes drifting from her name badge to the shape of her breasts beneath the chemist uniform.

If the teenage shop assistant minded, she certainly didn't show it. 'It's £30 for the kit, Mr Hanlon,' she said, placing a package on the counter. 'You take the mouth swabs, up to eight if you have multiple specimens to assess, and then send them away in the self-addressed container. It costs an extra £130 to get them processed in the lab, which can take up to seven weeks. But if you're really desperate to know the results, there's a twenty-four-hour option for £340.'

Hanlon whistled. 'They really rob you, don't they? I'll just take the £130 version, doll.'

Mags was slightly crestfallen. Like everyone in Ruckhouse she had fantasised about what it would be like to win Harry's jackpot. She dreamed of not having to worry about the price of anything, but here was the man himself, complaining that £340 was too much to pay.

Harry took a thick wad of notes from his pocket and began to thumb them out on the counter. When he was done, he told Mags to 'keep the change', which earned him another look of disapproval from the pharmacist in the back of the premises.

'What's the matter with old iron knickers back there?' Harry asked Mags, who desperately tried to stifle a giggle. 'And by the way, doll, if you're ever passing the Woodchopper, pop in. The drinks are on me. You can even bring dour face, too … if you must,' he said, indicating towards Elizabeth Smart again.

'Thank you, Mr Hanlon. I'll do that some time.'

Mags was still smiling as Harry staggered his way out of the chemist. But her smile soon vanished as she counted out the money only to realise that the £100 million lottery winner had given her the exact money. There was no tip, not that 'iron knickers' would have allowed her to keep it anyway.

OUTSIDE, Connor clocked Harry leaving Saltire. It was the fourth chemist Connor had visited in Ruckhouse that day and was by far the busiest. It was also the only one with a lottery-winning customer. His journalistic instincts told him Saltire required further investigation.

37

Game plan
MAY 22ND

'So what now?' Chief Constable Eric McNeil asked in the confines of his office, while pouring himself a large whisky. DCI Crosbie noted how his boss was drinking larger measures whenever they met. He didn't offer his deputy Mike Bruce or Crosbie a dram, not that the detective wanted to drink at 11 am anyway.

'If we charge the triplets, it will be all over the six o'clock news. Just one look at these three little girls and no one will believe they killed their father. Paul McFadden will turn it into a shit storm,' Crosbie ventured.

'I agree,' Bruce said. 'They'll think we're barking up the wrong tree. That we're persecuting a grieving family.'

'But their blood was on the knife?' McNeil said, more in hope than to add anything to the discussion.

'It's been planted, sir,' Crosbie said.

'Then let's charge, test our case in court on them and see if we can flush out the real culprit. What do you think?' The chief knew how hollow that sounded. His suggestion was met by silence from the two other men in the room. He answered his own question for them: 'Who am I kidding? The fiscal wouldn't take this anywhere near a courtroom. This is fucking hopeless.'

'All is not lost,' Crosbie said encouragingly. 'I will keep the Macarena under surveillance. Something will give, sir.'

'But when? That's the problem, I need to know when,' McNeil said, the panic starting to rise in his voice. Just then his mobile rang. 'It's the First Minister again,' he said, pouring himself another large whisky before his guests took their leave.

'Poor bastard,' Mike Bruce said out of earshot. 'I've seen this picture before.'

'Me too, sir,' Crosbie replied. 'But at least the case is finally moving.'

'I just hope it moves fast enough to save him from the bottle … and that ball-busting bitch.'

Crosbie didn't ask, but he reckoned the deputy chief constable was no fan of the First Minister.

38

The sales

FEBRUARY 1ST

'I saw Harry Hanlon yesterday, leaving a chemist,' Connor told April as he slung his jacket over the back of a chair in the Peccadillo. 'I was looking for the busiest pharmacy in the Ruck and there he was.'

'Uch, he takes so many pills he rattles,' April replied. 'I've asked him what they're for but he wouldn't say.'

'High blood pressure, I'd imagine.'

'And all the rest of it. Talking of which, did I tell you I took a dizzy turn in the shops the other day?'

'Nope.'

'I had spent half the day with Harry at the Woodchopper, unable to make head nor tail of his rambling stories...'

'I know how he feels,' Connor murmured.

'...when I decided I needed to buy myself another winter jacket, as I've been wearing this fur one to death in this weather. So there I was, rummaging away, when suddenly my vision went all blurred and I started to feel faint and sick. I thought I was having a stroke.'

'Really? Who'd have thought you'd have been at risk of a stroke,' Connor said with perfect timing as Martel served up April's daily portion of salt, saturated fat, pork and dairy products that passed for a traditional great Scottish fry-up.

'I had to sit down and everything.'

'On the floor or a chair?'

'A chair, and will you stop interrupting? I ended up with a member of staff holding my hand when I realised that everything was perfectly in focus through one eye but blurred with the other. That's when I figured it out.'

'You'd finally lost all your marbles?'

'No, I'd lost one of my contact lenses.'

'And that's it? What about all the dizziness, needing a chair and causing a scene? You're lucky they didn't call you an ambulance.'

'Ah, yes...' April said, trailing off as her face turned red.

'They did call an ambulance, didn't they?'

'Yes. But by this point I knew it was just my contact lens, though obviously I couldn't tell the staff as they were fussing all over me.'

'So...?' Connor urged her on, dreading what would come next.

'So while the kind lady went to get me a glass of water I kind of made my excuses and left.'

'You legged it?'

'Well, yes, as fast as I could, anyway.'

'Why didn't you just ride it out? You've got high blood pressure anyway so the ambulance crew would suspect that's why you had a dizzy turn.'

'I didn't want to be taken out of there on a stretcher, not just for a missing contact lens. How humiliating would that be?'

'So then what?'

'I drove home half-blind. I could only use my good eye to steer.'

'Your good eye? Marvellous. And what about the store?'

'Last I saw, on my way to the car park, was a blue light arriving. I won't be able to shop in there again. Pity, they have good sales.'

'So the next time I call you an ambulance-dodging, blind, old bat, I will be factually correct?'

'Apart from "bat",' April replied, through a mouthful of food.

'Why are you wearing contacts, anyway?' Connor said,

studying April's face. 'What happened to the gold-rimmed specs and neck chain?'

'Harry kept borrowing them.'

'Borrowing?'

'Yes, to read the puzzle section.'

'While you were trying to interview him?'

'Precisely. I started wearing contacts so he wouldn't bury his head in the paper when I'm speaking to him.'

'And he won't buy himself a pair of reading glasses?'

'He won't buy himself anything. And he never goes anywhere except that bloody pub. Then the chemist. Then home. Imagine what you would do with that money. Where you would go? The things you could experience? And all Harry Hanlon is doing is spending his time in the bloody Woodchopper. What a waste. I hate going up there now. I fear I've bitten off more than I can chew with this project.'

'Every writer hits this phase while doing a book. Just keep writing. Even if it just becomes observational about him trying to read the paper with your glasses. His story will all come out in the end, probably when you're least expecting it.'

'A bit like my contact lens,' April mused.

39

Irn-Bru
MAY 23RD

DCI Crosbie groaned when he saw the caller ID on his phone. It was his sister.

'Are you about tonight?' Linda Crosbie said, with no greeting at all.

Crosbie had often berated his older sibling for her appalling manners, which included a total incapacity to use the words 'hello' and 'goodbye' at the start and end of telephone conversations. He wasn't about to let her off lightly. 'And hello to you, too, sis.'

'Aye, whatever. Can you look after Damien tonight? I've got an extra shift on.'

Crosbie gave an involuntary shudder. His nephew Damien was one difficult kid. He had attention deficit hyperactive disorder, which Crosbie was convinced was a term made up to keep the therapy business ticking over. As far as he was concerned, Damien was just full of energy, as Crosbie himself had been as a kid. That was why he dreaded looking after him – he saw too much of himself in his nephew.

'I'm kinda busy,' he replied meekly, knowing Linda wouldn't take no for an answer.

'You haven't seen Damien since Christmas and I know you're working in the Ruck as I heard it on the news. They said you'd taken over the Hanlon case.'

Crosbie had left Ruckhouse long ago. Linda never did. As a single mum, she had been moved into a smart housing association home with Damien on the outskirts of the scheme. She actually liked living in Ruckhouse and had no intentions of ever moving. She also grafted hard for a living, being paid minimum wage working split shifts for meals on wheels, feeding elderly residents at home. She admitted that it mainly involved bunging something in the microwave then moving on to her next call. But Linda didn't care; she was proud to say she wasn't in debt and could always afford a two-week family holiday abroad with Damien every year.

'I start at six and should be done by ten. He'll need fed, so you might want to bring him a chippy. But remember: no Irn-Bru.'

'How could I forget?' Crosbie replied. Damien had some sort of weird reaction to Scotland's ginger-coloured equivalent of Coca-Cola. Just one sip was like giving the kid an adrenaline shot. He was therefore banned from drinking it by not only his mother, but also his school and the family doctor. Crosbie had made the mistake of giving his nephew a can of the drink one rare night he was babysitting and hadn't been able to get him to sleep until 5 am. And that was only after physically restraining him in bed.

The detective checked his watch. 'I'll be there by six,' he said without enthusiasm.

40

The stakeout
FEBRUARY 2ND

Connor hated stake-outs. The older he got, the less patient he became. He also found he would inevitably need a pee, especially in the cold, and the dashboard temperature reading said it was minus 12°C outside. He was with the *Chronicle*'s photographer Jack Barr, who was as legendary for his incredible ability to hold his water as he was for taking pictures of people who didn't want their pictures taken. It wasn't even as if he dehydrated himself – quite the opposite: he would knock back several cans of Diet Coke, leaving his empties to litter the back of his works van. Jack had come to the conclusion long ago that two 'workies' sitting in a battered old transit attracted less attention than a couple of journalists sitting for hours in a car, and he was right. His specially installed tinted rear window also allowed him to point his long telescopic lens at his targets completely undetected.

Their eyes were trained on Saltire Pharmacy. From where they were parked, they could see straight through the glass front to the methadone counter, used to supervise addicts as they swallowed the heroin substitute in front of the pharmacist. Many other chemists had a private room for methadone consumption, to protect what was left of the addict's dignity, but not Saltire, where the procedure was conducted in the full glare of the shop's fluorescent lights and fellow customers.

Barr was able to get clear shots of all the addicts as they came and went. But the cheap take-away coffees they had drunk the hour before were now playing havoc with Connor's waterworks.

'I really need to pee.'

'Amateur,' Jack scoffed.

'What's your personal best?' Connor asked, referring to Jack's bladder control record.

'Twenty-three hours and thirty-three minutes,' he replied proudly.

'That can't be good for you. I'm surprised your kidneys didn't explode. I think I need a catheter. Maybe I could find some friendly nurse to insert one.'

'My brother-in-law's a nurse. Hands like shovels. I could ask him for you.' Jack smiled.

'Not really what I had in mind.' Connor got out of Jack's van, with the intention of heading for the Manhatten Bistro three doors along from the chemist. The use of the word 'bistro' signified the owner's brave attempt at establishing a classy joint, despite the grim location, but they had hopelessly fallen at the first hurdle by the misspelling of Manhattan.

'Want a bagel with smoked salmon and cream cheese?' Connor asked Jack.

The snapper shot his colleague an incredulous look.

'Okay, if they don't have anything from New York, do you want a roll and sausage instead?'

'Yeah, I think you'll have more chance of that. You actually might get your head kicked in asking for a bagel around here,' Jack warned.

Connor entered the Manhatten and immediately had a newfound appreciation for the Peccadillo. He'd always thought his usual haunt was a bit shabby, but compared to this joint it was a palace. He took his place in the queue of workmen in their high-vis vests, ready to fuel up on calories and carbohydrates. Connor had gone gluten-free a year ago, not because he was coeliac but as a lifestyle choice. He scanned the chilled counter full of various sticky-coated pastries filled with plastic foam – or cream from an aerosol can, as it is better known. He didn't think there was a single item for sale that wasn't packed with wheat and gluten. The young woman behind the counter wore an expression that suggested she would rather be anywhere else on the planet, and when it was Connor's turn in the queue she just looked at him, with her pen and notepad at the ready, but didn't say a word. He took that to mean she was ready to take his order.

'A roll and sausage, please.'

'Sauce?' the girl barked back.

'Yes, please.'

'Colour?'

'Brown, thanks,' Connor said, while thinking this girl had the same way with words as Martel. 'And do you do a salad box?'

The request seemed so alien to the girl; it was as if she had just been asked for something in Swahili. 'Can ye dae a salad boax?' she shouted towards the kitchen.

'Aye,' came the reply.

'Salad cream?'

Connor hated salad cream. 'No, thanks.'

'Drinks?' the girl asked now. She really did not believe in the art of conversation.

'One large coffee and one small.' Quickly adding 'Both white' before she barked 'Colour?' again. 'And where's the toilet?'

'Doon back, on the right.'

Connor almost congratulated her on completing a whole sentence, but thought better of it. The toilet was as disgusting as he had imagined, with a slippery floor from all the layers of grease. He rinsed his hands in cold water – there was no soap – and then shook them dry as the hand dryer was, predictably, broken.

After settling up for the food and two coffees, Connor attempted to engage with the stony-faced waitress, purely out of devilment. 'Do you do bagels?'

'Whit?'

'Bagels? It's like a roll with a hole in it. They do them in the real Manhattan. With an "a".'

'Naw. If we did rolls with holes in them, aw the food wid faw oot.'

'Good point,' Connor had to concede. He'd never thought of bagels having a fundamental design flaw until now. He left the Manhatten with more than just food for thought.

———

SIX O'CLOCK WAS FAST APPROACHING and Jack and Connor didn't expect any more addicts. They knew that the pharmacist Elizabeth Smart would close the doors of Saltire precisely on time – she looked the type that, if someone failed to follow all the rules and regulations to the letter, heaven would fall from the sky and society would descend into chaos.

Jack sipped his giant coffee, which looked like it contained at least a litre of liquid, as if goading Connor over his fluid intake.

'Honestly, mate, I think you need to see a doctor about that. It's not natural how long you can hold it in.'

'Ah, Elvis, you are nothing but a weak-bladdered fool.'

By the end of play they had counted forty-nine addicts who had approached the methadone counter. Most were easy to spot, with a haunted, pinched look to them. And if their appearance didn't give them away, then the fact they left the chemist and made straight for the cut-price supermarket directly across the street to buy the cheapest booze available, certainly did. Methadone was designed to release its sedative effects more evenly throughout the day, rather than the sudden rush from heroin. To achieve a proper 'high', addicts needed to take it with strong painkillers or alcohol, or preferably both.

'I need to go undercover tomorrow. Ask old grey bun there to let me on her methadone register,' Connor said.

'Will you clear it with the desk?' Jack asked. 'They kinda frown on a whole day's stake-out now. Never mind four in a row. They also have me down for studio time tomorrow with some band.'

'Shit,' Connor said, knowing the picture editor would insist that Jack do the studio job which guaranteed a front page and inside spread for the Saturday magazine, rather than sit on another wait-and-hope long shot like a potentially corrupt chemist.

'I know, Elvis,' Jack said. 'There was a time I could be sent on a stake-out for a month and no one would bat an eyelid, even if it all fell through.'

'It's fine,' Connor replied, while his demeanour said it was anything but. 'Tell you what, if you can Dropbox me pics of all forty-nine methadone users, then I can identify them by myself when I'm here tomorrow.'

'It's hardly ideal though, is it?'

'No, but what is, these days? The paper is full of internet stories, Twitter spats and nude celebrity Instagram pictures. Who needs to pay for a stake-out when they can get all that shit for free?' Connor said glumly.

'And they wonder why the circulation is going down the crapper?'

'Now you're starting to sound like me.' Connor was used to constantly moaning about newspapers' many shortcomings to April, so he always felt vindicated when a fellow professional held the same views.

'Did you know all the contracted snappers have been asked to take a pay cut?' Jack asked. 'And that's after they've had a pay freeze for the last fifteen years.'

'Makes me feel guilty for moaning about our one per cent staff increase this year.'

'I know. The snappers are furious. But what can you do? You'd need to have your head buried in the sand not to see what's going on around you. Hardly any of our stuff gets used, and the papers are so small these days too, there's no space for all our photos anyway. If we can eke another five years' living out of this, I think we'll be doing well. Let's be honest, we're just lucky to still have a job.'

Connor let out a long sigh, resigning himself to tomorrow being an all-day stake-out conducted entirely by himself.

'Just don't drink anything, Elvis,' Jack warned. 'You can't do a stake-out from the toilet.'

41

Taser

MAY 23RD

DCI Crosbie arrived at his sister's house just as she rang his mobile to check if he was going to be on time.

'I'm right outside, Linda,' he said, cutting her off before she started shouting about where he was. As he got out of his car, a water balloon exploded at his feet, soaking his shoes and the bottom of his trousers. He looked up to see Damien laughing from an upstairs window.

'I'll kick your arse,' Crosbie shouted, only to receive a middle-finger response from his nephew. This was going to be a long night.

He was met at the front door by Linda, who brushed past him on the way out. 'Damien will need fed. There's a pizza in the freezer.'

'It's okay, I brought him a chippy as you suggested.'

'I didn't think you'd have the time. Just make sure you don't give him any Irn-Bru,' Linda warned again, before shutting her car door and driving off.

'I'm not insane,' Crosbie mumbled to himself and stepped into the mayhem of his sister's home. In the hallway, every picture frame was hanging at an angle, no doubt the result of his nephew playing football indoors, despite repeatedly being told not to. He found Damien standing in the kitchen, glugging straight from a two-litre bottle of forbidden Irn-Bru.

'Where the fuck did you get that?' Crosbie demanded, snatching the plastic container from the youngster's hand. He had drunk about a third of the contents, when just one glass was enough to send him over the edge.

'I nicked it from the shops. To wind you up. You can't tell me what to do – you're not my da,' Damien shouted while jumping up and down on the spot like a Tasmanian devil.

'Listen, you little scrote. You're not supposed to drink this stuff. It makes you mental. More mental than usual.' Crosbie emptied the remainder down the plughole, where it fizzed and gurgled, leaving a ginger scum around the kitchen sink.

Before it had been fully emptied, Damien tried to swipe the bottle, sending the remaining liquid splashing over his uncle's already wet shoes and trousers. Now they would also be sticky.

'Why, you little bastard!' Crosbie shouted as Damien ran out of the kitchen. The detective found a dish towel and tried to dry himself off when suddenly his nephew returned, brandishing a large potted cheese plant that took both of his little arms to carry.

'Here, catch, Uncle David.'

To Crosbie's utter astonishment, Damien launched the vegetation in his direction. He failed to catch it as instructed. The terracotta pot smashed into smithereens as it hit the tiled floor, sending earth and leaves scattering everywhere. Damien danced on the spot, holding his crotch as he tried not to piss himself laughing.

Crosbie pulled his Police Scotland standard issue Taser X2 gun from the holster attached to the back of his belt and pointed it at his eleven-year-old tormentor.

'You wouldn't fucking dare.' Damien smirked, taunting his uncle. 'My ma would kill you.'

Crosbie briefly glanced over his shoulder for any would-be witnesses before pulling the trigger, firing two prongs into his nephew's leg, sending fifty thousand volts coursing through his young body.

The rest of the evening passed off without incident; Damien remained more or less unconscious, lying on the couch where his uncle had laid him under a blanket. He finally came to his senses shortly before his mother was due to return.

'You alright, Damien son?' Linda asked, as she hung up her jacket. 'He's really quiet, David – what have you done to him?'

Damien thought about telling all, but had second thoughts when Crosbie showed him a flash of the Taser gun behind his mother's back.

'Nothing at all, sis. The wee man was as good as gold, eh Damien?' Crosbie said.

'A-aye, ma. G-good as g-gold,' his nephew stuttered, still feeling the after-effects of the unorthodox electric shock treatment.

42

Fishy

FEBRUARY 3RD

'You're a bit underdressed this morning,' April said, inspecting Connor's clothes as she arrived at the Peccadillo. He was wearing a pair of ripped jeans and a frayed old sweater more suited for lounging about at home.

'I'm going undercover,' he replied without elaborating.

'Oh, how exciting,' April said. 'Is that why you're here so early?'

'Yes, I've got to be somewhere for 9 am.'

'You'll catch your death in those ripped jeans. It's freezing out there.'

'I know, Mum.'

'Well, I've been doing a little bit of investigating myself after I discovered Harry has been seeing a psychic,' April said, beaming.

'Why's he doing that?' Connor asked, and silently mouthed 'Coffee' to Martel, who shot a dirty look straight back at him.

'I don't really know,' April said, taking a slurp of her sugary tea. 'But I think he's worried about something.'

'Heart attack? Diabetes? Stroke?' Connor said, thinking more about April's health again than Harry Hanlon's.

'He hasn't said. He doesn't say much. But when the psychic arrived at the pub he looked a bit worried. They went off to a function suite for some privacy and I was dismissed. I asked Harry about it the next day and he said he needed to know "something". I asked if it was to do with his money, but he said it was more important than that.'

'That is weird. I didn't think there was anything more important to Harry than money,' Connor said as Martel clattered his mug of coffee down on the table in front of him.

'Anyway, being the good journalist that I am...'

'A nosy cow,' Connor interjected.

'Precisely. I managed to find out who the psychic was. Mystic Matt. Turned out he used to be a fishmonger before working with the spirit world.'

'From fish to pish.'

'Exactly. I called him up, told him who I was and that I was working with Harry every day, and would he kindly let me know what Harry was so concerned about, as it may help with my research. He told me that was a complete no-no. It would breach psychic–client confidentiality.'

'Been watching too much *L.A. Law*.'

'I know. I told him not to be so ridiculous and that I wasn't looking to embarrass Harry, I was only concerned for him. He thought about it for a moment then told me, "I can't say much, except it's a matter of life and death." He sounded really worried when he said it, too. I asked if he felt Harry's life was in danger and he said, "Most definitely," and then hung up.'

'A psychic has predicted someone might die? Where do they get their superpowers?' Connor said sarcastically.

'You didn't hear the way he said it. It was spooky. Chilled me to the bone.'

'There's a lot of layers to get through to your bones.'

'It was quite unsettling.'

'Well, how about settling the bill? I've got a date with the Ruck.'

'Me, too,' April replied. 'I just hope the psychic hasn't spooked Harry too much. It's hard to get him talking as it is.'

43

Revenge
MAY 24TH

It was past 1 am when Crosbie finally left his sister's house and spotted the souped-up boy racer's car parked under a lamppost with its engine idling. It was the same car he had seen the day he broke Wise Guy's wrist with his cuffs. They had shouted obscenities at the detective back then, but they didn't see him now.

Plumes of smoke billowed from the open windows, and even from a distance Crosbie could detect the overpowering stench of cannabis skunk. The occupants were all laughing and joking from inside the smoke-filled car, completely oblivious to the detective, who stuck to the shadows. Crosbie got to within just a few feet from them, crouching down behind the rear of his targets' car. He took out his can of Police Scotland issue CS spray and smacked the top off on the kerbstone before lobbing it through the driver's side window.

The can immediately emptied its entire contents into the vehicle, causing the driver to floor the accelerator in a panic, only to realise he'd been blinded. Crosbie watched in amusement as the car screeched off, swerving several times before it smashed into a lamppost further down the street. The street lamp buckled then began to topple, lazily at first before it gathered pace and landed in a shower of electrical sparks on the roof of the written-off car.

All four occupants fell out of the doors, covered in blood and howling in pain. Crosbie started up the engine of his own car before calmly driving past the carnage flicking the V-sign to the young men writhing on the ground in agony. With their customised car now out of commission, at least the residents of Ruckhouse would get a decent night's sleep.

44

Method acting
FEBRUARY 3RD

Connor went straight from the Peccadillo to Saltire Pharmacy, getting there just before opening time. He had been practising acting in an agitated manner, and when the first staff members turned up for work he immediately began harassing them for methadone. His pleas were interrupted by the arrival of the pharmacist Elizabeth Smart, who demanded to know what Connor wanted. She then asked if he had a doctor's prescription.

'No, missus. No' yet,' Connor replied in his best broad Glaswegian.

'No prescription, no methadone,' Smart took great delight in telling him.

'I will get a prescription, missus, but I need my methadone now. I'm begging you.'

But Connor's pleas fell on the deaf ears of someone clearly used to dealing with desperate addicts. 'Our methadone register is full,' she said. 'You will have to get your prescription and try another chemist.'

'How can it be full, missus? Come on, just one more name won't hurt anybody.'

'It's full. You'll have to go elsewhere.'

'Full, full, full, that's all I'm hearing. How many is full?'

'We have a limit of one hundred and fifty on the register.

Try the one down the road. They may have some spaces left on theirs. But get your prescription first. It's against the law for a pharmacist to issue so much as paracetamol without a prescription.'

Connor retreated out of sight to his car, which was parked several blocks away. He called Jack Barr, who was busy in the studio. 'We counted forty-nine junkies yesterday,' Connor said, 'but the pharmacist tells me she has one hundred and fifty on her register. That's a hundred and one short. It's not as if a junkie can take a day off from being a junkie.'

'Some could have moved, been jailed or died,' Jack said over the background chatter of what was clearly a full studio, with some new band convinced they were the next big thing and acting like it already.

'I know there's a margin of error, but a hundred and one patients can't suddenly have gone missing,' Connor replied. 'She said the register was full. If some had moved on or died, she could have added me to the list. But she was emphatic. The list was full. I smell a scam.'

'Look, I better go. These prima donnas are getting restless,' Jack said, hanging up.

Connor decided to call April's retired pharmacist neighbour again, Ken Stirling.

'If you were a crooked pharmacist, how could you screw the methadone programme?' Connor asked.

'Very easily, I'm afraid,' Ken replied. 'For starters, even though most chemists are effectively the branch offices of a bigger organisation, they are entirely self-auditing. So anything that goes missing can be "sorted", if you know what I mean.'

'Wait a minute, are you telling me that all the medicines aren't heavily regulated?' Connor asked.

'In theory, yes. And especially in hospital wards where they carefully monitor the morphine since so many of the staff were developing addiction issues of their own. But chemists are pretty autonomous. It would take a whistle-blower to have HQ send in the auditors to do a stock check.'

'And what about the methadone itself?'

'It's made into liquid form onsite by the pharmacist, then

dispensed in 40 ml to 100 ml cups, which the person on the programme takes at the counter.'

'Do any addicts get to take the dose home with them?'

'Yes, some are trusted to do that.'

'So could a pharmacist dispense a week's supply for the addict to take at home?'

'No, they still have to appear in person every day, but some might have stomach problems and say they prefer to take it at night after a meal or whatever. In cases like that, and if the addict physically looks to be improving, they will be trusted to do just that and hopefully they don't sell it on.'

'Is there a market for methadone?'

'It's certainly a very lucrative market for the pharmaceutical industry.'

'Okay. Tell me one last thing, Ken: if a pharmacist says they have a hundred and fifty people on their methadone register but I only count forty-nine and fifty turning up over two consecutive days, what would that mean to you?'

'Some could be dead, although there's such high demand to get on the register that the pharmacist would strike them off as soon as possible. Others may have moved chemist if they've been caught shoplifting on the premises because, believe it or not, heroin addicts do occasionally steal things. But, taking that into account, I would say that only around a dozen maximum would fail to appear on a daily basis.'

'How about a hundred and one?'

'Impossible. What you have there is a scam, my friend.'

'That's exactly what I thought.'

'Which chemist have you been watching?'

'Saltire.'

'Ah, Saltire. There's been rumours about them before. As far as I know, they were audited at some point but nothing ever came of it. Of course, they won't be able to pull off a fraud by themselves.'

'Really?'

'They'll also need a compliant doctor. Dead patients. Real prescriptions. Split the proceeds. A rogue pharmacist and GP in Ruckhouse could make an absolute fortune, of that you can be assured.'

'Thank you, Ken. You've been more than helpful.'

Connor now knew beyond a shadow of a doubt that he was on to a good story. He also had a theory why the pharmacist Elizabeth Smart was always the last member of staff to arrive at the chemist in the morning. Tomorrow, he would put that theory to the test. And this time he would need Jack Barr for a new set of snatches. Now Connor desperately needed to find himself a whistle-blower.

45

Under the skin
FEBRUARY 3RD

April also headed to Ruckhouse after breakfast in the Peccadillo, to interview Robert 'Shifty' Hanlon. She had thought his father was a difficult interviewee, but Harry was, in fact, practically a chatterbox compared to his eldest son.

April could not bring herself to address him as 'Shifty' and called him Robert instead. He had wanted to meet at his girlfriend Angie Wyper's house and had reluctantly texted April the postcode for her satnav on the third time of asking. April took her place by Angie's breakfast bar while she rummaged around in her bag for her digital voice recorder and notepad, remarking how breakfast bars had been all the rage in the late '70s and '80s. But Robert wasn't interested in any small talk. He had only agreed to be interviewed after an idle threat from his father that he would be frozen out of the will. So now April was left with a reluctant subject who treated their chat as if he was being quizzed by the police.

At first, April felt like banging her head against a wall, or preferably his, out of sheer frustration. But then she decided to do what she had done throughout her career and write herself out of trouble. She turned his monosyllabic answers into a game of cat and mouse, and since she couldn't even get a straight answer to 'Have you seen your mother recently?', she decided to ask more pressing questions – including what he did for a living, as it was clear he did not have a job but seemed to be a man of means even before his father's windfall.

'I'm no' answering that,' Robert replied, drawing on a cigarette.

'You've been meeting some businessmen from Manchester called the Gallachers, I believe. I read about it in the newspaper. What sort of business are you doing together?'

'I'm no' answering that, either.'

'Are you a drug dealer?' April asked.

She expected Robert to erupt in fury. Instead he let out a laugh, before stubbing out his cigarette butt. 'I'm a businessman,' he said, giving his most detailed answer yet.

'What sort of business?' April pressed further.

'Business, business,' Robert said more forcibly, letting her know that's all she would be getting from him.

'Who are your business partners, then?'

'I have many business partners.'

'What can you tell me about the Gallachers?'

'You've been misinformed.' He smirked.

'What's your trading name?'

'What?' He looked slightly confused.

'Your business name? Robert Holdings? Shifty Services?' April asked mockingly, in revenge for a morning of non-cooperation.

'None of your business,' Robert replied huffily.

'Your business is none of my business? It's okay, I will check with Companies House later today. I'll see what business is registered at your home address and take it from there.'

'There's no business registered at my address,' Robert said, his face now reddening with anger.

'You're not a businessman, then. So how do you earn a living?' April asked again.

This seemed to flummox him, and he did not wish what he really did for a living to appear in print. The best he could think of to say was: 'I get money from my dad.'

Robert looked rather pathetic as he picked up his packet of cigarettes and plodded upstairs like a stroppy teenager. The local hardman, who swanned around Ruckhouse as if he owned the place, was reduced to saying he was reliant on his father's bank balance.

April knew Robert wasn't telling the truth, but she would write their exchange in a way that left it hanging; she'd let the book's readers decide what to make of Robert 'Shifty' Hanlon for themselves.

46

Fluke
MAY 29TH

'A Taser? You used a fucking Taser on your own nephew?

'The little rat,' Crosbie muttered feebly.

'He's not a rat. He just let it slip that he's feeling a lot better since his Uncle David shot him. I honestly can't believe this. You're a detective chief inspector. If I can't trust a high-ranking officer with my son then at least I thought I could trust my brother. But you shot him. Shot your nephew. With a TASER.'

'Listen, sis, I know it sounds bad when you say it like that, but I couldn't think of anything else to do. He'd done a third of a bottle of Irn-Bru then hurled the pot plant at me. I have seen people high on crack cocaine who weren't as manic as Damien.'

'So you shot him? With a Taser?' Linda said again.

'Yes, I did. I didn't zap him for long.'

'Just long enough for him to fall unconscious?'

Crosbie paused before replying in the softest tone he could muster: 'I'm not proud of myself, sis. But you have to admit it's had a remarkable effect on his behaviour.'

'You could have killed him.'

'Unlikely. Tasers hardly kill anyone,' Crosbie said, instantly regretting how heartless he sounded.

'Hardly? I really can't believe my own brother did this.'

'Look, sis, has your life improved or not since the ... incident?'

'Since you Tasered him, David. Say it. Tasered him.'

'Okay, has your life improved since the ... Tasering?'

'Since you shot your nephew. Yes, life has improved.'

'He's doing better at school?'

'Yes.'

'And he's been a quieter, more attentive boy at home?'

'Yes, he has. Since you shot him.'

'So, really, it was for the best.'

'That's not the point. You could have seriously injured your own nephew.'

'That's the worst-case scenario, sis.'

'But you could have,' she continued.

'But I didn't. Look, we're going round in circles here. I know I shouldn't have Tasered Damien. It was a stupid and reckless thing to do. But out of that moment of madness I have made both my nephew and sister happier.'

'By pure fluke.'

'Some of the best things ever invented were by fluke. Penicillin, for example.'

'So you're now comparing yourself to Sir Alexander Fleming?'

Crosbie forgot that, for all her roughness, his sister was well read. 'Granted, that's probably a bit of a stretch. But I have helped, haven't I?'

There was silence down the line broken by the sound of his sister sobbing gently. Crosbie felt terrible.

'I'm so sorry, sis. I've always had a bit of a screw loose. You know that.'

'I do. But Damien looks up to you. He thinks his big important detective uncle is fantastic, and yet you shot him.'

'I'm sorry. That's all I can say. I'm so sorry.'

'The weird thing is, he still thinks you're amazing. He told me not to cry as the Taser has made him "a better boy". Can you believe that? An eleven-year-old trying to reassure his mother that being shot was good for him.'

'How can I make it up to you both?'

'Damien wants you to look after him again. Do you think you could manage that without electrocuting him this time?'

'Of course,' Crosbie said enthusiastically, sensing redemption. 'Anything else?'

'Can you get my car serviced? It'll be about £150 but I just don't have the money this month.'

'Consider it done. Now, let's never mention the "incident" again – deal?'

'Deal. As long as you leave the Taser at work.'

'Absolutely. Bye now.' After hanging up, Crosbie patted his Taser gun and said, 'Don't worry, pal, I'm not leaving you anywhere.'

47

Ruse

FEBRUARY 4TH

Connor could remember his first doctor's surgery when he was growing up. It had been on the ground floor of a tenement building on Radnor Street, just before Sauchiehall and Argyle Street merged into Dumbarton Road outside the majestic Kelvingrove Art Galleries and Museum. The surgery's waiting room was constantly cold, although that could have been because the only time he visited was in winter.

Once, he had taken a bout of viral meningitis and remembered the kindly Asian GP visiting the room and kitchen where he lived with his mum, Annie. It was the mid-'80s and long before Connor had ever experienced central heating, not that they could have afforded it anyway. Each morning he and his mum would fight for space above an electric hall heater while they got dressed in a flat where you could see your breath and ice forming on the insides of the windows. The doctor had taken one look at Connor, noticing his extreme sensitivity to light, and immediately phoned for an ambulance. He remembered thinking that Bram Stoker must have based Dracula's aversion to sunlight on meningitis, as a single beam coming through a chink in his curtains felt like it was searing his skin.

He had welcomed the week-long stay in hospital, which

was luxury compared to home, even though he'd had to endure a lumbar puncture. He could still recall the crack as a sturdy needle burst through his spinal column, and the queasy feeling of a fluid sample being drawn out.

The Ruckhouse Medical Partnership couldn't have been more different to his childhood GP practice. It was a modern, two-storey, cube-shaped building with a flat roof and electric doors that were in near-constant use from the stream of patients coming and going. The local health authority had spent a small fortune on the building in an attempt to improve the health of people from the Ruck. Connor felt their good intentions were doomed to fail, judging by the number of patients standing defiantly in the freezing temperatures in front of the *No smoking* signs, puffing on cigarettes or vaping. He always wondered how people in poverty-stricken areas could even afford to smoke, given that cigarettes were so unbelievably expensive.

The journalist spotted the pharmacist Elizabeth Smart walking purposefully through the snow in what appeared to be expensive hiking boots. Her greying hair was tucked under a woolly hat, but she still held her head in a haughty manner, looking down her nose at all she surveyed.

He was relieved that the picture desk had assigned Jack Barr to the job again. The snapper had expertly fired off a couple of test frames of her from behind as she entered the building, readying himself for when she exited. Connor, meanwhile, followed the pharmacist into the surgery. He watched as she brushed past the lengthy queue at the reception desk to a side window, where she gave a weak smile as a member of staff handed over a thick pile of prescriptions, which she tucked into her black leather handbag. She turned on her heels and marched out, deliberately paying no attention to anything or anyone, as if even being in such close proximity to the people of Ruckhouse offended her senses.

Connor took his place at the end of the queue, fully confident Jack Barr would capture Elizabeth Smart exiting the building. The reporter deliberately danced from foot to foot, trying to give his best impression of an agitated addict as he neared his turn at the window.

'How can I help you?' the middle-aged receptionist asked when it was finally his turn.

'I've just moved to the Ruck, right, and I'm needing my methadone, but I spoke to a woman in the chemist yesterday and she said she's got her full quota or something like that. To be honest, she was a bit of a snooty bitch, if you'll forgive my French.' Connor definitely detected the beginnings of a smile on the receptionist's face at that comment. 'Anyway, she says I need a prescription, right? But the problem is, I'm no' registered with any doctors here 'cos I just got out the Bar-L, you see.'

The Bar-L was Barlinnie Prison, an imposing Victorian-built jail in the east of the city where they still hanged prisoners until 1960.

'I can give you an emergency appointment with our locum GP.'

'Locus what?' Connor said, feigning ignorance.

'Locum. It means a temporary doctor.'

'Like a substitute teacher?'

'Precisely. Or, if you can wait just a little while longer, I can try and find you a slot with our addiction specialist?'

'How long for the specialist?' Connor said, once again hopping from foot to foot.

'As quickly as possible. If you've moved to Ruckhouse, I recommend you wait to see the specialist.'

'Then I'll be able to get my methadone?' Connor asked with fake urgency.

'Then you'll get whatever appropriate measures the doctor deems fit.'

'Aye, alright then. As long as it's no' all day.'

'It won't be. And in the meantime, can you fill in this form, please?'

The receptionist handed over a clipboard and Connor took his place in the waiting room. He now had to decide upon a name. If he used his own, the database would show his real address in Glasgow's West End – a far cry from the deprivation of Ruckhouse. He decided to use the name and address of his contact Stevie Brett, who had died the year previously. Stevie had had a myriad of health problems, mostly around his asthma, but no history of substance abuse as far as Connor knew. He was just going to have to wing it and hope the NHS Central Register hadn't been updated with Stevie's untimely death. In Connor's experience, patients passing away usually took the most time to be entered on health records, despite it being their most important detail.

Connor didn't have Stevie's ten-digit identification number, but most patients don't know theirs anyway. Instead, he retrieved Brett's postcode from the contacts in his phone. The next thing he needed was Stevie's date of birth. This left Connor stumped for a moment until he remembered he had recently been sent a notification of Brett's birthday on Facebook, which also wasn't aware of his demise. Connor was now feeling more confident – if Mark Zuckerberg's multi-billion dollar company didn't know about Stevie's death, he doubted the poor old NHS would, either. He was basing his theory on a community nurse he had once dated who needed four different log-ins for the computer systems at various doctors' practices she worked at, despite the fortunes the NHS had spent to try to simplify their IT systems.

He handed the completed form back to the receptionist while going through his addict routine, ringing his hands and shifting constantly from foot to foot.

'Thank you, Mr Brett. I'll enter your details into our system. It shouldn't be too long now.'

Whilst he waited, Connor remained in character: an impatient patient, fidgeting constantly in his seat and pacing a patch of floor between his seat and the reception. Eventually, an automated voice announced, 'Ste-ven Br-ett. Doc-tor Mar-ran. Room fifteen.' Connor momentarily failed to respond before realising he was now Mr Br-ett.

He made his way quickly to room fifteen. He just hoped he could pull off his ruse and the doctor didn't discover that the real Stevie was dead.

48

Comings and goings
MAY 29TH

Dugdale was back in the empty council flat keeping the Macarena under surveillance yet again. DCI Crosbie wanted him to stake out the Hanlons' home during daytime to monitor the movements of all the siblings.

First to leave was Michael, pushing his brother Billy in the wheelchair in the direction of the day centre. The youngest Hanlon returned less than fifteen minutes later by himself, to retrieve a heavy backpack that Dugdale correctly guessed would be full of university textbooks as Michael made his way to the local library to prep for the start of medical school.

Shortly after 11 am, Kendal arrived in her silver Mercedes. She was only there for approximately half an hour before she stormed out with her older brother Shifty in tow. It was clear they were having a heated row as there was a lot of finger-pointing between the pair before Kendal shouted, 'Fuck off – business is business,' loud enough for the whole street to hear. She drove off at speed, spinning her wheels as she went.

Ten minutes after that, Shifty lived up to his nickname as he scoured up and down the road on the lookout for any potential threats, perhaps from his sister, before he roared off in his BMW X6 in the opposite direction from Kendal.

The triplets left the house together at precisely midday,

dressed in matching summer floral dresses, driving off in unison in their red, white and blue Minis.

Dugdale texted his boss to let him know the Hanlons' movements and what Kendal had shouted to Shifty.

Good stuff, Crosbie texted back. *I think it may be time I pay Kendal a visit. We go way back – I'll see how far back she remembers.*

Dugdale couldn't be certain what Crosbie meant, but he could hazard a guess.

49

Porsche

FEBRUARY 4TH

The young doctor was dressed in a sharp silver designer-label suit, with a tie-less pink shirt. He was handsome with an unnaturally deep mahogany tan that Connor knew was probably the result of a regular date with a sunbed – which for a doctor was quite remarkable as it meant he was happy to risk his health for vanity.

Before the doctor could introduce himself, Connor launched into his act: 'Thanks for seeing me, doctor. I've just moved here, you see, and I don't have my methadone. I went to that chemist but the snooty woman wouldn't give me any. Full up, she said. One hundred and fifty maximum, or something. I'm desperate. I need a hit. I don't want to go back on the smack. That's how I ended up in the Bar-L in the first place, right? I'm climbing the walls here.'

'Okay, Mr Brett, take a seat and we'll see what we can do for you. I am Dr Marran.'

'Marran? Where's that from, then?'

The doctor gave an easy smile. 'Romania, originally. It means marine. We were once a family of sailors.'

'Did your family sail here, then?' Connor asked, causing the doctor to laugh.

'No, we flew. It's faster. Anyway, Mr Brett, I am the addiction specialist for this practice. So I'll be your point of contact here while you're living in Ruckhouse.'

'And you'll get me my methadone? Today?'

'Yes, I'll get everything sorted for you today. Now you said you've been on a methadone programme but I don't have any record of it here on the system.'

'That's 'cos I was in the Bar-L.'

'It doesn't matter where you were, it should be on your NHS records.'

Connor inwardly cursed himself for not realising that would be the case.

'No matter,' the doctor said, 'can you remember how much you were on?'

'Er, 40 mls, I think.'

'That sounds about right. And how are you otherwise? I see you have chronic asthma too, so we will also need your inhalers on prescription. Can you roll up your sleeve, please?' The doctor began attaching his blood pressure pump to Connor's arm.

'When can I get all this, doc?'

'As soon as you leave here.'

'But that snooty cow won't take me.'

'I'll have a word with Miss Smart' – the doctor had no need to ask who Connor was referring to – 'I'm sure she can find a space on her register for you.'

Connor could see the doctor subtly checking for any needle marks on his arms, while inflating the blood pressure pad.

'120/80, you have textbook blood pressure, Mr Brett. Very good.'

Connor thought his running regime had blown his cover. 'I've been trying to keep fit. Just need to keep clean as well.'

'That's the spirit. You could end up as a marathon runner, Mr Brett.'

Connor was a marathon runner, but if Dr Marran was suspicious he never showed it, and he spent the next few moments tapping at his keyboard before a small printer sprang into action, spewing out a pink prescription slip.

'That your motor in the car park?' Connor asked, deliberately changing tack.

'Which one?' Dr Marran replied while finishing off his notes on the screen.

'The red Porsche.'

'Guilty as charged,' the doctor said with a broad smile.

'How much?'

'Are you wanting to buy it from me, Mr Brett?'

'No, but I bet you didn't get much change out of £100,000.'

'Try £150,000,' the doctor said, handing over the pink prescription. 'I've booked you in for another appointment next week to see if it settles your anxiety. And keep up the running or whatever it is you're doing to keep fit. You're in fine health, otherwise. Nice meeting you, Mr Brett. I'll call Miss Smart now. Everything should be sorted out by the time you walk over to the chemist.'

Connor left the surgery with a nervous sweat sticking his shirt to his body. But if his cover had been blown then he certainly wouldn't have been issued with a prescription. As for Miss Smart, the doctor clearly had a hotline to her. After all, calling a chemist was the work of a receptionist.

Connor stood outside and Googled the red Porsche 911 turbo, which was parked directly across from the main entrance, perhaps so the reception staff could keep an eye on Dr Marran's pride and joy, or maybe because he wanted to show off. Search results said the model cost around £145,000. Not much change from £150,000, just as the doctor had said. Connor felt it was crass for the vainglorious Marran to flaunt his wealth in a community that had none, bar its famous lottery winner. By whatever means, the doctor was making a small fortune from Ruckhouse, reminding Connor of the old phrase, 'where there's muck, there's brass'.

50

Temptation
MAY 29TH

Kendal's home was a smart semi-detached new-build clad in yellow sandstone and rough cast. It was typical of the new estates that spring up with alarming speed all around the country. They are usually given grandiose names like The Meadows. Hers was called Woodland Views, on account of a tiny smattering of trees on its perimeter which the house-builders had originally wanted to chop down to erect more units, only to be denied by the council. So they had decided to make a virtue of the name instead.

In reality, the rows of identikit houses were sandwiched between a railway line and giant electricity pylons, and you could actually hear the power humming through the cables. Their dominance made the estate look like it was in the throes of some sort of apocalyptic *Day Of The Triffids*-style attack. Funny to think that this was seen as the 'posh' end of Ruckhouse.

Crosbie found Kendal's house, which had her Mercedes Coupé sitting outside. The DCI hoped she had calmed down after her heated doorstep row with her brother an hour earlier – he remembered how volatile she had been as a teenager.

He knocked on the door and waited. There was no answer. He was about to try again when he heard footsteps on the stairs inside. The locks were undone and Kendal opened the door wearing a dressing gown and a towel around her hair. She looked tiny without her heels.

'You would have to call just when I was taking a shower. Impeccable timing, Bing.'

'Can I come in, Kendal?'

'Well, I don't want the entire neighbourhood gawping at my tits,' she said in her typically brusque manner.

'Thanks,' he said, stepping into her home. She showed him into the front room and sat down on the couch opposite. Her dressing gown rode up, showing her muscly fake-tanned legs, while her cleavage was emphasised by the gown's belt tied tightly beneath her breasts. Crosbie needed all his self-control not to indulge in admiring the sight in front of him that had been denied to the neighbours.

'I'm not supposed to see you without a lawyer,' she said. 'Strict instructions. Especially after your questioning of my sisters.' But her smile said she wasn't going to be calling Paul McFadden anytime soon.

'What else could we do after we found the triplets' blood on the murder weapon?'

'Planted it, more like,' Kendal replied coolly.

'Not on my watch. And the Kendal I knew didn't take strict instructions from anyone.'

'People change.' She smirked.

'Not always,' Crosbie remarked dryly.

'Well, you've changed. Used to be a right scrawny thing. Just another boy from the Ruck. Never thought you would end up as a copper.'

'At least you didn't say "pig".' It was Crosbie's turn to smile.

'I thought about it. So how can I help you, Bing?'

'I am trying to find your dad's killer, but I find it strange that his family don't want to help.'

Kendal laughed out loud before answering, 'Can you blame us? Our dad wins £100 million, then six months later he's murdered. The triplets' DNA is found on the knife when everyone knows they couldn't harm a fly. Even you lot must have figured that out or you would have charged them. So who's going to be your next prime suspect? Me?'

Crosbie chose to remain silent and expressionless.

'So knowing which way the finger of suspicion was going to point, we decided to get "pro-active" – or fight fire with fire, as I prefer to call it,' she said. 'That's why we brought in the best lawyer that money can buy. And, as you know, money isn't really an issue for us anymore.'

'But surely you would want your father's killer brought to justice?'

'Justice?' Kendal scoffed. 'And since when have the people from the Ruck ever had justice? You surely haven't forgotten everything from your time here. It's always been a question of what the cops can make stick rather than who actually did it. And the cops have always hated the Hanlons. That's why they sent you. The local boy who can try and screw whatever you can out of us. Your bosses can't wait to pin it on one of us. But they're barking up the wrong tree. We're all innocent. That's why we can't break ranks. So what you call non-coop-eration, we call survival.'

'It looks guilty,' Crosbie observed.

'I don't give a fuck how it looks,' Kendal snapped, turning the atmosphere distinctly frosty.

Neither spoke for several moments, until Kendal decided to soften her demeanour.

'Look, Bing, I don't know who killed my dad. But the last thing we want is your lot doing your usual divide and conquer thing, trying to get us all to turn on each other. That isn't going to happen. So you are just going to need to solve this one all by yourselves.'

Her reaction was not typical of the recently bereaved, but Crosbie knew the Hanlons were far from typical. 'Will your father's money be split evenly between all of you?'

'That's definitely venturing into "needing a lawyer present" territory, Bing.'

'I was just curious,' he said truthfully.

'Yes, but curiosity can lead to accusations. Look, if there's nothing else, I would like to get this hair dried before it turns into a frizz ball.'

'Of course. Thanks for your time, Kendal.' Crosbie made

his way to the door, but what Kendal said next almost floored him.

'You could always come upstairs while I get ready?' she offered, walking towards him.

Crosbie felt an instant stirring in his loins. Before he could answer, Kendal pulled his head towards her, their lips locking passionately. She pushed one of her bare legs between his, feeling how he was now almost fully aroused.

He pulled away. 'I would love to Kendal, but this case is fucked up enough.'

'Just thought we'd get it out of our system. Unfinished business and all that.'

'Thanks, I'm flattered. Truly, I am.'

'Well, I'm not going to beg,' Kendal said.

Crosbie felt his willpower wilting in the heat of the moment. His chief constable had told him to do 'anything' to solve this case. Perhaps this could be looked upon as being in the line of duty.

Kendal made the decision for him, untying her robe, with only her hardened nipples preventing it from falling all the way open. She took his hand and led him upstairs, saying, 'By the way, if you think this will help with your case, it won't. I don't do pillow talk.'

Right at this moment, the murder of Harry Hanlon was the last thing on Crosbie's mind.

51

Bad batch

FEBRUARY 7TH

'No one is interested in the death of another junkie,' Connor Presley's news editor, Big Fergie, barked down the line.

'I know that, but that's the ninth this month. It's got to be worth a couple of door knocks?'

'For what? To get a sob story from some poor old dear who thought her junkie son or daughter would have got clean if only they'd got the help they needed from the NHS? Save it, Elvis. No one gives a fuck about a dead junkie. Not the cops. Not their local communities and certainly not us. Have you got anything else?'

'Not right at this moment.'

'Well, find something. And it better not involve needles,' his news editor demanded before bringing the conversation to an abrupt end.

Connor knew his boss was right. This wasn't a newsworthy story for the *Daily Chronicle*. He suspected Big Fergie was also right about the police and their lack of concern. He called Police Scotland's communication department to speak to one of the more friendly PRs, Gail Firth, nicknamed Gale Force by her friends and colleagues. Although she could blow hot and cold, she was actually the rare type of public relations professional you could ask a question and expect an honest answer.

'Hi Gail, Connor Presley.'

'Elvis, how the devil are you?'

'Surviving, just. Any more cutbacks and my editor will have to start calling you himself for stories.'

'Tell me about it. They're making two compulsory redundos in here, too.' Gail sighed.

Connor forgot that it wasn't just the newspaper industry that faced the constant threat of job cuts nowadays. 'Really? How many will that leave you with?'

'Fourteen, in total. Just enough to man the rota as long as no one gets sick or decides to get pregnant.'

'You not up for the latter, then?'

'Way past that, Elvis, in case you're offering.'

'Always.'

'Anyway, it's a bit early for that kind of chat. What are you up to? Another "bungling cops" story?'

'Nah, I'm bored of them. I'm on for some advice.'

'"She looked sixteen" is no defence.'

'Not that kind of advice. See these drug deaths? Are they being investigated?'

'Investigated? In what way?' Gail asked suspiciously.

'I just thought nine deaths in a month was worthy of more interest.'

'Elvis, are you writing something on cops not doing enough?'

'No, not at all. I just read about another death and it got my spidey senses tingling. I figured there might be more to it.'

'Well, your spidey senses are way off, Elvis. They're junkies. They inject shit into their veins. Only, there must be a bad batch doing the rounds. We have put out a general health warning to all GPs to alert the addicts to the danger. But what more would you expect Police Scotland to do? Post-mortems have been carried out: they all said death by overdose. Procedures have been followed to the letter.'

'Whoa. I'm getting the full Gale Force Ten here,' Connor said, trying to defuse the situation. He forgot how wound-up Gail could get while defending the police.

'I haven't even started yet,' Gail fumed.

'Look, genuinely, I am not fishing for anything. I just thought I might be missing something.'

'You're not. And anyway, I wouldn't have thought your editor would be interested in dead junkies.'

'He isn't. Listen, I've got to go, but thanks. I always enjoy our chats.'

'Me, too,' Gail replied.

'That's what I love about you: from a hurricane to a soft summer breeze in almost the same breath.'

'I bloody wish it was summer. This winter seems like it will never end. Anyway, take care of yourself, Elvis.'

Connor sat in his car pondering the two back-to-back conversations he'd just had about how no one cared about dead addicts. But their families cared. Connor cared.

52

Busted

MAY 30TH

'I'm told you had a meeting with DCI Stuart Urquhart?' Crosbie said, as Dugdale entered his office. The colour drained from the young trainee's face. Before he could answer, Crosbie added, 'I thought I gave you express instructions not to speak to any of the previous investigating team.'

'You did, sir, but...'

'But you ignored me?' Crosbie said.

'Yes, sir, I did.' His mentor must have spies everywhere. Dugdale knew it was pointless trying to defend himself. He had gone behind his boss's back and was well and truly busted.

'What did that old windbag have to say for himself?' Crosbie asked.

'He had tried to find the missing DVR, sir. He had the house searched and the family followed, but came up blank. He's convinced one of them smuggled it out of the Macarena somehow. He reckons that if they went to such lengths, it means that something incriminating has been recorded, sir.'

'Urquhart was always full of himself,' Crosbie said dismissively.

'He has a point though, sir,' Dugdale replied.

'Don't get lippy with me, Duggie, you still disobeyed a direct order.'

'I learned from the best, sir,' Dugdale said, chancing his luck.

Crosbie burst out laughing. 'Okay, youngster. You're off the hook. But don't go speaking to that twat again. He'll only try to recruit you.'

'Yes, sir.' Dugdale thought it was best to keep DCI Urquhart's job offer to himself.

'I need you to head up to your wee hiding hole again. I want you to follow the Hanlons when they leave. See where they go. Pick a new Hanlon a day and report back to me.'

'Yes, sir,' Dugdale replied.

'And by the way, a prick like Urquhart will promise you the moon, but why have that when you can spend all your time in the Ruck, thanks to me?' Crosbie asked rhetorically.

Dugdale was starting to think he had made an unwise career choice.

53

Death knock
FEBRUARY 7TH

Nancy Clarke had that heart-broken look Connor had seen so often on the doorstep before. She was a tiny woman with sloped shoulders and grey skin that matched her cropped grey hair. She looked in her seventies but was probably much younger. Her red eyes could barely meet Connor's – the grief wore so heavily on her. She stepped aside in the hallway before he had even finished his introduction.

'My Gerard was a good boy.'

As Connor knew from experience, mothers always thought their sons were 'good boys', even if they were murderers or paedophiles. He reckoned if he'd been able to doorstep Adolf Hitler's mother, she would have also declared her son had been a 'good boy'. He followed Nancy into her flat, which was well-kept but with meagre possessions. He suspected her son had sold off anything of value that his mother owned.

'He was trying to go clean,' Nancy said as she reached the kitchen. 'He really was. He'd been on the methadone. He was sticking with it, too.'

'But he overdosed on heroin, Mrs Clarke.'

'Aye, son. He was sent it in the post.'

'Sent what, Mrs Clarke?'

'Drugs. He got a card the morning he died. My son only ever got letters from the fiscal.' Scotland's public prosecutor, the Procurator Fiscal, was always just referred to as 'the fiscal'. 'Then he gets a letter. Like a birthday card, and he's all happy about it. But it wasn't his birthday.'

'Do you still have the card, Mrs Clarke?'

'Aye, son. I offered it to the police but they weren't interested. Just wanted an open-and-shut case.'

The card had a simple design of a purple orchid on the front – it was one of those cards that could be ordered over the internet with a personalised printed message. Connor held the card by its edges, treating it like potential forensic evidence. Inside, it read, *For old time's sake.*

'The smack was inside the card,' the woman said. 'It was a wee brown package. Gerard couldn't help himself. He'd been on the methadone programme for six months and had been totally clean for the last three weeks. But when someone puts drugs right into his hand like that, he couldn't resist. It killed him. Too pure, they said. His body wasn't used to the drugs anymore. It stopped his heart. I found him sitting on the sofa with the needle still in his hand. No mother should have to see their boy like that.'

Nancy started crying, her sobs bringing on a rough-sounding cough from the depth of her lungs that painfully wracked her small, frail body.

Connor asked softly, 'How did you know the drugs were in the card, Nancy?'

'He hadn't gone out that day and I'd only gone to the bookies. I've got a wee cleaning job, just doing the toilets and hoovering up before it opens. I gave him the card before I left. I was suspicious. I wanted him to open it but he was still sleeping. He must have opened it when I'd gone.'

'So you didn't actually see the drugs inside?'

'No, son. But that's the only way he could have got them. No one comes to visit him anymore. I wouldn't allow his old pals in. They're the ones who got him started on the junk. He was living a quiet life … until this.'

Nancy returned to the kitchen drawer to retrieve a small brown packet. 'I found this scrunched up in my bin. He must have put it there while cooking up in the kitchen. I asked the cops to test it for me. Know what the cheeky bastard said to me? "This isn't *CSI*, missus."'

Connor could just imagine a young cop acting like a prick.

'Could you get it tested, son?' Nancy said, with hope in her eyes.

There was a time when his company wouldn't balk at spending £800 having samples tested at a laboratory. But those days were long gone. And his news editor had also explicitly warned he didn't want any stories with needles. 'I'm sorry, Nancy. My paper wouldn't pay for that.'

The hope that had briefly flickered in the grieving mother's eyes faded away. Her hand with the packet slumped by her side.

'I'll take it. See what I can do,' Connor said, having no idea what he'd do with it next. He reckoned his only chance was to convince DCI Crosbie to have it tested, but Police Scotland's budgets were under as much pressure as newspapers.

'Thank you. My son was murdered. Please find who killed him. They deserve to be brought to justice for what they've done.' Nancy then broke into those sore, uncontrollable sobs again.

Connor would try his best but knew it was a big ask.

54

Normal

MAY 30TH

So that's what's called going under cover? Xx.

DCI Crosbie looked at the text he'd received from Kendal Hanlon and again felt a pang of regret at compromising his whole case.

Not under cover, I was strictly off duty. It was nice seeing you again, Kendal.

Crosbie knew his reply sounded stilted and unnatural. But he was trying to imagine the exchange being read out loud in court or in front of a police complaints panel. He knew it wouldn't save him from dismissal but it might just prevent the Hanlon investigation collapsing around his ears.

Alright, Mr Detective, no need to be so formal. I'm about tomorrow night if you want to come over to the house again? Xx

Crosbie felt a tingling down below. Kendal Hanlon was one heck of a turn-on. But he also knew she was either using him or setting him up. Probably both. Tomorrow night would give her enough time to fit secret cameras in her bedroom, if that was her plan. Then the main police officer investigating her father's death would be in her back pocket.

I'm busy right now – got a big murder case to try and solve. You may have heard about it, he messaged back.

I heard you're getting nowhere with that. The playful message was not one Crosbie would expect from a daughter supposedly still grieving. *Don't keep me hanging on too long. Unlike you, I do have options*, she added.

Crosbie was very tempted, but he knew he was playing with fire. And his carnal desire was immediately shattered by a call from his sister. He knew it wouldn't be pleasant.

'You'll be pleased to know Damien is doing fine since you shot him.'

'Nice to hear from you too, sis.'

'His teacher is just off the phone. Apparently, he managed to sit through the class for the first time ever without fidgeting or getting out of his chair and causing a disruption. He "engaged" in some group discussion and made "worthy contributions".'

'Maybe he just needed a manly presence around the place.'

'A manly presence? You shot him.'

'Well, it seems to have worked.'

'Yes, it has, lucky for you,' his sister said, hanging up and leaving Crosbie genuinely amazed by the miracle powers of his impromptu use of electroshock therapy.

55

Scatter pad
FEBRUARY 7TH

Connor had left Nancy Clarke's home to chap the door of another council flat, this time right in the heart of Ruckhouse. It was known as a 'scatter pad', the unofficial term for emergency temporary housing for victims of domestic abuse, recent releases from jail or drug addicts evicted because of repeated anti-social behaviour. It was one such addict called Martin Young who had been found dead on the premises the previous night. Police had already issued a press release saying there were no suspicious circumstances nor were they seeking anyone in connection with the death. In other words, it was just another junkie overdose. Case closed.

The door was answered by a woman in her mid- to late-fifties in cleaning overalls. Connor had already clocked the small, battered blue van parked outside with the faded name of a cleaning company on the side. The council obviously wanted any remnants of the deceased eradicated before their next emergency arrival, who would no doubt be left standing on patches of still-damp carpet.

The cleaner asked, 'Can I help you, son?'

'I hope so. I'm Connor Presley from the *Daily Chronicle*.'

'It's more than my job's worth to speak to the press, son.' Although she was defensive, she was still being nice about it. Connor felt encouraged to press on.

'I know, and I wouldn't want to get you in any bother. I'm just wondering if you came across a card or a letter while clearing up?'

'I did find a card, as a matter of fact,' she said, rooting about in a bin bag marked *Hazardous Material*, wearing her thick, industrial-strength gloves. 'I thought it was strange as you never find cards in a scatter pad, son. They're not the type of people to get sent cards, if you know what I mean?'

'I do,' Connor assured her.

'Here it is. Don't touch it until I get you a pair of gloves,' and she disappeared into some corner of the apartment and returned with a set of latex surgical gloves much thinner than her own. 'You don't want to touch anything from inside these flats, son. They leave needles, shit, piss – excuse my French – just lying around. And that's just the ones who live. When they've been dead for a few weeks, it's a right mess. Luckily, that poor boy was still fresh.'

'Fresh' seemed a hugely inappropriate description, but given the woman's line of work involved all sorts of smells, Connor could understand why she differentiated various kinds of deaths.

He had great difficulty pulling on the gloves as they were meant for much smaller hands.

The woman watched him and smiled. 'Bet you don't have problems pulling on the other sort of latex.'

Connor chuckled. He had not expected any smut talk but he imagined in her job she would take the laughs wherever she could find them. The gloves fell short of his wrist but would do. The card had the same simple design of a purple orchid as he had seen before. He opened it to read the printed message:

Marty – just a little present from an old friend. Enjoy.

'Didn't make much sense to me,' the cleaner said.

'What's your name?' Connor asked.

'Now don't be going and putting me in your paper, son.'

'No, I wouldn't do that. I've just enjoyed chatting with you.'

'It's Agnes, son. Agnes Hutchison.'

'Agnes?'

'Aye, alright, that's my Sunday name. Everyone calls me Senga.'

Connor had no idea why at some point in the dim and distant past someone had decided to spell Agnes backwards to come up with Senga, which was a truly horrible name.

The cleaner seemed to read his thoughts. 'Here's a tip, son. If you ever have a daughter, don't call her Agnes. She'll only end up as a cleaner like me.'

'Looks like you're doing alright. That's your van out front, isn't it? So you've got your own business.'

'Aye, and I haven't had a holiday in two years. It's knackering, son.'

'Never thought of taking on anyone?'

'Why, you after a job? I could do with a bit of eye candy.'

'The way newspapers are going, I might need to take you up on your offer. Here, Senga, if I gave you my card, would you send me a text if you get any more cases like poor Marty?'

'What's in it for me?' she asked, but didn't really mean it.

'You'd be doing a great public service. I'm specifically after drug deaths and any cards like this. Please keep them for me. It could be important.'

Senga suddenly looked worried. 'Listen, son, I don't want to be dragged into anything, you understand? I've got to work in the Ruck.'

'I know. But I'm not after anything but these cards. You only come in after the cops have been, am I right? So you wouldn't be taking anything from a crime scene. You are literally throwing out the trash. I just want one little bit of trash to come in my direction.'

'Alright, son. I'll do that,' she said, studying his card. 'Chief Investigations Editor,' she said, reading it out loud. 'Very grand.'

'It would be if I headed up a huge department. But I don't. It's just me.'

'You're a loner, just like me then?' Senga said, liking his honesty. 'Okay, deal,' she added, pocketing his business card. 'Knowing the Ruck like I do, I don't think it'll be long before you're hearing from me.'

56

A day in the life
MAY 31ST

It was the last day of May and another 'scorcher', as the tabloids would call it, although after a month of glorious sunshine, even the newspapers had relegated their weather coverage from the front pages to inside. Not that Dugdale cared as he was still cooped up in the empty council flat overlooking the Hanlons' monstrosity, the Macarena. He decided just to follow the first members of the family to emerge, to release him from his urine-soaked confines as quickly as possible. But Billy and Michael left first, with the younger brother pushing the older in his wheelchair towards the day centre for learning disabled adults. Dugdale decided it would be a waste of time to follow them as he could see the day centre at the end of the road from his vantage point anyway.

He didn't have long to wait until the next of the Hanlon family came out of the house: the triplets left in unison, done up to the nines, with their make-up and hair extensions. Their police file noted that the Border Agency had recorded twelve visits to the US in the last three years alone. The previous investigating officers from DCI Stuart Urquhart's team had discovered the girls were working for a subscription porn site. The officers had obviously studied the site extensively, as the file said that the girls mostly 'performed with each other' but latterly men had been introduced on screen for the girls to 'engage with'.

Dugdale was amazed the powers-that-be had even considered charging the petite triplets with the murder of their father. They were tiny. One theory was that Harry Hanlon had got them involved in the porn industry and they had killed him in revenge. But you only had to look at them to realise their only chance of killing a man of Harry's stature was with a gun, not the brute force required with a knife.

The triplets each got into their red, white and blue Minis and drove off. Dugdale followed at a discreet distance. He was in no particular rush; finding three Minis in the Ruck would be easy enough. Five minutes later, Dugdale located the cars parked near the row of shops containing the Manhatten Bistro, Saltire Pharmacy and four competing hair and nail salons. He could see the three sisters through the giant window of one of the salons having their nails painted. Dugdale took note of the date, time and location, with the observation *Had their nails manicured*. An hour later, the girls filed into the Manhatten for lunch, where the trainee detective noted that they had eaten alone. After that, they drove back to the Macarena. And that seemed to be the extent of their day.

Dugdale had always imagined the excitement of taking part in a stake-out, but the reality was almost too boring to bear.

57

Intruder

FEBRUARY 8TH

'Is that you?' April asked Connor in hushed tones.

'There's no proper way of answering that,' he replied, checking his bedside alarm clock. It had just gone 5 am. He knew April didn't normally surface until much later. 'Why are you calling now? You had a funny turn again?'

'No. It's just, I can hear someone talking.'

'In your head or in your house?'

'My house. It sounds like an American. An American woman.' April's voice sounded a little panicky, but she remained silent while listening out for the voice again. Then there it was. Connor had even managed to hear it down the phone.

'Did you hear that?' she asked.

'Yes.'

'Someone's definitely in my house.'

'But why would they be talking to themselves? Stay quiet and hold the phone up high so I can hear it again.'

April did as she was told while Connor pushed his ear as close to his iPhone as possible, trying to speak and listen quietly so he didn't wake Anya in the bed beside him. He could hear April's rapid breathing, but nothing else. Then the voice spoke again. A smile began to form on Connor's lips.

'Been anywhere new recently?' he asked.

'What?'

'Have you visited anywhere new lately?'

'What on earth are you on about? There's someone in my house and you want to know if I've had a day out?' she said in a barely concealed whisper.

'What I want to know is, have you been to a new address recently? Somewhere you haven't been before.'

'Yes, I visited Robert Hanlon at his girlfriend's the other day. So what? There's someone in my house, you idiot!'

'Did you use your satnav?'

'What?' She nearly shrieked with incredulity.

'Your satnav. Did you use it?'

'Yes.'

'And does that satnav speak with an American accent.'

'Yes,' April said more quietly.

'And is that satnav now sitting on your hall table.'

The penny finally dropped and Connor could hear April's bedsprings creak as she got out of her pit. It was followed by her heavy footfall as she made her way downstairs. The voice was much louder this time: 'You have reached your destination,' it said in its tinny, American accent.

'Oh, my. I nearly jumped out of my skin there. It's been lying on the hall table for the past couple of days doing absolutely nothing then suddenly bursts into life?'

'A bit like yourself.' Connor laughed.

'Just when I think I'm finally tech-savvy, this happens. Why does technology hate me so much?'

'I have no idea. But there's certainly never a dull moment when April Lavender's about. Well I may as well get up and go for a run. I guess I'll be seeing you at the Peccadillo shortly.'

'Oh God yes, I'm starving.'

58

Inconsequential
MAY 31ST

DCI Crosbie had decided to work outside this morning to enjoy the glorious conditions. It reminded him of spring at school when the teacher would take class outside on exceptionally sunny days. He took with him the rough draft of Harry Hanlon's autobiography, ghostwritten by April Lavender. It had supposedly been studied by the previous investigator DCI Stuart Urquhart, who was looking for any clues in the manuscript about the killer's identity. April had also been interviewed but, despite spending weeks with the subject before his death, was unable to offer a single name as a suspect.

Crosbie could see Urquhart hadn't thought much of April's book: he had signed his name and printed his rank on the front cover, under the comment *INCONSEQUENTIAL*, which he had written in bold ink. DCI Crosbie had ignored anything Urquhart said or thought all his professional life, so he was not about to start taking heed of him now. He began reading the opening chapter, which was about the moment Harry realised he was £100 million richer than the previous day.

Crosbie could tell he was going to enjoy this book, even if Urquhart thought it added nothing to the ongoing inquiry.

59

Rough day
FEBRUARY 8TH

Connor rubbed the sleep from his eyes as he sat inside Jack Barr's van and watched the young shop assistant in the chemist. He had joined April briefly at the Peccadillo for a strong cup of coffee before heading to meet up with the photographer for the stakeout. And now Connor couldn't stop yawning, after his unexpected early morning alarm call. But he appeared to be having a better day than the shop assistant being chastised by the pharmacist Elizabeth Smart, who was picking up items from the shelves and placing them where they were obviously meant to go. To compound the young girl's misery, it was being done in clear view of the other customers, which would have only added to her embarrassment.

At closing time, the assistant was the first to leave. It looked like she couldn't wait to get out after a horrendous day at work. She didn't have a car so Connor followed her on foot, trudging through the thick snow, which was falling yet again. He didn't have far to walk as she entered a block of flats that had recently been renovated by the local housing association. Along with new double-glazed windows, two-tone red and white roughcasting had been added, to cover the drab, grey breeze-block structure.

Many locals had tried to maintain their little part of Ruckhouse with tidy, well-manicured gardens. One neighbour had even added hanging baskets, which made Connor wonder how often they'd had to rehang them after the local youths had kicked them around the street in the name of fun. But the shop girl's apartment block wasn't one that tried to keep up with the Joneses: its small communal front garden was strewn with litter and broken bottles.

Connor watched a light going on in the right first-floor flat. The new door entry system was broken, as per usual, and he walked up the stairs to knock on the shop assistant's door. Loud music was already blaring from within the flat. She really had had a rough day. He knocked loudly several times before the thumping dance music was finally turned down a notch. Eventually, the young girl opened the door, peeking out from behind the security chain.

'My dad's not home,' she said.

'I'm actually here to speak to you.'

'What about?'

'That cow you work with.'

The shop assistant stared at Connor quizzically, before saying, 'You better come in then, but we only have twenty minutes before my dad comes home.' She introduced herself as Mags Cheyne and showed Connor to the front room, where he explained he was a journalist looking into the drug deaths of local addicts.

'I don't want to get into any trouble. I'll lose my job and my dad will go mental.'

'You won't, and your dad doesn't need to know.'

'You're the junkie from the other day,' Mags suddenly realised. 'The one who couldn't get served.'

'Correct. I was undercover.'

'What do you want?'

'I need a list of everyone who's on the methadone programme. Your boss Elizabeth Smart told me she has a hundred and fifty addicts on the list, but I only ever count a third of that coming into the chemist.'

Connor knew he had struck a chord when Mags replied, 'I asked her about that, too, and she told me to mind my own business. But she has a list with names on it and we're to tick off everyone who has been in for their methadone. There are always loads who haven't appeared, but Miss Smart ticks all boxes anyway, even though I know they haven't been in.'

'Can you get me that list?' Connor asked.

'No, because she puts it away in her own files.' Mags thought for a second and added, 'I could take a photo, though? She takes forty minutes for her lunch and the list is just left under the counter.'

'Perfect, Mags. I think your boss is committing major fraud and I would like to see her answering for her actions.'

'I would like to see that, too.' Mags beamed. It was the first time she had smiled all day.

60

Shadowing Shifty
JUNE 1ST

It was the first day of June and the headline news was that weather forecasters were predicting that Scotland's unprecedented heatwave would continue for at least another month. Some expert then told the BBC that this was a result of global warming. Dugdale couldn't help but think that global warming was a price worth paying after the long winter the country had just been through.

He was back in the commandeered council apartment overlooking the Macarena, with intentions of following Robert 'Shifty' Hanlon as he went about his business.

As always, it was Michael and Billy Hanlon who left the family home first. Dugdale watched as the younger man pushed the large frame of his older brother in his wheelchair in the direction of the day centre, where he diligently took him every day of the working week. Their police file said that Michael had been accepted as a medical student at the University of Glasgow, starting in September. He wondered what would happen to Billy then, as Michael seemed to be the only member of the Hanlon clan who helped his disabled sibling.

It was almost midday before Shifty Hanlon emerged from the Macarena, wearing a scowl along with a tight-fitting sweater. His phone was glued to his ear. He threw his gym bag into the back seat of his car, and Dugdale guessed he was going to work off some of his frustrations by pumping iron down at the private health club that was in an area where the average house prices were quadruple that of Ruckhouse.

He followed Shifty's BMW and found a spot at the furthest point of the club car park. It was the type of place with floor-to-ceiling windows so the outside world could see their patrons working out. Dugdale was no stranger to a gym himself, but he wondered if the sight of unsmiling, straining and sweaty bodies put off more people than it encouraged to become members. Shifty was lifting some huge weights with his steroid-assisted physique, before taking to a running machine to help improve his cardiovascular. Shifty constantly glanced in the direction of his mobile, which Dugdale could see was placed in a phone holder on the running machine, as he waited on a message or a call that didn't come.

At the end of his hour-long workout, he checked the mobile once more before disappearing to get changed. If Shifty headed back towards the Macarena then Dugdale would hazard a guess he didn't receive the message he had been waiting for. Twenty minutes later, the eldest Hanlon got back in his BMW and drove home. He didn't leave again for the rest of the day.

61

The early bird
FEBRUARY 10TH

April parked her car outside Kendal's house. She had proved to be the most elusive of all the Hanlons, cancelling or postponing arranged interviews at the last minute. April got the distinct impression the eldest Hanlon daughter had absolutely no intention of ever speaking to her, but she had managed to catch her unawares when she called at 8 am while waiting for Martel to serve breakfast.

'The early bird catches the worm,' she said to herself after putting Kendal on the spot and insisting she would be stopping by her house in half an hour.

April didn't care much for the new housing estate where Kendal lived. 'Bloody rabbit hutches. Give me a draughty old Victorian house any day,' she said within the confines of her car.

She looked along the street at the other cars parked in various drives. There was the odd works van here and there, but most of the homeowners seemed to have very smart vehicles indeed. The average wage in Scotland was around £30,000 per year, yet people seemed to have money to spare for their smart little houses and their two cars in the driveway, she thought. Some had four-by-fours parked next to expensive German cars like BMWs and Mercedes-Benz. She wondered how on earth they could afford them. Even if both people in the household were working, that was still only a household income of £60,000. She had earned something like that at the *Chronicle*, yet she could only afford beaten-up old bangers for years before finally spending some of her redundancy money on the smart convertible she had now. She always told everyone it was a Renault but in fact it was a Peugeot, and even Connor had given up correcting her.

'Put it on the never-never.' April sighed to herself, remembering the words of her dear departed mother who had bought everything 'on tick' and died in debt. April was allergic to debt. She hated the thought of owing anything to anyone. But she guessed everyone must be doing it now, borrowing money and living outwith their means to afford their little box houses and fancy motors.

She knocked on Kendal's door. 'Oh, it's you,' Kendal said by way of a welcome. She didn't exactly look thrilled to see April. Her demeanour was even frostier by the time they got to the kitchen.

'What time is it?' Kendal asked as she put the kettle on.

'It's just gone ten past nine,' April said breezily.

Kendal was wearing a skimpy dressing gown, which did little to conceal her chest. She was pretty but April reckoned she would be a lot prettier if she smiled once in a while. The layers of make-up also gave her a hard look.

'Got any fags?' Kendal asked.

April was about to say no, but then reached for the emergency pack in her bag. They each lit up a cigarette.

'I don't really smoke, you know,' April protested, earning a suspicious look from Kendal.

'You could have fooled me,' Kendal replied.

'I mean, I have given up. Well, trying to give up, but then the weight just piles on.'

Kendal blew a plume of smoke from her mouth as she looked April up and down.

The journalist read her thoughts. 'I was once like you, skinny with curves in all the right places. But then I discovered my true love: food,' April said with her trademark cackle.

But Kendal was losing patience. 'Look, what is this book about? I'm busy.'

'I just wanted to ask what life was like for you before the big win. And about your mum, too.'

It was Kendal's mother that April was most interested in. She had learned from Harry that her name was Kristine, but relations between them had been strained, to say the least. In fact, Harry didn't have a good word to say about his ex-partner. April, being the nosy person she was, wanted to know more.

Kendal weighed up April's words, deciding whether this was something she was prepared to discuss or not, before taking a seat at the kitchen table. Her dressing gown partially fell open, revealing the tattoos on her long, fake-tanned legs. April wondered why people insisted on ruining their lovely bodies with horrid ink doodles.

'There's not much to tell. We were broke before, but I got by.'

'Got by, how?' April said as she switched on her dictaphone and placed it on the table.

'Ways and means,' Kendal said coolly.

'Can you elaborate?'

'What?'

'Explain what you mean by "ways and means"? If you wouldn't mind?'

Kendal thought about how she would reply before shrugging. 'It doesn't matter now. But by the time I hit fourteen, everyone wanted to ride me. It helped I had these,' Kendal said, opening her gown to reveal the most perfect pair of breasts.

'Wow,' April said genuinely, 'they're magnificent. Are they real?'

'Sure are,' Kendal said proudly. 'Every horny bastard in the Ruck wanted to get their hands on them,' she said, covering up again. 'That's when I figured it was going to cost them.'

'Cost them?' April replied naïvely.

'A pound a go. They could feel them – nothing more – for a quid. If they wanted to get their dirty mitts inside my bra, it was two quid. It was easy money. And when you had fuck-all, it felt like a fortune.'

April had been skint but never that skint. She wondered if she would have done the same. Either way, she couldn't help admire the Hanlon girl's will to survive and the ingenuity of her sliding scale fees.

'Did it ever move beyond the breasts?' April couldn't believe she had asked, but she was curious.

Kendal blew out another cloud of smoke. 'Not at first, but by the time I was sixteen…'

'By the time you were sixteen or before you were sixteen?'

Kendal laughed. 'Alright, Miss Marple, busted. Before I was sixteen. If you put that in your book, there will be a lot of nervous people in the Ruck. But I wasn't a prossie, okay? I want you to make that clear. I wasn't doing drugs, like the other little skanks. I was just doing it for the money.'

April was pretty sure that was the dictionary definition of a prostitute. 'How much were you charging?' she asked.

'Enough. I could earn fifty quid a day – and that was without parting my legs. I was taking home more pay than the teachers.'

'Did it progress from there?'

'Progress?'

'Did you start having sex? Intercourse?'

'Intercourse? I've never heard it called that before, grandma. But no, they didn't get their hole.'

April visibly recoiled at the word 'hole'. She couldn't think of a more repugnant name for sex.

Kendal sniggered at her discomfort. 'Sorry, do you not like that word? I shall try to put it more politely. I didn't let anyone get a poke. Better?'

'Marginally,' was all April would concede. 'What about your mother?'

Kendal's smile quickly disappeared. She asked April for another cigarette as she gathered her thoughts. Eventually, she said, 'My dad and her were always fighting. She had left him – for the millionth time – but then she heard about my "business" at school and turned up in the playground one day. She caught me at it. Thumped me senseless.'

April could imagine the scene.

'She was calling me a little whore in front of the whole

school. But I wasn't a whore – it was just blowies and hand jobs. But she wouldn't listen. The whole school was watching. Eventually the police came and took Mum away and I went into care.'

'So you were still fifteen at that point?' April checked.

'Yeah. Nearly.'

So she was fourteen, April thought to herself, but decided not to challenge Kendal any further.

'The worst part was, I had saved up nearly a grand,' Kendal continued. 'Hid it under a floorboard in my room. But then when my dad heard I'd been turning tricks, he figured out I'd have a stash somewhere. He found it and pissed it all away long before I was even allowed back home. So all my hard work had been for nothing.'

April actually felt sad for her. It had been work – not in the conventional sense, of course, but work all the same. Then Harry Hanlon spent it.

'After that, I told myself I would never go through that humiliation again,' Kendal said.

'What did you do?' April asked as she lit up another cigarette herself.

'The care home helped me get a job at the chemist. General dogsbody but still, it was something,' Kendal explained.

'I hate to be cheeky, but were you doing anything else on the side?' April probed.

'No, I learned you could make a man pay more than cash. You just have to be smart about it.'

'How?'

Kendal thought for a moment before she smiled at some memory. 'Well, say some fella is always desperate to see you on a Wednesday night. You meet him the first few Wednesdays but then say it's too much hassle, what with work and all that. So you then suggest how it would be so much easier to get to his flat if you could drive. But first you need driving lessons. Then a car. Nothing fancy. Just something to get from A to B.'

A to bed, more like, April thought to herself.

'So you suggest all that casually just before he's shot his

load and after you've told him what a great ride he is. Before you know it, I've passed my test and I've got a car.'

April knew it was cynical but also understandable, given what she had been through. 'I can't imagine there are many men from the Ruck who can afford to buy spare cars?'

'Only the drug dealers. The rest are junkies. I know them all as I had to dish out their methadone every morning in the chemist.'

'You must've been a popular girl,' April said, managing to prevent herself from adding 'in more ways than one'.

'Yeah, everyone either wanted me for my body or my drugs.' Kendal chuckled.

'How long did you work at the chemist?'

Kendal took her time before replying, 'Years. I quit when all this happened.'

'Why?'

'Thought it was time for a change.'

'Did your father give you any of his winnings?' April asked.

Kendal laughed, before composing herself. 'That's not really how Dad works. If you want any money, you've got to pick the right time to ask, usually when he stumbles home pissed from the Woodchopper and before he passes out in his armchair. Then and only then are you likely to get something out of him. But my dad isn't the something-for-nothing type.'

'What do you do for money now, if your dad isn't helping you out? Surely you have a mortgage to pay on this beautiful house?'

'I'm looking for another job. I've got an interview next week at another chemist. Hopefully, I'll get that; if not, I'll apply somewhere else.'

April couldn't believe how casual Kendal was when it came to securing a job. If April had been out of work with a new house, she wouldn't have been able to sleep from the worry. But Kendal was very blasé. It was almost as if she didn't have any money concerns at all.

'And how's your relationship with your mum now?'

'We're good,' was all Kendal would say as she narrowed her eyes ever so slightly.

'Would she speak to me for Harry's book?'

'Ha, I don't think you could print half of what she has to say about my dad.'

'I would still like to talk to her. Without putting too fine a point on it, she is the woman who divorced a man with nothing who went on to win £100 million. I know I'd be livid to be left with nothing after putting up with all his shit for years.'

'She'll probably say no,' Kendal said, picking up her iPhone to send her mum a message, 'but I can always ask. I'll let you know what she says.'

Kendal obviously believed she had said enough. 'Look, I've got stuff to do, but we could meet up again soon, if you have more questions.'

'Yes, that would be good. And you'll let me know about your mum?'

'Sure,' Kendal said, showing April to the door.

62

FOI

FEBRUARY 15TH

Connor ripped open the manila envelope lying on his desk. He knew a Freedom of Information request response when he saw one. As the envelope was thick with paper inside, he also knew that his request had not been rejected. The government had taken almost the maximum twenty business days to process his request, just as Connor had predicted.

Connor scanned the needlessly long-winded legalese – *Having received your request dated ... we have agreed it falls within the remit ...* – before his eyes came to the headline figure of £19,820,039 paid out by the Scottish Government to private pharmacies to administer the methadone programme.

'Fuck me,' he said out loud, 'they make almost £20 million a year just from junkies – and it's all legal.'

The following sheets of paper contained a region-by-region breakdown of methadone users, the number of prescriptions issued by individual chemists and the amount they were paid.

Saltire Pharmacy was one of the highest paid in the country, reclaiming a total of £306,052.50.

Connor found another chemist in Ruckhouse that was paid £168,339, while one on the scheme's boundary made over £113,968.

'More than a half-million pound industry in the Ruck alone.'

He turned the page to see the government had also provided a breakdown on the charges, as he requested. The Scottish Government was being charged between £4 and £6 for each methadone prescription. The chemists paid £1.99 to the pharmaceutical companies for every 500 ml of methadone.

Connor checked his notes from his conversation with April's retired pharmacist neighbour, Ken. *Addicts received between 40 ml to 100 ml a day*, he had written. *If they got 40 ml then that one prescription would last around 12 days. The heaviest dose would need a renewed prescription every five days*, he had quoted Ken as saying. *The chemists then charge £2.16 for every dose dispensed, including 10p for each container and £1.34 for supervised administration.*

Connor totted up the figures on his phone's calculator. 'They're making £3.60 on top of every dose,' he said to himself. 'That's a 180 per cent mark-up.'

He called April, switching his phone to loudspeaker so he could talk while using the calculator function at the same time.

'How are you?' April said cheerily.

'Got the FOI in for the methadone users. Saltire is making over £300,000 a year.' Connor started tapping at his screen. 'And that's just from a hundred and fifty junkies.'

'Right,' April said, struggling to keep up as her mind always went blank when confronted with a barrage of figures.

'That's 54,750 prescriptions per annum. The profit is almost £200,000 for one pharmacy. But get this: the chemists are also paid £11.44 for each item on every prescription. So Saltire got an additional £626,340, which doesn't even come from the methadone programme, but straight from the government's coffers for their free-prescriptions policy. This is a veritable goldmine.'

'Wow,' April replied, feigning understanding of what her former colleague was actually banging on about. Connor saw right through her, as usual.

'Okay, for those at the back of the class, that means that

Saltire is making more legally out of heroin addicts than the drug dealers are.'

'Ah,' April said, finally cottoning on, 'but how can they do that?'

'All they have to do is cook the books. Your neighbour told me that every pharmacy is autonomous. Saltire is only treating around fifty addicts but all they would need to do is tell head office they have one hundred and fifty on their books, make sure the drug companies are paid for the doses and skim the rest from the government's never-ending methadone gravy train.'

'Can they do that?'

'They are doing that. I know they're doing it. It's a scandal.'

'Then you've got yourself an old-fashioned scoop.'

'No one says scoop, except in the movies, you should know that.'

'True,' April conceded, 'but it sounds good.'

However, something was bothering Connor. Even though the figures involved were impressive, he felt they still weren't impressive enough for someone like Colin Harris, especially after any corrupt pharmacists and GPs had taken their cut. There must be another angle. A scam on top of the scam. Maybe this was why Harris was feeding him all that helpful information about Shifty and the Gallacher brothers. Maybe he was trying to divert attention from the good thing he had going on here, right in Shifty's own backyard.

Connor knew he was finally on to something huge. He could feel it in his bones.

63

The interview

JUNE 2ND

Dugdale watched from his urine-soaked observation point as Kendal Hanlon arrived at the Macarena. Her silver Mercedes Coupé pulled up just as her brothers Michael and Billy left to make their way to the day centre. She exchanged a few brief words with them both but did not crack a smile or offer to drive them to their destination, probably figuring it was too much hassle to fold Billy's wheelchair up and put it in the boot for such a short distance.

Dugdale knew his boss had already questioned Kendal at her own home, hinting that he had done more than just talk, but Dugdale was still intent on following her, especially today when she was dressed more conservatively than normal, as if she were attending a job interview.

Again the trainee detective had no troubles tailing such a flash car in a rundown area. Kendal drove all the way to the ring road before pulling off at the junction for the neighbouring housing scheme of Stonylee. It was another deprived district but not nearly as bad as Ruckhouse, from what Dugdale could see – it possessed more shops and amenities, for starters.

He watched as Kendal pulled up outside a chemist just before 11 am and figured this was her proposed new place of work – though it seemed hard to believe that someone in her position needed a job. He saw her walk in and receive a warm handshake from the tall, middle-aged male pharmacist. It was the first time he had seen her smile all morning and even from a distance it made Kendal instantly more beautiful. The pharmacist was clearly taken by her too: he shared a joke before showing her into a back room with his hand placed lightly on her shoulder. Dugdale doubted whether the prospective employer would ever lay a finger on Kendal if he knew she had once stabbed a man in the neck with her stiletto heel just for accidently bumping into her in a nightclub.

After half an hour Kendal left with yet more smiles and another warm handshake – it would seem she had got the job. Dugdale tailed her back to the entrance to her housing estate before deciding to drive back to police HQ, where he hoped to give his report directly to DCI Crosbie. He needed a break from the vacant council flat as he was beginning to smell its pungency in his sleep.

64

Content
FEBRUARY 22ND

Connor had to wait days before he was able to get a private meeting with his news editor in the confines of his special investigations office-cum-broom cupboard. All senior management had been away on a training course, which meant they would come back spouting pointless new jargon. Connor had noticed a direct correlation between the newspaper's worsening circulation figures and the increased number of these spurious courses.

He knew his boss was becoming increasingly frustrated by his lack of productivity, but Connor knew it wasn't personal – Big Fergie was no doubt constantly having his ear bent by the acting editor Gordon Gault for his staff to produce more exclusive 'content' for print and digital. Connor hated that term. It was so banal. The story he was working on wasn't just 'content' to fill a page or a screen – it was an exclusive that would have their rivals scrambling for a follow-up, that could win him 'Scoop of the Year' at the annual Scottish Press Awards. Connor did not produce 'content'; he composed copy. And he would continue using the old dyed-in-the-wool newspaper terms until he was inevitably made redundant.

'What's up, Elvis?' Big Fergie asked.

Connor thought his boss looked tired. He seemed to have

aged since the last time they'd met. 'I thought you're supposed to come back from these management courses refreshed and re-energised?'

'Fucking load of shite,' Fergie harrumphed.

Connor was glad to see they shared one another's views on that point. 'Look, I know you've been pissed off by the amount of time I've been spending in the Ruck, but I'm working on a good one,' he assured his boss.

'What have you got?'

'A methadone scam.'

'Oh, for fuck's sake, Elvis. I told you: no one cares about bastarding junkies.'

'I know that.'

'So why are you wasting your time on it?'

'Because people *will* be interested in where £20 million of their taxes is going,' he said, waving the Freedom of Information results in his direction.

Big Fergie was suddenly all ears. 'Go on.'

'The government are forking out an absolute fortune every year on methadone and it's almost completely unregulated. They're not even sure how many addicts are on the books or whether the programme works or makes them worse. What's more, there seems to be a black market between a crooked doc and a pharmacist. And I'm sure Colin Harris is involved in some way, too.'

'So what's happening, exactly?'

'The chemists bill the government for the number of methadone prescriptions they issue. But I know that they are cooking the books. Does this look like a methadone user?' Connor produced a picture of an elderly lady bent double as she pulled her tartan shopping trolley along the street behind her. 'According to Saltire Pharmacy, she's on their methadone programme.'

'How did you get the list?'

'A whistle-blower.'

'That's illegal now.'

'So is large-scale fraud.'

Big Fergie thought about the public interest defence for a moment, before adding, 'And the GP?'

'Dr Marran. Drives a very flash car,' Connor said, showing his boss another photo on his phone, this time of a red Porsche with spoilers.

'Lots of doctors do. They're doctors,' Big Fergie said, deliberately playing devil's advocate.

'This one has a habit of writing prescriptions for the recently deceased. He also consistently forgets to notify the chemist of any deaths of those on the methadone programme. And as you know, there have been a lot of drug deaths lately.'

'An admin error?'

'That's what he'll no doubt claim. But we can show that he was the same doctor who signed many of the death certificates days before he writes their methadone prescriptions. Again, he can claim it's an oversight. But it's still there in black and white looking dodgy as fuck.'

'So he must be getting a kickback from the chemist?'

'Yes, and Colin Harris.'

'Where does Harris come into this?'

'I believe he's taking the dead junkies' unused methadone and selling it on.'

'So the pharmacist and the doctor are getting two bites of the cherry?' Fergie asked.

'Exactly. One from the government and another from Colin Harris Esquire. It's a beautiful piece of business that Harris no doubt has plans on expanding.'

'Fuck me, this is just like the old days, Elvis. It's an old-fashioned investigation. Uncovering corruption. It's marvellous.' Big Fergie beamed.

'It'll be marvellous when I get it all stood up.'

'Take whatever time you need. Use whatever snappers you want. But I love it, Elvis. Fucking love it. This will run for days.'

Big Fergie suddenly looked several years younger, as if the weight of running a news desk with an ever-decreasing budget and the spectre of yet more redundancies had been lifted from his shoulders, albeit temporarily.

Connor knew that the only thing which truly made journalists happy were great stories. His next steps would be to confront the doctor and the pharmacist. But at some point he was also going to have to speak to Colin Harris – even ruthless gangsters have a right to reply.

65

The nightmare ex
FEBRUARY 23RD

April's troublesome satnav took her to a part of Ruckhouse she had never been before, talking her through each turn along the way in that tinny American voice she hated so much, but could somehow never manage to change on the settings.

She had received the postcode and address from Kendal for her mum, Kristine, who had finally agreed to speak. April would be the first journalist to interview the woman who divorced Harry Hanlon just months before his incredible windfall. At the time of Harry's lottery press conference, he assured the media that all his family would be taken care of, including his ex-wife. It was a kind gesture that had endeared him to the general public.

Kristine's apartment was close to the Hanlon family home, situated on the ground floor of a three-storey block of council flats. Like much of Ruckhouse, a lot of money had been spent modernising the apartments and they would have been considered desirable if they had been almost anywhere else than the middle of a deprived Glasgow housing scheme.

Kendal's mother was standing outside, finishing a cigarette, when April pulled up in her convertible. She would have been able to spot Kristine anywhere as she was Kendal's craggier double.

April took her time getting out of her car and carefully made her way up the icy path. 'I see the council don't grit your pavements, either?' April said, by way of introduction. 'I don't know when I'll get a chance to take my top off in this weather.'

Kendal's mother sniggered at the unfortunate turn of phrase.

April's face reddened. 'Sorry, I meant take my top down – oh, that sounds even worse, doesn't it? I meant on my car.'

'I know what you meant,' Kristine replied.

'I'm April,' April said.

'Yeah, I guessed that.' Kristine crushed the butt of her cigarette under her heel, leaving the dowt beside a pile of others.

Kristine did not offer April either a cigarette or her hand as a welcome. She was a small, squat and hard-looking woman, who April imagined had been good-looking just like her daughter, many moons ago. She turned and walked into the building without saying a word, presumably just expecting April to follow. Inside, tea or coffee was not forthcoming, with Kristine simply taking her place in what appeared to be her favoured armchair. April sat down in the couch opposite and busied herself retrieving a tape recorder and notepad from her bag.

'This is nice,' April said, scanning the sparse room. But there were only two ornaments on the fireplace, and no photos of any family at all.

'Aye, it's alright,' Kristine said, lighting up another cigarette, which made April wonder why she had stepped outside for the other one. Again, there was no offer of one for her guest, but April now knew why: Kristine was broke.

'When did you move in?' April asked.

'Six months ago, when I was getting divorced from *him*.'

Him. April reckoned Harry's ears would be burning by the end of this interview.

'How long were you and Harry together?' April said, switching on her dictaphone, her pen poised over her notepad.

'On and off since Kendal was born. What is she now? Thirty-seven? Thirty-eight?'

They clearly weren't as close as Kendal made out as her daughter was actually thirty-nine and soon to turn forty.

'And married?' April added.

'About ten years,' Kristine replied, taking another draw of her cigarette. April would have to double-check all these time frames, because if this woman couldn't get her own daughter's age right, she doubted anything else would be accurate.

'Was it a happy marriage?' April said, deliberately asking a loaded question, knowing it would light the blue touchpaper.

'Are you fucking kidding me?' Kristine spat. 'That bastard beat me black and blue. And he hit his kids, too. He's a drunken, womanising, wife-beating child abuser.'

April only wished she was back on a daily newspaper – this would be an instant splash. It still would be whenever the book eventually came out, but then the buzz would be long gone.

'When did the trouble start?' April said, pushing further.

'From the beginning. He was always quick with his fists.'

'Did you retaliate?'

'Only to defend myself. I had to stick up for myself, and the kids, too.' She puffed nervously on her cigarette, though whether her anxiety was from the memories or from lying, April couldn't tell.

'Is that why you moved out?'

'Aye, it was either that or the women's refuge. The council had to give me something.'

That was true, although April wondered why she'd been given a flat less than two miles from her abuser's home, if she really had been in that much danger. 'At Harry's lottery press conference, he said he would look after all his family, including you. Did he?'

'Fuck off,' she spluttered. 'That bastard didn't give me one fucking penny.'

'So why didn't you speak up? I know I tried to approach you when I was with the *Daily Chronicle* but you didn't say anything about what he was putting you through?' April knew that something wasn't ringing true.

'I was waiting to see if he would weigh me in,' Kristine said.

But April thought that a woman like Kristine wouldn't just meekly sit around in silence waiting for Harry to pay her. She would shout, scream and threaten him, and if that didn't work she would have humiliated him in the press. However, she chose to stay silent. Of course, if she was a victim of domestic abuse she could be scared, but Kristine didn't look the type who frightened easily. 'I see the name Hanlon is on your door. Have you not changed your surname?' April asked out of curiosity.

'I can call myself whatever I want,' she replied defensively.

April now knew for certain she was lying. Why would any woman want to keep the name of her abuser after being legally separated?

'You should speak to Kendal again,' Kristine offered, taking the lead for the first time since they started the interview. 'She will back up what I've said. She also has other things to tell you, too.'

Kristine was a bad actress. Her well-rehearsed line was stilted and unconvincing in its delivery. 'I'll do that,' April replied, now knowing the pair were definitely in cahoots. She wondered what they had dreamt up between them. She had no doubt that Kendal would make contact first – and she didn't have long to wait after leaving Kristine smoking her umpteenth cigarette of the morning.

66

Update
JUNE 2ND

DCI Crosbie had allowed Dugdale to have the rest of the day off after he had delivered his report on Kendal attending a job interview. He was keen to return to Harry Hanlon's autobiography anyway and wanted peace to read.

Ironically, he had just finished the chapter about Kendal turning tricks at school for money. Crosbie had remembered it well, not that he could afford to pay her for a grope, but he could recall the day her mum arrived and battered the crap out of her daughter in the school playground. There was a huge commotion with the police and it was the last he had seen of Kendal until they had sex at her place a few days previously. He had not paid for the privilege but he suspected there would still be a high price to pay for their dalliance.

Like the rest of the school, Crosbie had been shocked by the ferocity of Kristine's attack on her daughter. He remembered the nervous looks on the faces of some of the teachers who may have paid the underage Kendal for her services. And now, reading her own account of the incident in her dad's book, he realised just how utterly tragic it had all been. Kendal had spent the next year and a half of her school life in care. She had been a tough nut before becoming a subject of the state, but being taken from her home had made her even harder.

He could now see she had become a product of the system. Kendal was not the type to ask for or illicit sympathy, but Crosbie felt sorry for her nonetheless. He wondered what she could have become if only she had been given a better start in life – if she had escaped the Ruck as he had done. He liked to believe she would have been a successful business-woman rather than one of seven siblings suspected of the brutal murder of their father.

DCI Crosbie couldn't tell if he was enjoying the Hanlon biography so much because he knew the cast of characters and locations, or because it was such a damn good read. Either way, he thought April Lavender might just have a best-seller on her hands one day if her book was ever published.

67

Right of reply

FEBRUARY 23RD

Elizabeth Smart left the doctor's surgery with the day's prescriptions stacked away neatly in her black leather handbag. Everything about her was neat and proper, from her greying hair tied in a tight bun to the tweed coat fastened almost all the way to the top over her starched white blouse and three-quarter length skirt. This was a woman who liked order in her life. Elizabeth walked smartly, too, in a perfectly straight line, making her way to Saltire Pharmacy, where she arrived at precisely 8.50 am today and every day.

Connor had observed her routine on many occasions. She hadn't even broken her stride when one morning a local attempted to stop her to ask the time. Instead, she had pushed past with the stinging remark, 'Buy a watch.'

He would never forget the contemptuous look she had given him when he had posed as an addict pleading for help. She seemed to have enjoyed his desperation and misery, like a Nazi concentration camp commandant toying with doomed prisoners before sending them to their deaths. In fact, the more he thought about it, the more he could envisage Elizabeth as a willing member of the Third Reich.

Connor was going to thoroughly enjoy fucking up her day.

'Miss Smart. Elizabeth Smart,' he said as he approached her. The pharmacist went to walk by, but Connor stood in her way. 'You probably won't recognise me as I'm wearing a suit today. I'm Connor Presley, the special investigations editor for the *Daily Chronicle*.' Connor loved how grandiose that sounded on these occasions. 'The last time we met I was posing as a heroin addict trying to get on your methadone programme,' he added with a smile, which was met by a scowl.

'And how can I help you?' Elizabeth Smart replied sharply.

'Well, it's not really your help I require this time, Miss Smart – it's more that I'm giving you the right to reply. I'm running a report in the newspaper about how you, Dr Marran and the gangster Colin Harris have been running a methadone scam.' Connor pointed his dictaphone in the direction of her mouth, its red record light flashing ominously.

'How preposterous,' Elizabeth said as she went round Connor, her head down as she made a beeline towards the sanctity of her workplace.

'I know, I'd have thought that, too – someone as respectable as yourself and, of course, the good doctor. But I've spent weeks gathering evidence' – Connor was keeping pace with the pharmacist – 'and it doesn't look good for you.'

'Is that so?' Elizabeth replied with a nasty tone.

'I believe that you and Dr Marran have exaggerated the number of addicts you dispense methadone to. You said you had a maximum of a hundred and fifty on your books, but each day I've only counted fifty-odd receiving the drug from you.'

'Not everyone needs supervision.'

'Indeed, but you have continued to dispense drugs to dead patients. Some have been dead for months.'

'If that's the case then that's an administrative oversight. I shall look into it immediately.' Elizabeth had stopped walking by now, apparently confident she was back in command.

Connor decided to play his trump card without putting Elizabeth Smart's employee Mags Cheyne in the frame. 'You also have people on your methadone programme who are not recovering addicts. Several people. One seventy-six-year-old woman gets treatments for her arthritis but was aghast when I told her she was also on the methadone programme. I believe this to be more than an administrative oversight. I believe this to be deliberate fraud.'

'I will sue you for every penny if you print a single word of these lies,' Elizabeth warned, trying to retain the upper hand, but the steely edge had gone from her voice.

Connor went in for the kill. 'What's more, I believe that the unused methadone from these bogus claims is then being passed on to Glasgow businessman Colin Harris, who sells it on the black market. I put it to you, Miss Smart, that you are an integral part of a conspiracy to defraud the NHS and the Scottish Government of several hundred thousands of pounds each year. What is your response to that?'

'You'll be hearing from my lawyer,' Elizabeth responded as she broke into a trot.

'You'll need a very good lawyer, Miss Smart, when the police coming calling,' Connor shouted towards the back of her head. He could have easily caught up with the pharmacist, but he had told her the allegations and given her a fair right to reply. Pursuing her along the street could be seen as harassment, and he wanted everything done by the book for the fallout that would no doubt ensue.

And anyway, Jack Barr – inside his beaten-up old van at the end of the street – would have captured every moment of Elizabeth Smart's discomfort with his long lens. Connor looked forward to seeing the photos.

68

Allegations

FEBRUARY 23RD

April had only just returned to her car, when she received a text from Kendal Hanlon: *Have you got time to talk? I'm at home.*

April texted straight back. *Sure, on my way.*

The snow had come on heavy again, meaning the gritted roads were becoming nearly impassable and her convertible would be slipping and sliding all the way to Kendal's house. 'What was I thinking buying a convertible in Scotland?' she asked herself before she remembered telling Connor how much she had been looking forward to driving with the 'sun on my face' – only for Connor to add, 'and the wind blowing through your chins'. He was a cheeky swine but he did crack her up. She missed working with him. Now all she was doing was moving from Hanlon to Hanlon and that was no fun at all.

Kendal showed April into her kitchen again. She also failed to offer her guest a cup of tea, coffee or a cigarette.

Like mother, like daughter, April thought.

Kendal got right to it. 'You know how I told you my dad wasn't the something-for-nothing type?'

'Yes, I do,' April replied wearily, feeling this conversation was about to get very dark, but she pressed on regardless. 'What did you have to do, Kendal?'

'Usually just a wee hand job would be enough,' she said,

puffing on her cigarette in an almost identical fashion to her mother. 'He's normally so pissed he doesn't even know who he's getting it from. Not that he cares.'

'And what did you get in return?' April asked.

'Money. Recently, it has been fifty quid. But before it was just whatever he had in his pockets.'

'Before? What age did this all start, Kendal?'

'When I was still at school.'

'But you were taken into care at fourteen.'

'Fifteen.'

'You were fourteen, Kendal, I checked. So was this before or after then?'

'After, I think, but definitely when I was still underage,' Kendal replied vaguely.

'Did he make anyone else do the same? The triplets?'

'Not that I know of.'

'And you never discussed with your brothers or sisters what your father made you do?'

'It's not the sort of thing you just bring up, is it?'

'Do you have any proof?' April asked.

'What sort of proof?' Kendal said defensively.

'Eyewitnesses? Photographic evidence?'

'It's hardly a spectator sport and it's not the kind of picture you want for the family album.'

But it would be an ideal photo for blackmail, April reckoned, which she believed Kendal was more than capable of.

'Can anyone verify your claims, Kendal? Have you told anyone else at all apart from me?'

'Just my mum. Sorry, kinda ruins your book a bit, doesn't it? Not the happy-ever-after fairy tale ending you were hoping for.'

April felt drained. It certainly wasn't the story she had wanted or promised the publishers. Instead, she found herself in the middle of a family feud. And now there was this, a clumsy attempt to frame Harry Hanlon. Although, what if the allegations were true? Or at least had a grain of truth?

'You should go to the police,' April said grimly.

'Are you kidding?' Kendal scoffed. 'I'm not a grass.'

'I really think you should. I can't use this in Harry's book,' April explained.

'You were in newspapers, weren't you? Take it to them. Expose the pervert for the dirty bastard that he is.'

'But it will only be you and your mum's word against his. That won't be seen as impartial. It will be viewed as revenge by a woman who had the misfortune of divorcing a man shortly before he won £100 million. You would be accused of collaboration.'

'Collaboration?' Kendal said, becoming aggressive.

'Colluding. Making it up.'

'I'm not a fucking liar, okay?' Now Kendal was getting downright threatening.

'Then you will have to go to the police. These claims are nothing unless they are being officially investigated.' It was April's duty to give this advice, as she had done so in the past when an interviewee came to her with allegations of sexual abuse. The fact she didn't believe Kendal was neither here nor there.

'I will then, see if I don't,' Kendal said without conviction. She stomped to the front door and opened it for April to leave. Manners were clearly not Kendal or her mother's thing.

April sat in her car. The blizzard had stopped and the sun was making a rare appearance, forcing April to reach for her sunglasses to protect her eyes from the snow glare. She even contemplated putting the car's top down until she remembered it was minus 7°C. But these thoughts were just a distraction from the turmoil she now felt in the pit of her stomach. How could she finish writing a book about a man who could be a child abuser? Thank God it was the weekend. She needed a rest from all the Hanlons.

69

Showdown
FEBRUARY 24TH

Connor ordered a bottle of Les Preuses Grand Cru from the Portman's barmaid Mary and made his way to Colin Harris's usual booth.

'I'll bring the glasses,' Mary said as she followed the journalist past the deadbeats on their stools to the other side of the pub, which always gave Harris more privacy for his 'business' meetings. 'Is Colin expecting you?' Mary asked suspiciously, as she took a corkscrew from a side pocket to open the bottle.

Connor noticed that the corkscrew was one of these multi-tool affairs, which also contain a sharp-looking blade, longer than the type on a Swiss Army Knife. 'No, I thought I'd surprise him.'

Mary arched her heavily drawn-in eyebrows. 'He's not the type who likes surprises, son.'

Connor thought it was funny being called 'son' by people roughly his own age. 'I know, but I need to speak to him and I thought it'd be better face to face.'

'On your head be it,' Mary said ominously as she headed back to the bar, where she poured another pint for one of her regulars, before fishing out a packet of cigarettes from her bag to head outside for a smoke. Connor noticed she also took her smartphone with her, no doubt to alert her boss to his presence.

Connor studied the label of the £160 bottle of wine, which he had no intention of paying for, and started to feel angry. Harris may have been a good contact for him over the years, but he was still scum. Highly intelligent and engaging, but scum nonetheless, who grew rich off the abject misery of others.

A little over ten minutes after Mary had returned from her smoking break, the door flew open and a harassed-looking Colin Harris entered, making straight for Connor. 'What do you want, Elvis? I'm busy.'

Harris had never been so curt with him before, so Connor didn't bother with any pleasantries. 'Methadone,' was all the reporter replied.

'Is work that bad? Or did you pick up nasty habits from all the time you've spent hanging around the Ruck.'

'You're right, I have spent a lot of time there of late. How did you know?'

'I saw you asking for a bagel in the Manhatten one day. With an "e". Its illiterate owner wouldn't do well on *Just A Minute*.'

Connor could kick himself for not spotting Harris in the café. But that was typical of the gangster: on the outside he was so bland he just blended in.

'The Ruck is a real shithole, isn't it?' Harris continued, still not taking a seat or his jacket off.

'Made all the more shitty by crooked GPs and pharmacists,' Connor replied. The phrase hung between the two men for an uncomfortable length of time before Harris finally relented.

'So investigative journalism is still alive and kicking, is it?' Harris replied. He took off his chequered suit jacket and slung it over the back of a chair, before taking his seat. He then poured himself a large glass of Chablis and topped up the journalist's glass.

'It started off with a report on Radio 4, and you know how much I love my Radio 4, Elvis.'

Connor nodded as he sipped his wine.

'Some university professor had done years of research on Scotland's methadone programme and concluded it was an "out-of-control black hole" where addicts just disappeared. Now I'd have thought that every penny of taxpayers' money spent on any NHS scheme would be tightly controlled – especially when it's costing the country over £20 million a year – but not so according to the professor on the radio. And get this: the professor said there were still no accurate figures of how many addicts were even on the programme. I mean, just imagine that. £20 million a year being spent and you don't even know how many customers you have.'

Connor noted how Harris used the word 'customers' for addicts, as that's exactly what they were to him.

'What's more, the professor said that once addicts are on the methadone programme, they're just parked there forever. "Indefinitely", was the word he used. Yet, the NHS doesn't know anything about them. They don't know if they come off drugs all together, get worse, nothing. All they do is sign the cheque every year. It's just as the professor said: it all disappears into a black hole.'

Connor could guess which way the conversation was going; all he had to do was give it a little push. 'So you stood on the edge of the black hole, stared into the abyss and saw a business opportunity?'

'How poetic, Elvis. You always did have a way with words. All this unaccountable government cash was just swirling around in space. The amazing thing was, it was limitless. £20 million this year, £21 million the next. What politician in their right mind would ever cut the methadone programme and leave unmedicated junkies to run rampage amongst their constituents?'

Harris had replied to Connor's question, although, like a skilful politician, he hadn't answered it directly. 'But you weren't the first one to spot this business opportunity, were you?' Connor pressed on regardless. 'It was Kendal Hanlon who was involved at the start, wasn't it? She's the one who got the ball rolling. She would have noticed that when a junkie died they still stayed on the books. Perhaps she even pointed out this flaw in the system to Elizabeth Smart. Maybe had a little joke about sharing the profits – that's how these plans can start.'

'Come now, Connor, if you've ever met Elizabeth Smart then you know she's not the joking kind,' Harris replied, which at least confirmed the gangster knew the pharmacist.

'Okay, but perhaps she's just a cold-hearted business-woman. Maybe she mulled over Kendal's suggestion, ran a few figures and thought, "Why shouldn't I make extra money for having to work with the scum of the earth?" That probably fits her character profile more accurately.'

Harris said nothing.

'Then I'm wondering why Kendal didn't just get her brother Shifty to sell on the excess methadone – because they would have been awash with the stuff every day and no doubt would have aroused suspicion if they started dumping it. So why not sell it on? Increase their profit margins yet again. But someone as street-smart as Kendal wouldn't want Shifty to be involved in such a lucrative arrangement. She knows an idiot when she sees one, even if it was her own kith and kin. So she came to you and she ends up with a nice house and a nice car. Then you suggest she moves on to another chemist, and then another, setting up and establishing your network as she went from chemist to chemist. Recruiting everywhere she went. Perhaps the plan even led to tension between her and Shifty. A sibling rivalry that saw him try to outdo her and get in with the Gallachers to take over Ruckhouse and then Glasgow. But he was too late. You already had it sewn up. But the Gallachers still created a problem.'

'No one likes uncertainty in any line of business,' Harris replied coolly, still not confirming or denying anything.

'But junkies continue to die,' Connor said, staring directly at Harris.

'I have news for you, smokers smoke, drinkers drink and junkies take junk.'

'And reporters write stories. I've already fronted up Elizabeth Smart, by the way, but since she clearly hasn't told you I suspect that means she and Dr Marran are trying to cover their tracks. My news desk has a snapper and a reporter waiting to speak to the good doctor when he leaves the surgery, but I guess he won't have a lot to say. He might even decide to sail back home. Or they might even decide to pin all the blame on you, Colin, as they have reputations to maintain and you don't.' Connor noticed a flicker of doubt in the gangster's eyes.

The bodyguard at the door had an exchange with someone standing outside the bar's entrance, before turning to his boss and emotionlessly waiting for instructions.

'Let him in, Bill,' Harris said, as the bodyguard allowed a middle-aged man in a suit to enter the bar.

'Lawyers, Elvis. You know how it is. I have to meet him now, I'm afraid.'

'You're going to need a criminal specialist soon, Colin.'

'For now I will stick with the corporate suits. Bye, Elvis. I'll enjoy reading your story.'

The lawyer completely ignored Connor as he shook Harris warmly by the hand. He then placed his brown leather briefcase on the table, opened it up and laid out a selection of documents for his client to sign.

As Connor made his way to the door, Harris shouted, 'And Elvis, you need to get out of the Ruck. It'll drag you down. The place is full of junkies.'

Connor turned around to see Harris smirking back at him. He was now more determined than ever to wipe that smile off his face.

———

BACK ON THE STREET, Connor checked that the digital voice recorder in his pocket had captured the conversation. He suspected Harris knew he was recording him as he had said absolutely nothing that was incriminating, bar hinting he had met Elizabeth Smart. He would have to park any connection between Harris and the methadone scam for the moment. But Connor vowed he would return to it again as soon as he had any solid evidence.

70

Book club
JUNE 2ND

DCI Crosbie had just read the chapter about the Hanlon triplets working in the porn industry in America.

DCI Urquhart's team had already discovered the subscription website they regularly appeared on and had given in-depth descriptions of the films they appeared in, which he imagined would have been a dream assignment for one of Urquhart's young detectives. But April's journalistic instinct had seen her question the triplets about who had got them started in the adult film industry. She obviously reckoned it was unlikely the Hanlon sisters had any contacts Stateside and therefore suspected that one of the other Hanlons had been exploiting the girls.

April's line of thinking interested Crosbie. He was looking for a murder motive, and the triplets were still the only suspects with a direct DNA link to their father's murder weapon. In any other case that would have been enough to charge them, but this wasn't any other case. And he feared he would have as much luck getting any answers out of them as April, who had written how she had been met with 'coy looks and giggles' when she asked them directly who had introduced them to the porn industry. Also, April had been able to speak to them without the omnipresence of the family lawyer Paul McFadden, a privilege that would not be extended to DCI

Crosbie, which meant he wouldn't even get coy looks and giggles – he would just be treated to a 'no comment' interview again.

But a burning resentment at being forced to sell their bodies for other people's sexual gratification, and the humiliation of performing for the camera, may just be enough of a motive for murder – if it had been their father who got them started in porn. However, Crosbie knew Harry's social circle remained steadfastly within the grim confines of the Woodchopper. The man had rarely ventured anywhere further than Ruckhouse, never mind California.

The detective was grasping at straws, but at this moment straws were all he had.

71

Disillusioned

MARCH 1ST

Connor arrived at the Peccadillo to see April muttering to herself as she flicked through her notepad while writing on a sheet of A4 notepaper. She had a full cup of tea beside her that was obviously untouched as it didn't have her customary smear of pink lip gloss around the rim. He placed beside her that day's copy of the *Daily Chronicle*, which had a photograph of the pharmacist Elizabeth Smart and Dr Marran on the front page under the headline '*SCOTS GOV'S DRUGS SCANDAL*', along with the subdeck 'We expose dodgy doc and crooked chemist's methadone scam'.

April normally devoured her breakfast while immersed in the newspaper at the same time. But not this morning.

'Are you ill?' Connor asked while taking his seat. April barely looked up as she continued to do whatever it was she was doing. 'I said, are you...'

'Yes, yes I heard you. And no, I'm not ill.'

'Then why no fiesta of food, as usual?'

'Because I'm busy.'

Connor mouthed the word 'coffee' to the surly waitress Martel, who did a marvellous impression of barely acknowledging his existence as usual. 'Busy doing what?' he asked. 'Going mental?'

'I feel like I'm going mental trying to work out the bloody

Hanlons. Harry is more interested in his bloody crossword clues than helping me finish the book. I've got the super-intelligent Michael Hanlon, who I can't trust as he thinks he's far smarter than me.'

'So he'd be right there.'

'He may have all the knowledge but none of the sense. Then there are the triplets, who are just weird. I'm sorry, but they freak me out. And all that porn stuff, yuck. While Robert is a total idiot, but clearly a dangerous one.'

'Correct,' Connor replied.

'Then we come to Kendal and her equally conniving mother, Kristine. They're both nasty pieces of work. Kristine is full of tales of being a battered wife who is scared of Harry. I have interviewed several women over the years who have been both physically and mentally abused by their spouses. They are broken people. But not the bold Kristine. She's as feisty as they come. She had lots of claims about being beaten up, but none of the detail. No dates, no nothing. She couldn't even get her daughter's age right. Then minutes after I'm finished with that charade, I'm summoned to meet Kendal who is now full of claims of sexual abuse, and being made to turn tricks for a few pounds from her dad. The only one I could trust is Billy and that poor boy doesn't know any better. I wish I'd never got involved with them. I'm not enjoying this book at all. I've written a load of crap. I'm not even sure what's true anymore.'

Connor let his former colleague vent off, without his usual quips. He may never show it but he hated to see her stressed like this.

'Look, every writer hits that point where they think it's all pointless,' he said, having had the experience of writing his first true crime book the previous year. 'You think, "Why would anyone read this shit, never mind buy it?" It's what happens when you've become immersed in a project. Not being able to see the wood for the trees. But all that's really changed is Kendal and Kristine's allegations. So stick your journalist's hat back on and put their claims to the test with Harry.'

'It's not exactly the sort of stuff you expect to read in a biography though, is it?' April sighed.

'This is not exactly an ordinary biography though, is it? It's more like a documentary. Think of it like that. As if you're making a TV documentary. The diary of the lottery million-aires. What happens to a dysfunctional family after such a huge windfall?'

'You're right about dysfunctional. There is nothing ordi-nary about the Hanlons.'

'And that's what will make your book so interesting. So finish it, then worry about it being crap afterwards.'

Connor may have had a direct way with words, but he had once again given April the pep talk that she needed.

'Thank you. I will. You've even put me in the mood for breakfast. Then I'll see Harry.'

'That's more like the April I know and love.' Connor laughed.

'You love me?' she asked.

'Of course not,' he replied.

72

Boom time
MARCH 2ND

Robert 'Shifty' Hanlon was a worried man as he sat in his car outside the Woodchopper watching his father get into a taxi and leave. He considered following him home but knew it was futile; he had already asked his dad for the money inside the bar. When that hadn't worked, he had tried threatening Harry. And when that failed, he had resorted to pleading.

'Dad, they're going to kill me if I don't give them a million pounds by the end of the month.'

But his own father had laughed in his face. 'But you don't have a million pounds, son.'

Shifty had just received another menacing message from the Gallachers and the situation was now critical.

We've brought the fucking merchandise, now where's our fucking money? they had demanded.

Shifty knew they weren't kidding around. The brothers had thrown hand grenades into pubs, cars and houses in the Greater Manchester area in order to wrest control of their home city's thriving drug trade. Shifty had wanted to emulate their achievements here in Glasgow, but his plans to bankroll his ambitions had slammed into a large blockage in the shape of Harry Hanlon.

And that's when things got truly pathetic: 'Please, Dad, I'll pay you back. Please.'

Shifty's begging caused much sniggering amongst the regulars of the Woodchopper. They all knew he was trying to establish himself as the local drug kingpin and hard man, but they also knew a coward when they saw one.

However, it was his father who laughed the loudest. 'Son, you haven't paid me back a single penny in all these years. Not once. And I'm now supposed to believe you'll pay me back £1 million? I've heard some jokes in my time but that's hilarious.' He then placed his arms around Shifty's shoulders as if doling out some fatherly advice. 'You should never promise money that's not yours. You'll get your share when I'm dead. You all will, but not a minute sooner. Until then, I'm afraid you're on your own.'

'When I'm dead' couldn't come soon enough for Shifty and he now gave it some serious thought. But he knew any inheritance would take time to sort out and time was something he most certainly didn't have. He hadn't replied to the last text message from the Gallachers and now they had taken to calling him instead.

'Where's our fucking money, Shifty?'

'Hi, Liam,' Shifty replied meekly. 'I will have the money soon. I promise. I just need to get it from the bank.' He knew his feeble response wouldn't cut it with the brothers but he didn't have the intelligence to think of anything else.

'If the Bank of Dad doesn't open its vaults soon then it'll be BOOM time,' Liam promised.

'Sorry, I will get it. You just have to give me some more time. I know I've already missed the deadline but I will get it.' But he was speaking to himself. Liam Gallacher had already heard enough.

Shifty knew that his father's death might be the only viable option left.

73

Clue
JUNE 5TH

It was just a single line as part of a long-winded chapter where Harry Hanlon ranted about the importance of family, but it leapt off the page at DCI Crosbie.

April had been speaking to Harry about his ancestry, which he had obviously researched as he gave detailed descriptions of the life and times of his forebears right back to when his great-grandfather left Ireland for a better life in Liverpool, before migrating north of the border. Like many people of advancing years, or coming to terms with their own mortality, Harry's heritage now meant a great deal to him.

Family should always know where they come from. Family should always stick together, no matter what. There is nothing more important that your ain folk (own kind). April had helpfully written the last bit in brackets, with one eye on attracting an international market for her Hanlon memoir. *That's why I had all my weans (children) DNA-tested*, Harry/April concluded.

And there it was in black and white: the first clue in forty thousand-odd words of reading. Crosbie looked at the letters *N/A* – 'not applicable' – written in red pen in DCI Stuart Urquhart's handwriting, which he had marked on every page after studying the memoir's contents.

'You always were an arrogant son of a bitch, Urquhart,'

Crosbie said to himself. If Harry Hanlon had DNA-tested his own children then the detective had a good idea where he would have had it done.

74

Confrontation
MARCH 10TH

April had been unable to track down Harry for over a week. She had been told by the barman that father and son had had a heated confrontation in the Woodchopper and since then Harry had not been back. She had checked in at the pub every day as Harry's mobile was permanently switched off and his voicemail so full it wasn't accepting any more messages. She had routinely checked the Macarena, but only ever got Michael, Billy or the triplets. They claimed they hadn't seen their dad, either.

But finally here he was, sitting in his usual booth. He looked like he had aged since the last time they had met, as if worry was wearing him down. April hated to compound his misery.

'You're a hard man to get hold of at the moment,' she said, taking her coat off as she took her place next to him.

'I've been busy.'

'Doing what?'

'Are you my fucking wife or something?'

April knew she had overstepped the mark. She needed to change tack. 'Sorry, Harry, I've been worried about you.'

'I needed some time on my own. I stayed in a hotel. I needed time to think,' he explained.

'Harry, I know you seem to have been under some pressure of late, but I need to speak to you about something. I have been to see Kendal and Kristine.' April spent the next ten minutes going through their allegations. Harry didn't say anything or even show a flicker of emotion until she had finished speaking.

'I've never touched the lassie,' he finally said. 'She's a conniving cow, just like her mother.'

April had expected Harry to deny Kendal's allegations. Now she was just waiting for him to blame the victim. Most paedophiles do. Real ones, that is. 'She says you would make her perform sexual favours for money.'

This caused Harry to laugh. If he was guilty, he hid it well. 'Oh, this is rich.' He smiled.

'What do you find so funny?'

'It's not funny. It's ironic. I used to pay her mum for a quick go, everybody did. She'll know that.'

'So you're saying you paid Kristine for sex but not Kendal?'

'I've never touched any of my kids. Maybe the odd clip around the ear when they deserved it, but what parent hasn't?'

April instantly recalled the shame she'd felt for raising her hands to Jayne. She knew being an overworked single mother had not been an excuse. She was glad the Scottish Government had outlawed smacking altogether as it removed any doubt about it being wrong. 'Kendal was most specific in what she said. That sometimes you'd come home drunk from the Woodchopper and ask for a "hand job" in return for money. That's why she eventually left the house for a place of her own.'

'Oh, is it a hand job she's settled on, then?' Harry scoffed.

'Pardon me?'

'When she came in here trying to blackmail me, she said it would be a blow job. She obviously thought that reflected worse on her than me.'

'Are you saying Kendal's a liar?'

'Like mother, like daughter. They're in cahoots. Both lying through their teeth.'

April felt the same way, but she was duty-bound to put these allegations to Harry, all the same.

'They've come up with this together,' he continued. 'Kristine is still pissed off because all she ever charged me was a tenner. I thought that was the going rate, but I heard she'd turn tricks for half that amount if you pleaded poverty.'

'Was this going on before you got Kristine pregnant with Kendal?'

'This was going on all the time. She considered it her job. She was still doing it when she had Kendal until she got busted for "soliciting" and social work threatened to take her precious daughter away. That's when she came banging on my door. Telling me I had to take them both in.'

'And did you?'

'Aye, I took them in, even though I knew.'

'Knew what, Harry?'

'Nothing. We'll save it for later,' he said, picking up the *Daily Chronicle* to look at his crossword.

'Harry, she's going to go to the police with her allegations. Then the newspapers,' April warned, trying to regain his attention.

'So she told me. Hope she gets done for wasting police time. And if the papers print anything, I'll sue them for everything they've got.'

'Are you a paedophile?' April pressed on, studying Harry's reaction closely.

'No. I am not,' he said, putting his paper down to stare directly at April. 'I am many things. I drink too much. I've been a shit dad and I was a crap husband, but I am not a paedophile. Ask yourself this: would Kendal have stayed so long if I kept making sexual demands? She's only been in her new place about six months. So if it was true then don't you think someone as cunning as her would have evidence?'

April had thought it suspicious that Kendal had no proof at all.

'If I was always pissed, as she says, she could have videoed me or taken a picture and I'd have been none the wiser until I was lifted by the cops. But she has nothing like that, because it didn't happen. Believe me, if Kendal or her lying cow of a mother had anything on me they'd have demanded a million upfront. They'd have even brought a suitcase to put it in.

Then when they'd blown that, they'd be back for more. They're peas in a pod. I have to protect myself.'

'Kristine also claims you beat her,' April added, but her heart wasn't really in it.

'I'm not proud of it but I only gave as good as I got. No more, no less.' He looked ashamed.

April now knew she would believe Harry's version of events over that of his daughter and his ex-wife.

'Listen, I need to see what you've written so far. Could you print it off and send it to me?' he asked.

His request took April aback. He had never shown any interest in the book until now. 'Look, Harry, if you're worried about all the Kendal and Kristine stuff, I can…'

But Harry cut her off: 'I'm not interested in that pair. Just send me what's been written. I need to check some things.' And with that, he picked up his puzzle page again.

April knew that was the end of today's interview. She also knew his winnings had been a curse on the whole Hanlon family, each in its own individual way. She wondered if the lottery operators ever thought of that when they handed over those oversized novelty cheques in front of the cameras, or if they ever warned the winners that great fortunes could also bring great misery.

75

Deaf ears

JUNE 6TH

'I'm sorry, officer, but all official requests have to go through head office,' the young, smiley Asian chemist from Saltire Pharmacy explained to DCI Crosbie and Dugdale after they had requested sales records for the purchase of a DNA kit by Harry Hanlon.

'I understand that, but I was just wondering if you would use some discretion?' DCI Crosbie asked, more in hope than anything.

'I would help if I could, but I'm sure you can understand after everything that has gone on …' She was, of course, referring to Elizabeth Smart's suspension following Connor Presley's exposé in the *Daily Chronicle*. 'It shouldn't take head office any more than a week to process your claim, especially since it's police business.'

'I understand, but I don't really have a week. This could help a major murder inquiry,' Crosbie continued in vain.

'I'm sorry,' the pharmacist replied. 'I wish you all the best with your inquiry, DCI Crosbie. I really would help if I could.'

Crosbie turned to leave when he spotted the name tag of the young shop assistant loitering by the counter. Her eyes were trained to the ground, but her ears would have been on red alert to the conversation.

'Mags Cheyne,' Crosbie said to Dugdale when they were back in the car. 'Unusual surname for these parts. I bet her dad is Geordie Cheyne – I used to go to school with him. Let's pay the Cheynes a visit.'

76

Prophecy
MARCH 14TH

April had arranged to pick up Harry to drive him to the Woodchopper again, but was informed by the nosy neighbours he had left early today.

She planned to show him the extra chapter she had written about Kristine and Kendal's allegations, although she wasn't even sure if the publisher would even use it. In truth, she wasn't sure about anything anymore, but she had tried to give their claims and his rebuttal equal length. Nevertheless, she feared that Harry would now pull the plug on the entire biography.

When April arrived at the Woodchopper, Harry's psychic – Mystic Matt – was just leaving. He kept his head down and his collar up as he made his way quickly to his car, without acknowledging April. Inside the bar, Harry seemed more agitated than usual.

'I can't get the last one,' he said in frustration as he re-read the final crossword clue from the *Daily Chronicle*. 'It doesn't make any sense. *Red Rum races backwards to the collective name for feathered friends you stone.*' Harry read it once more before smacking the paper down on the table.

April waited to see if more was coming, and Harry said, 'You've got to watch them like hawks.' His eyes moved shiftily from side to side, and a deep frown created a wave effect on his meaty forehead.

'Watch who, Harry? Kendal? Kristine?'

'Every bastard,' he replied, taking a long swig from his whisky and coke.

Getting sense from Harry was difficult enough at the best of times, but with an added dose of paranoia April found him almost impossible to follow. 'Sorry, Harry, I'm not with you. Please explain to me who is after you.'

But Harry withdrew into himself and said no more. April was taking her notepad, pen and digital recorder from her bulging bag when, without warning, Harry placed his hand on top of April's. His palm was surprisingly soft, completely devoid of any calluses. She suspected that was because he hadn't done a hard day's work in years.

'If something happens to me, April, don't let anyone but the police have the book,' he said, pushing a bulging A4 manila envelope across the table. April guessed it was the copy of the manuscript she had given him after his unusual request to read it.

'Oh my, Harry, you're speaking like a cryptic crossword,' April said, taken aback but trying to keep the atmosphere light.

'I'm serious. They'll come looking for this. Keep a copy and keep it safe. And don't edit anything out of it.'

'Are you happy with it, Harry?' April asked tentatively. She had learned a long time ago never to go fishing for compliments as it was usually a path to disappointment.

'Happy with what?'

'The book. Are you happy with everything I've written?'

'Aye, aye, it's fine,' he said, finishing his whisky with a tremor of the hand she hadn't noticed before. 'I've made a couple of corrections. Make sure they're kept in exactly as I've written them.'

April was pretty sure Harry hadn't read the entire rough draft, which meant he must have been looking for something in it. Something he wanted to make sure she had included. Something he had corrected.

'Would you like another drink?' April asked, as she began

to shuffle along the bench to head to the bar. But Harry stopped her in her tracks.

'No. I've got stuff to do. We'll continue tomorrow.'

April was dumbfounded. She suspected this was the first time in his adult life that Harry Hanlon had turned down a free drink.

He manoeuvred his large frame with great difficulty from the booth and left with a grunt when April bade him farewell.

'Well, that was short and sweet,' April said to herself. She scanned the pub but there was no one else except the bored barman. She looked at the manila envelope sticking out of her handbag, and, with Harry's words of warning still ringing in her ears, she began flicking through the bundle of A4 sheets. So far, she had written almost seventy thousand words. Another ten thousand should do it. The problem was, she didn't know how to bring it all to an end. She kept thumbing through the manuscript until she came to the chapter where Harry was talking about his love of crosswords. It was a filler chapter and she suspected it would be ditched at the very first edit. But Harry seemed to have read her mind, for at the top right-hand of the page he had made an asterisk and a note written in his red bookie's pen: *KEEP THIS CHAPTER IN!*

'Thanks, Harry,' April mumbled to herself. 'You've just made a boring book even duller.'

She flicked through the chapter until she saw he had made a minor correction to one of the cryptic clues that he had boasted of creating on his own. Instead of *A watery gateway to a wilderness, which can leave a minty taste*, as April had written, Harry had changed it to *Gateway to the Lakes leaves a minty taste*. He had also added *Across (6)*, meaning it was a six-letter word. April concluded that she had transcribed it incorrectly because she hadn't understood it at the time, and she still couldn't work it out, but it was obviously of great importance to Harry.

He had added a comma to another of his clues – *Brickwork repairs at the end of the pier, the last face some saw as the end came near* – with *Down (11)*, for an eleven-letter word, which began with an 'E' from the first clue.

The last one was *Family background, occupation and date of birth, not of mine*, with *Down (7)* beside it. That was another clue April hadn't been able to fathom.

She was flummoxed. Life was complicated enough without turning everything into a riddle. That's why she would always fundamentally hate crossword puzzles. But, still, she was curious. She needed to figure out what point Harry was trying to make.

April began packing up her unused digital recorder and notepad when her eyes drifted towards Harry's copy of the *Daily Chronicle*, which was folded open at the puzzles page and his unsolved crossword clue. *Red Rum races backwards to the collective name for feathered friends you stone.* She repeated it, as Harry had done, and then she had a light-bulb moment. 'Stone the crows. The collective noun for a group of crows is "murder". Red Rum backwards is "murder". I really am getting better at these.'

But her smugness soon vanished. 'Oh no. I hope that doesn't prove to be a prophecy.'

77

Home visit
JUNE 6TH

Crosbie and Dugdale watched as Mags Cheyne arrived at the first-floor flat where she lived with her dad, Geordie. They allowed her five minutes alone in the house before they came knocking.

'Hey Mags, I'm DCI Crosbie and this is DC Dugdale, may we come in?'

'I can't say anything. I'll get in trouble.'

'Don't worry about your work. They don't need to know,' Crosbie assured her.

'It's not them I'm worried about. It's my dad. He told me I better not lose my job. He was furious when I spoke to that reporter.'

'Reporter?'

'Callum, or Connor, or something?'

'Connor Presley?'

'That's right.'

'What did Elvis want?' Crosbie asked.

'I can't say. My dad told me not to talk about it again.'

'Your dad's Geordie, right? I went to school with him.'

'I didn't think cops came from the Ruck,' Mags said in slight amazement.

'All the best people come from the Ruck,' Crosbie said, laying on the charm. 'I remember Geordie well. Cracking footballer. I'll have a word with him if you're worried. Are you scared because you helped Connor with his story that got your old boss sacked?'

'Please don't tell anyone,' she pleaded. 'I will lose my job and my dad will kill me for being a grass.'

'You won't lose your job. I promise. And I don't care if you helped that reporter bust your boss. Sounds like she deserved it. I just want to know if Harry Hanlon was on any medication. His autopsy report said they found traces of an anticoagulant, because he had something called Hughes Syndrome.'

'That's right,' Mags said. 'Sticky blood. It can be hereditary. I'm studying to be a pharmacist myself. Saltire are paying for my training. It costs a fortune. That's why my dad has warned me not to say anything again.'

'I just need to know if he'd ever been on anything else that we didn't know about. Was he taking any anti-anxiety pills or something for depression? All we're trying to do is build a picture of what was going on in Harry's life before he was murdered. Any clues, Mags?'

'Nothing like that. But he did come in and buy a DNA kit.'

Crosbie already knew that from April's book, but he had wanted Mags to offer up the information first instead of pushing her for it.

'It cost £30 and had enough mouth swabs for up to eight samples. The standard cost of processing is an extra £130, but I remember being really disappointed as he wouldn't pay the extra £340 to get them back in a day.'

'Disappointed because the old miser chose the cheapest option?' Crosbie asked.

'Yes, and the fact he said he had left me a tip when he hadn't. Not that my boss would have allowed me to keep it, anyway.'

'Do you know if he got the results?'

'I presume so. They would have been sent to his home, not the chemist, but because he chose the cheapest option it could have taken up to seven weeks.'

'Can you remember when he bought the kit, Mags?' Crosbie asked.

'Yes, it was the last day of January.'

'January 31st? And you remember this how?'

'Harry Hanlon is the most famous person I've ever met. He was also the richest. I took a note of it on my phone's calendar,' she said, retrieving the entry and showing it to the officers. 'I like to keep a diary.'

'Can you take a screenshot of that entry, Mags, and send it to my email address,' Crosbie said, handing over his card.

Mags Cheyne emailed the screenshot and gave the DCI back his card, adding, 'I don't want my dad knowing you were here.'

'I understand, Mags. But if your dad gives you any crap, just tell him Bing called.'

'Who's Bing?' she asked.

'Me. It was my nickname at school. Because my surname is Crosbie. So they named me after Bing Crosby.'

'Who's Bing Crosby?'

'A singer. *White Christmas*? *Silver Bells*? *Silent Night*?'

The nineteen-year-old looked at Crosbie vacantly.

Crosbie sighed. 'Just tell your dad to call Bing if he has any issues. Thanks, Mags. You've been brilliant.'

⸺

BACK IN THE CAR, Dugdale asked his boss, 'What does it mean, sir?'

'It means, Duggie, that the youngsters today have no idea what good music is. I was going to ask her if she knew who Frank Sinatra was, but I suspect I would have got the same blank reaction.'

'And the DNA kit, sir?'

'Harry was checking if all of his kids were actually his. Which means he had his suspicions. That's why his lawyer didn't want me cross-checking all the Hanlons' DNA samples. That slippery bastard McFadden knows one of them isn't Harry's biological kid. Then there's the date he bought the kit, January 31st. If he had them all swabbed that night and sent off to the lab, it would take seven weeks to get the results.'

'That would take us right up until March 15th – the night

he was murdered,' Dugdale said, the excitement rising in his voice.

'Exactly, Duggie. If we find who's the cuckoo in the nest then we'll find his killer.' Crosbie knew it was their first major breakthrough in a long and arduous case.

78

Dead straight

MARCH 16TH

'Harry Hanlon is dead.'

'What?' April shouted down the phone. She was still in bed and didn't know the time, or even what day it was.

'Murdered,' Connor said. 'Found floating in his hot tub.'

'Shit, shit, shit, wait a minute...' April fumbled for her glasses and the bedside light switch. She sat up, disturbing the cat, who gave her owner the evil eye as usual. 'Right, come again,' April said, now propped up on her pillows.

'Harry was discovered this morning. Face down in the hot tub.'

'Couldn't it have just been a heart attack?'

'Yes, that's possible. But he most likely died from the big fucking knife sticking out his back.'

'Oh my.'

'Oh my, indeed. The cops will most definitely want to speak to you.'

'Shit. What will they want to know?'

'For starters, were there any threats on his life?'

'Not that I know. But remember I told you that psychic warned his life was in danger.'

'Yeah, but what about the family? Shifty? Kendal? Her mum?' Connor asked. 'The cops will ask you about them, too. If you had to put money on it, who would it be?'

April thought long and hard before she replied, 'All of them. I think absolutely all of them had a motive to murder Harry Hanlon.'

'Shit,' Connor said. 'I need to go. I have a splash to write.'

79

Predictions
MARCH 16TH

Connor Presley had interviewed half a dozen of the Hanlons' neighbours, many of whom were still wearing their pyjamas. Only one of them, a bald man who seemed to be perpetually hanging out of an apartment window opposite the Macarena despite the bitter cold, was prepared to be named and photographed for the paper. The bald man had duly informed Connor that the house was party central and the only thing of note from the night of the murder was how unusually quiet the Macarena had been. In fact, he had only seen the family come and go that day after Harry had returned from the Woodchopper shortly before five, with a bag of takeaway food.

All these trivial details made it into Connor's copy, which he wrote on his iPhone and sent to the office within fifty minutes of his arrival at the crime scene. He deliberately left out the fact that April was in the midst of writing Harry's biography as that would make an excellent day-two follow-up story – which was just the way the mind of a seasoned journalist worked.

Connor's words, along with Jack Barr's photos of the forensics teams in their trademark white suits entering the Macarena, would be used almost immediately by the *Chronicle*'s digital desk. They would also form the main basis of the next day's front-page splash in the print edition, with a few extra added details, including the statement from Police Scotland that they were keeping an 'open mind' with the murder inquiry. That was a coded way of saying they didn't have a clue who had killed the lottery millionaire.

Connor then filed a colour piece about the state of the neighbourhood and how it had now lost all hope with the death of its most famous resident. It was bollocks and he knew it, but it was what his editor had asked for.

Knowing he would get absolutely nothing else from hanging around Ruckhouse for the rest of the day, he messaged April: *What was the name of that psychic Harry was seeing?*

The three dots immediately appeared, which meant April had been eagerly monitoring the news websites for updates on the murder.

Mystic Matt. Any news?

Harry's still dead, he replied before finding Mystic Matt's website. He also discovered on Google a local newspaper story about a woman who was suing the psychic for failing to pay for their son's maintenance. The aggrieved ex-lover had been quoted as calling him 'Mystic Prat', which Connor strongly suspected was fed to her by a journalist with a headline in mind. But the article contained his real name, Matthew McIntosh, and even more helpfully his address, which was still common practice in local publications.

Let me know any updates when you get them, April pleaded.

Will do. He'll probably already know this but I'm going to doorstep Mystic Matt, he wrote.

He's about as psychic as my kettle, she replied, which gave Connor his first laugh of the day.

80

Packing up
MARCH 17TH

Connor found Mystic Matt's apartment with a bit of difficulty. It was a small bungalow that had seen better days, with chunks of grey roughcast broken off the external walls to expose the bare brickwork underneath. Either the psychic business was experiencing a bit of a downturn or his ex-wife's lawyers had finally caught up with him about the missing maintenance payments.

Connor rang the doorbell, which didn't work, then clapped loudly. A moment later a man wearing a ladies' dressing gown opened the door. He had thinning hair, which he was in the process of dyeing, with a stained white towel wrapped around his neck.

'Can I help you?'

'Connor Presley from the *Daily Chronicle*. I need to speak to you about Harry Hanlon.'

'No comment,' Mystic Matt replied, and slammed the door shut.

Connor then did something he hadn't done in his entire career. He prised open the letterbox with his fingers and shouted through it, 'I am doing a story for tomorrow's paper that you gave Harry a reading shortly before his death. It's going in, with or without your side of the story. I would rather do it with you, though.'

The door was yanked open again and before Connor even had a chance to stand up straight, Mystic Matt said, 'Get in. Quick, before anyone sees you.'

If the exterior of the house had seen better days, the interior was decidedly shabby, with clothes scattered everywhere. Connor also spotted two open suitcases on the couch – Mystic Matt was leaving in a hurry. But if time was of the essence then why would the psychic be dyeing his hair? That's when the penny dropped. 'Looking for a new start, I see. And a new look,' Connor said, pointing at the psychic's head.

'Something like that. I'm getting out of the medium business. For good,' Matt said as he stuffed more clothes into the already full cases.

'What will you do?'

'I'd rather go back to being a fishmonger than this.'

'I hate to kick a man when he's down, but didn't you see this all coming?' Connor said with a hint of sarcasm.

Matt stopped in his tracks and looked directly at the reporter. 'Oh, but I fucking did. The moment I met Harry I knew he'd be killed. I couldn't tell him that at first – I had to make sure.'

'And this was all from your psychic powers, was it?'

'Yes. I was right, wasn't I?'

'Harry Hanlon won £100 million and still lived in the Ruck. You don't need to be a psychic to know he'd be a target,' Connor scoffed.

'Almost everything I've done in my life has been a fuck-up in one way or another. It's like I have a Midas touch, where all things turn to shit instead of gold. But I am psychic.'

Deluded fool, Connor thought. He actually felt sorry for Matt as he clearly believed he possessed mystical powers.

Matt stopped and stared at Connor until his gaze became uncomfortable. He then said, 'There are big career changes coming your way very shortly. You'll have a huge decision to make soon. If I was you, I'd take the chance for a change of direction. You won't regret it.'

Connor was momentarily dumbfounded, before deciding this was just all part of the medium's act. 'Thanks for the career advice but I'd rather talk about Harry.'

Matt returned to packing his case before saying, almost nonchalantly, 'As I said, I knew Harry would be murdered the minute I met him. And I knew it would be by someone close to him.'

Connor bit his tongue. He was tempted to say that statistically you are far more likely to be murdered by a close relative than a stranger. 'So what happened when you told Harry he would be killed?'

'He said he knew.' The psychic didn't elaborate as he continued to stuff clothes into the suitcases at a frenetic pace.

'So do you know who did it?' Connor pressed on.

Mystic Matt continued to pack in silence.

'Tell me the name, Matt. Tell me who you think killed Harry.'

'That name will never pass my lips. Got it? Not for you or the police.'

'That's withholding crucial evidence. You have a suspect's name and you won't repeat it out of some psychic-client confidentiality bullshit? Give me a break. Being a medium is not a profession. It's a con.'

Mystic Matt ignored the insult. It was only one of many he'd heard down the years. 'The only reason I will never repeat it is because no one will believe me.'

'What the hell do you mean?'

'People will say I'm wrong because the person couldn't possibly have killed Harry.'

'And why's that?' Connor asked incredulously.

'Because he was murdered by a child.'

'Matt, you're making no fucking sense whatsoever,' Connor said, losing his cool.

'The person who killed Harry Hanlon was a child. I had the same vision from the first time we met to the last. I don't have a name but a feeling that's as clear as a bell. The strongest and most powerful vision I've had in all my life, and it was the exact same one each and every time I saw Harry. It was on a constant loop in my mind: "Harry will be killed by a child ... Harry will be killed by a child".'

'But that's bollocks. Harry was killed with great force and violence.'

'I don't care, Mr Newspaperman. All I know is, he was killed by a child. That's all I'm going to say. Now, if you don't mind, I have a plane to catch.'

'Where are you going?'

'As far away from the Hanlons as possible. They're dangerous. They will stop at nothing to get his money, and I don't want to be collateral damage.'

Connor thought Matt was being overly dramatic but he left knowing he had a good follow-up story. He would quote the psychic from the dictaphone he had kept concealed in his pocket and use a photo of him from Mystic Matt's own website. The picture desk could worry about any copyright issues.

'A child,' Connor said, chuckling to himself. 'What a fruitcake.'

81

The funeral
MARCH 24TH

April wore her black dress she kept aside solely for funerals. She had been to so many in the last couple of years that the dress really could do with being dry-cleaned, especially with the soup stain she had slobbered down the front of it during the last purvey.

But she had not expected to be attending the funeral of Harry Hanlon.

April was still in a state of shock from his murder. She couldn't help thinking her book was somehow involved. Perhaps if she had never written it then Kendal and Kristine's abuse claims would never have surfaced, legitimate or bogus as they may be. But now Harry was dead. She should have left him alone. He had been happy drinking in the Woodchopper every day and doing his puzzles. *Then interfering April had to go and stick her big nose into his affairs*, she silently berated herself.

His cremation was taking place at the council-run crematorium. Harry's body had been delivered in a black hearse, which had looked out of place alongside the fleet of white Rolls-Royces that had ferried the mourners. The hired luxury seemed weirdly inappropriate for the occasion, more suited to weddings than to funerals, but perhaps it was a show of unity and defiance from the Hanlons that they all arrived together in the matching cars. They knew the media spotlight was on them, and that the police and the people of Ruckhouse believed one of them had murdered their father for his millions. But here they were, dressed head to toe in black, stepping from the brilliant white cars, mourning Harry Hanlon together, a family united in their grief.

Apart from the fleet of Rolls-Royces, this was like any other typical Glasgow funeral April had attended. Many of the older women had short, grey, mannish hairstyles, and all were smoking. Between the cigarettes and vape fumes, it looked like a dry ice machine had been set off. April recalled the service for her daughter Jayne's best friend Lisa, who had died at the age of thirty-three from Hodgkin's lymphoma. No one had smoked at her funeral and her generation of mourners all looked so fit and healthy, with their fake tans, good diets and gym workouts.

The only one who looked in that mould today was Kendal Hanlon, although even from a distance April could see she had overdone the fake tan and the make-up. Her face was set hard and her mother was only a step behind her. She wondered if either of them felt the same guilt over Harry's death as she did.

The mourners filed into the crematorium for the service, and April suddenly felt a presence by her side.

'Sorry for your loss.' It was Connor, dressed in a black suit and tie.

'What are you doing here?' she asked.

'Working. What do you think? Paying my respects?'

'Sorry, of course. I never thought. If you wanted an order of service, I would have got you a couple.'

Connor already had one, which featured a young Harry Hanlon on the front cover, laughing at an unheard joke, with a glass of whisky in one hand and a cigarette in the other. Connor would use the contents as part of his copy, along with the minister's words of condolences, recorded on the dicta-phone in his pocket. Covering funerals was a bit of a grey area journalistically. Unless the family specifically requested no press were to attend, they were technically public affairs, hence why Connor was well within his rights to be there. Any moral question about intruding on a family's grief was a debate for another day.

'He was rather handsome as a young man, wasn't he?' April said, looking mournfully at his picture.

'Sure,' Connor said, before adding, 'You do know you had nothing to do with his death?'

'It's kind of you to say that, but do you think we would be sitting here right now if I hadn't started his book?'

Connor went to answer April, but then decided to remain quiet. It was a good question and he took his time to think it over. 'Maybe not today,' he said eventually, 'but I believe one way or another we would have still ended up sitting here in the near future.' He activated his recorder for the start of the service, leaving his former colleague alone with her thoughts. He knew April was in a very dark place and he was worried for her, but right now he had a job to do.

The humanist service was conducted by a celebrant who had clearly never met Harry Hanlon. He waxed lyrical about him being a 'larger than life local character', which April thought could be code for just about anything. He droned on about his many attributes and how he revelled in his role of fatherhood. April could think of no such 'revelling' whenever he had discussed his brood, only fears and suspicions about them. Finally, and thankfully, the service came to an end with another flurry of lies and half-truths about how Harry's lottery fortune had meant an 'exciting new chapter' for the Hanlons, but 'what a pity Harry hadn't been around for long to fully appreciate his new-found fortune'. April wondered if the celebrant had read a newspaper in his entire life. Was he completely oblivious to the fact Harry had been stabbed to death and it was entirely likely that his murderer was sitting in one of these pews, a hanky clasped to their face to blot the crocodile tears or hide a knowing smile?

She turned round to silently remonstrate with Connor, but he was already up and heading for the exit when the closing music started and Harry's large coffin descended from view to be turned to dust.

April watched in a daze as Harry's close family members filed out to stand in line at the door and shake the hands of the departing mourners. April was dreading the prospect of looking any of them in the eye again. She'd had enough of the Hanlons to last a lifetime. They were also a living reminder of the book she had no intentions of finishing, despite the publisher's increasing irate demands to see her first draft.

The first to greet the mourners was Michael, his jaw set rigid and one hand on the handle of Billy's wheelchair, gently keeping his learning-disabled brother in line as he rocked back and forth. The youngest Hanlon could only muster a 'thank you for paying your respects' after April had wished him all the best at university. She then told Billy he looked very smart in his suit and how he would have made his father proud.

'Make my daddy proud,' he parroted back, a huge smile on his face.

The triplets nodded in unison when April told them she was sorry for their loss, while Robert 'Shifty' Hanlon looked a worried man, as if the proverbial weight of the world was on his shoulders. She wondered what was going through that limited brain of his.

Kendal was last in line.

'Sorry for your loss,' April repeated as she shook her hand, but Kendal didn't let go.

'Are you still going to write my dad's book?' she asked, a little too aggressively for April's liking. She didn't like either Kendal's tone or the mention of the biography.

'No,' she replied truthfully. 'I'm done with writing. I'm retiring. For good this time.'

'Good,' Kendal said, relaxing her strong, gym-honed grip. 'It's probably for the best, anyway. It would open up a whole can of worms, and who wants that?' Kendal then smiled. It was false, for sure, but it immediately softened her hard features and momentarily made her look pretty.

For April, it had felt cathartic to state publicly she was retiring for good. She wanted to retire and fade away. She wanted to have no more to do with the Hanlons and now she never would because April Lavender was out of the writing game forever.

82

No further forward
MARCH 29TH

Connor called Police Scotland's communication department, as he had done routinely every morning in the two weeks since Harry Hanlon's murder.

'Nothing to report, Elvis, enquiries are still ongoing,' the cops' PR Gail Firth had replied yet again. Gail had refused to elaborate, even off the record, on how the investigation was progressing. There were only so many follow-up articles Connor could write without any firm facts to move the story on.

He told his news editor Big Fergie that there was no update on the case. Fergie swore under his breath, and Connor walked back towards his broom cupboard office. After the successes of recent months, from the methadone investigation to working on the Hanlon murder, he now felt flat. April had also stopped coming to the Peccadillo in the morning so he was feeling isolated again, especially as there were hardly any colleagues to talk to at work anymore.

He tried calling April again, but she didn't answer. He didn't bother leaving a voicemail and resorted to messaging her instead, but there was no reply.

An email popped up on his screen from Big Fergie asking Connor to rewrite some press release based on spurious research promoting some product or another. With nothing better to offer, Connor resigned himself to the re-write. Now, on top of feeling flat and alone, he could add thoroughly depressed to the list of current emotions.

He feared today would be the shape of things to come unless Police Scotland suddenly made a sudden breakthrough in the Hanlon case, and he didn't see that happening any time soon.

83

Short fuse

JUNE 12TH

Shifty waited nervously in the car park of the Woodchopper for the Manchester crew to arrive. He still didn't have the money they required, but he had what he considered to be the next best thing, a copy of his father's last will and testament. A photocopy had been obtained as Shifty, the eldest member of the Hanlon clan, had been elected executor of his father's estate. It showed that he was in line for over £15 million from his father, less inheritance tax.

The passenger doors to his BMW all swung open at the same time as the Gallachers stepped into his car, Noel in the front and Liam in the back.

'Lock the doors,' Noel ordered, and Shifty fumbled for the key fob obediently.

'Have you got our fucking money?' Noel asked in his thick Mancunian accent. 'It's been fucking months and we've been very patient.'

'No, Noel, I haven't got it. But I've brought this, look,' Shifty said, waving the will under his nose. 'It says I'm to inherit £15 million. I will be able to pay you double if you can wait just a little bit longer. That'll be £2 million,' Shifty added hopefully. He was scared – he just hoped it wasn't too obvious.

'Ah, Shifty,' Noel replied with a condescending smile on his face, 'you always promise so much. How we were going to take over Glasgow together, how your dad's millions would help undercut Colin Harris and make us the biggest players in the market. Hell, I even thought it might be possible when Harris started scaling back his operations. You told us he was scared. But Harris wasn't spooked, was he, Shifty? He just moved into the methadone game. He out-thought you, Shifty. With your own sister, too. Shit, that must've been a mind-fuck: Kendal doing a deal with the enemy.' Noel tapped the side of Shifty's head. 'The junkies have been dying off. Harris has scorched the earth. We're left dealing with all the dregs while he moves on to fleecing the NHS. That's pure genius, Shifty. You will never have the brains to match a man like Colin Harris.'

Shifty was dumbstruck. The Gallachers knew more about Harris's business manoeuvres than he did. It was almost as if they had been in contact with him. That's when the penny dropped. 'I wouldn't trust a word Harris told you. He's always been a smooth talker, but he'll stitch you up, Noel. He's a grass, too. He has contacts with the police.'

'Any decent businessman should have contacts with the police. I know we do. I'm surprised you don't. How else do you find out what they're up to?'

'You'll be making a big mistake if you go with him.'

'Too late, Shifty, we already have. The thing about Mr Harris is, he lets his money do the talking. He's paid us up front. We're still waiting for our money from you.'

'When I get the money, will you think about going into business with me again?' Shifty hadn't realised how needy that would sound until he heard himself say it.

Noel gave him a sympathetic look a father might give a remorseful child. 'I've heard you killed your dad?' Noel asked.

Shifty didn't answer. He had hinted often enough that he was involved in Harry's death and was inwardly glad word had got back to the Gallachers.

'I hate to break it to you, Shifty, but if you're charged with your dad's murder then there's no way on God's green earth that you're going to be able to get your hands on your inheritance. No court in the land will grant that, no matter what you have written on that bit of paper,' Noel explained. 'So I wish you all the best, my friend, with whatever you do next. But stay out of business, would ya? You're not and never will be a businessman. You're just not cut out for it. Stick to pushing tenner bags on the street corners while there are still some junkies left. Now let us out and we'll leave you in peace.'

'What about the money?' Shifty asked.

'It's fine. Written off. Let's just put it down to experience.'

Shifty flicked his eyes to his rear-view mirror to stare at Liam sitting in the back seat. He then glanced back at Noel. He was waiting for a sucker punch, but none came. With the Gallachers' debt now written off, Shifty felt he had won the lottery himself.

'Nice key ring, by the way,' Noel remarked, admiring the gold key fob dangling from Shifty's car ignition.

'Like it?' Shifty beamed. 'It's real gold. A customised fob. Cost me nearly a grand,' he said, taking it out of the ignition and handing it to Noel.

'Yes, I like it a lot,' Noel said, turning it around in his hand, before pressing the fob to unlock the car doors. 'I'll have to get one for my Merc back home.'

'I got it online. You can have them done in silver and platinum, too. I'll send you the link, if you like?' Shifty was delighted about the unexpectedly friendly turn the conversation had taken.

'I do like,' Noel said, as he opened the passenger door and handed the fob back to its owner. 'Thanks, Shifty. Catch you soon.' The brothers stepped out simultaneously, slamming the doors behind them.

'Yes!' Shifty gave a fist pump. 'Ya fucking beauty.'

But his celebratory mood was cut short by the sound of the central locking system of his car being activated.

'That's weird,' he said, as he pressed the unlock button on his key fob again. But as soon as it was unlocked, he heard his doors lock again. 'Must be a fault,' he said, puzzled, as he repeatedly pressed the button, only for the same thing to happen again and again.

Unlock.

Locked.

Unlock.

Locked.

Shifty's dogmatic routine was interrupted by a sizzling sound, like a sausage cooking in a frying pan. The noise was coming from the direction of the passenger-side footwell. He reached over to find the source of the sound and picked up an American M67 grenade. It felt hot from the pyrotechnic delay fuse burning inside.

The spherical steel grenade had remained much the same since it was first deployed by the Americans during the Vietnam War. Its 180 grams of explosive produced a fatality radius of five metres, more than enough to prove deadly within the confines of a car.

Noel had asked for the key fob to unlock his car as Liam, sitting in the back seat, held a blank fob, which he'd set to 'remote programming mode' to make a copy of Shifty's device. Once they had stepped out of his car, Liam then repeatedly pressed the lock button, and they watched the confusion spread over Shifty's face from a safe distance.

Robert Hanlon wasn't the quickest, which unfortunately meant it took him valuable seconds to realise the seriousness of his situation. When he finally scrambled to manually open his driver's door and escape, it was all too late.

Noel and Liam were already pulling out of the car park of the Woodchopper when the grenade detonated, rocking Shifty's car on its axles and blowing out all the windows.

The copy of Harry Hanlon's last will and testament fluttered to the ground several metres from the wreckage, lightly scorched around the edges. The paperwork had survived but it hadn't saved the life of his son Robert 'Shifty' Hanlon.

84

The aftermath
JUNE 13TH

'Robert Hanlon would have been charged with the murder of his father, the lottery winner Harry Hanlon,' Chief Constable Eric McNeil said, addressing a packed news conference the day after the explosion in the Woodchopper car park that claimed the prime suspect's life. 'This was an extremely challenging case but diligent work by our investigating officers led to a breakthrough. We believe we had gathered enough evidence to have led to a successful prosecution. We may never know his motives and are not about to start speculating, but there is no doubt in our minds that Robert Hanlon murdered his father. '

I'm glad someone's feeling confident, DCI Crosbie thought to himself as he watched McNeil take centre stage, wearing the shiny brass of high office. McNeil was the fourth chief constable of Crosbie's career and he was amazed that, no matter their good intentions and bold promises made when they started out, they all ended up looking, sounding and acting the same.

The chief constable fielded several questions about the explosion outside of the Woodchopper, with Connor Presley asking directly if they had located and questioned Noel and Liam Gallacher. McNeil gave the generic response that they were pursuing a number of lines of inquiry, which was good enough to give Connor days of follow-up stories. Crosbie noted how pleased the *Daily Chronicle* reporter looked, obviously in the zone again, with the months of inertia finally being swept away.

McNeil again returned to the theme of Robert Hanlon and how he would have been charged with Harry's murder, making it clear that, while Robert Hanlon's murder case was open, his father's was well and truly closed.

Crosbie did not share his boss's belief that their evidence would have stood up in court. There were no forensics linking Shifty with the murder weapon – only the triplets' DNA had been found on the knife handle. He knew full well that the family lawyer Paul McFadden would have mercilessly picked apart the Crown's case stitch by stitch. He would have no doubt used the triplets' DNA match to exonerate Shifty and pin the blame on the identical sisters, knowing the Crown would be forced to abandon all hope of ever getting a conviction.

The press conference was concluded and DCI Crosbie was invited to join the chief constable and his deputy, Mike Bruce, for drinks. McNeil's PA, Joan, had made sure they had two bottles of Prometheus single malt, with a jug of water each. Earlier, she had given Crosbie a 'Well done!' kiss, throwing her arms around his neck. He'd asked if she wanted to meet up later, but she just waggled her wedding ring in his face.

McNeil and Bruce were full of backslapping bonhomie, with the chief repeating several times how the First Minister was absolutely ecstatic at the outcome. 'She says you've "saved Scotland's reputation".'

Crosbie thought that was overdoing it. They had named Harry Hanlon's murderer, who was conveniently dead and therefore couldn't contest their claims. He watched as McNeil poured another large whisky, steadily working his way through the bottle. He reckoned his boss must have developed a taste for it during his meetings with the First Minister. He'd seen it all before, a policeman on the make and their desperate scramble to the top, only to find it a miserable and lonely existence. Crosbie also knew from experience that cosying up to politicians would do you no favours in the long run. Any politician, no matter the party, would happily throw a chief constable under a bus if it saved their own skin.

But Crosbie still drank their expensive whisky and took the praise. He was the hero once more. His reputation fully restored. Funny how he didn't feel like celebrating.

85

Three months later
SEPTEMBER 5TH

A lot had happened since the murder of Robert 'Shifty' Hanlon to keep Connor Presley busy again. There had been the subsequent funeral, the official closing of the Harry Hanlon case, and the arrest, questioning and release of the Gallacher brothers, pending further enquiries. Meanwhile, the Scottish Government had wilted under sustained pressure from opposition parties and launched an inquiry into the NHS's methadone programme, sparked entirely by Connor's investigation. Elizabeth Smart had been charged with large-scale fraud, but the police investigation was still ongoing. Her accomplice, Dr Marran, had fled the country with a European Arrest Warrant being issued for his detention. He was still at large, but the journalist knew it was only a matter of time before he was found.

Connor was always at his happiest when he was busy. His news editor also had a spring in his step once more and had even suggested that his senior reporter take a couple of days off in lieu to recharge his batteries after all the extra hours he had been putting in.

'Go spend some time with that Russian girlfriend of yours,' Big Fergie had suggested, but it was another woman Connor had in mind.

April opened her door still wearing her pyjamas and a dressing gown despite it being just after midday.

'I never thought I'd have to do a door knock on you,' Connor said, by way of a greeting.

April could only smile meekly. 'At least it's not a death knock,' she replied as she welcomed him in.

Connor had not set eyes on his former colleague for three months and was amazed to see she had let her grey roots grow in. In all his years working with her, he had never once seen a single strand of grey on her head, as they never survived long enough before they were plucked or bleached. But here she was, looking distinctly dishevelled. She had also lost weight, which made her whole body look saggy.

'Do you want a cup of tea?' she offered. 'Although I may have run out of milk.'

Connor had seen enough already. 'Oh for God's sake, woman, what the hell is wrong with you? You stopped turning up at the Peccadillo. You've stopped taking my calls. You've clearly stopped washing your hair and I'd rather not think about it, but I bet you've stopped washing yourself, too. So what's going on?'

'I don't feel like it,' she said, her eyes on the floor.

'I don't feel like getting up in the morning, going to work in a converted broom cupboard by myself and paying my taxes, but I still do it. You can't just stop everything because you don't feel like it. What's happened to Harry's book?'

April almost winced at the mere mention of the unfinished biography. The publisher had now resorted to sending ever-increasing threats via legal letters demanding the completed manuscript. She had not even switched on her laptop since Harry's murder, never mind attempted to finish his book.

'I can't write it anymore. I don't know where to start or finish. It's a mess. The whole damn thing is a mess. My life is a mess. How can I write a biography on someone who was murdered by his own son?'

'Because you're a fucking journalist, that's why, and you're duty bound to tell his damn story. So go get a bloody shower and get the laptop fired up.'

'No, I'm retired. I'm not writing anymore,' she insisted.

'Bollocks to that. Writers never retire. It's in our blood. And your legal woes aren't going to go away by burying your head in the sand. So write yourself out of trouble. Stop wallowing in self-pity and finish the goddamn manuscript. You've been stuck since the Ides of March. So *carpe* fucking *diem* and move the fuck on. And dye your hideous hair. I'm off to buy some milk for the tea.' Connor left, slamming the front door behind him.

April sniffed under her arm, wincing at the smell that greeted her nostrils. Maybe Connor was right, after all. She knew she had retreated into her shell but nothing seemed to be able to break her out of her funk. Even her daughter Jayne had given up shouting at her. April walked towards the bathroom, where she leaned towards the mirror and inspected her head. It was Connor's 'hideous hair' comment that had finally struck a chord.

'Okay, I will start with a shower, and then my roots are getting a bleaching like they've never had before.'

86

Brothers in arms
SEPTEMBER 6TH

Both DCI Crosbie and his trainee, Dugdale, had been left deeply unsatisfied by the closure of the Harry Hanlon case.

DCI Urquhart and his team had been drafted in to investigate the murder of Robert Hanlon after the grenade explosion at the Woodchopper. It was felt that new investigators should oversee the homicide so it did not get 'confused' with Harry Hanlon's case. Crosbie knew what that meant: the chief constable had officially declared Harry's murder solved and he needed a kiss-ass like Urquhart to make sure any inconvenient truths uncovered during the course of the Robert Hanlon investigation would remain buried.

Crosbie had now been assigned a series of other bog-standard cases that took up little of his manpower or intellect, which is why he decided to send Dugdale back to the surveillance flat in Ruckhouse.

'What are you thinking, sir?' Dugdale asked his boss.

'Nothing, really. I just want to see what the family are up to now. Michael Hanlon must be starting university this week. I wonder what he is going to do with Billy.'

'I could ask social services, sir?' Dugdale suggested eagerly.

'You could, but the eyes never lie. I would prefer to hear it from you. Just tell me what the Hanlons get up to,' Crosbie said.

Half an hour later, Dugdale took up his position by the window of the abandoned council flat. Junkies had broken in during the intervening three months to use the empty flat as a shooting gallery – abandoned needles, bloody rags and dried faeces were scattered across the floor. It had done nothing to improve the smell of the place.

The trainee didn't have long to wait before Michael Hanlon emerged from the Macarena, pushing his older brother Billy in his wheelchair towards the day centre at the end of the road. Dugdale observed them both go in, before Michael left by himself. Crosbie must've been right about him starting university.

Dugdale decided to leave the surveillance apartment and walk to the day centre, taking the time to study the modern low-rise as he approached, with its sandy-coloured brickwork and colourful signage desperately trying, and failing, to give some character to the featureless building. The rim of razor wire around the roof was a reminder that there were always bad forces from the outside ready to rob and ruin the good work that went on within.

Dugdale rang the metal intercom system and was greeted by a cheery English voice. 'Can I help you?'

He could hear the noisy chatter of people talking and Radio 2 playing in the background, with presenter Ken Bruce doing his daily Pop Master quiz show. Dugdale checked his watch: 10.30 am. 'It's Detective Constable Dugdale here,' he said, deliberately omitting the 'trainee' prefix. 'I was hoping to have a chat with the organiser if they have a few minutes.'

'I hope it's not about my parking tickets,' the English voice replied, before adding, 'I'll let you in. Push the door when you hear the buzzer.'

Dugdale did as he was told and walked into the entrance hall. Whoever ran the place had made a damn good go of ensuring it was as bright, friendly and welcoming as possible. There was a giant mural on the main wall which greeted visitors. It was a work in progress from those who used the centre, and the artwork petered out as it snaked along the hallway. There were multicoloured uplights and the smell of coffee and toast coming from a kitchen area somewhere.

'Hi, I'm Becky Hardie. Would you like a cup of tea?'

'Yes, please,' was all Dugdale could think of to say. He was almost dumbstruck by the sheer beauty of the presence before him. Becky Hardie was the same height as Dugdale, with blonde, shoulder-length hair, blue eyes and an unbelievably pretty face. But it was that smile which truly captivated him. She positively beamed with her shiny white teeth. Dugdale was instantly smitten.

'And you are?' she asked, offering her hand to shake.

'Er, Dugdale. Detective Constable Dugdale, ma'am.'

'Well, Detective Constable, don't call me ma'am. It makes it sound like I'm running a brothel.'

Dugdale could feel his cheeks reddening slightly. He hadn't blushed like this since he was in high school.

'You're just in time for Pop Master. We're all pretty hopeless at it, but everyone seems to like the tunes.'

'I try to listen to it every day,' Dugdale said.

'Really? What's your best score?'

'Thirty-nine. I've had that quite a few times,' he said, hoping he didn't sound too bashful.

'Wow, maximum points! You should go on air.'

'I've thought about it, but they always say it's more difficult when you're on the radio. Also, I don't want my bosses to know I'm doing a pop quiz when I should be working.'

'I'm sure even a detective constable is allowed a ten-minute break.'

'It's actually Trainee Detective Constable. I don't think taking part in Pop Master will get rid of the "trainee" tag any sooner.'

'Ah, you didn't say you were a trainee.'

'Sorry, I should have.'

'Ha, don't worry. So tell me, Mr Trainee Detective, why did you want to be a policeman in the first place?'

'To catch the bad guys, I guess.'

Becky laughed. 'Well, that's as good a reason as any. If only everything in life was so black and white.'

'It is when it comes to the law. You've either broken it or you haven't.'

'Spoken like a true policeman. I doubt you'll be a trainee

for much longer.' Becky turned to address the half a dozen or so folk in the breakout area, seated around the radio with their various mugs of tea and coffee. 'Now, everybody, this is Trainee Detective Constable Dugdale. And he's here today to do Pop Master, then afterwards he's off to catch some bad guys,' Becky said playfully.

Dugdale felt his cheeks burning again. The way she made him blush was getting ridiculous.

'Becky, Becky' – a man with learning difficulties began waving his arm to gain her attention – is he going to arrest Andy Mulgrew? He punched my face and pulled my hair.'

'I know he did, Callum. But Andy has said sorry many times for doing that and has promised it won't happen again,' she replied patiently, despite obviously having tackled this topic several times before.

In a far corner of the room, Dugdale spotted Billy Hanlon in his wheelchair. He was paying the new visitor no attention whatsoever.

Meanwhile, Ken Bruce's dulcet tones introduced the first contestant, before asking him a series of general knowledge pop music questions, scoring three points for every correct answer and six for a bonus question. The disabled adults in the kitchen area shouted out various random and often hilariously wrong answers. But Becky just seemed happy most of them were participating, smiling that beautiful smile Dugdale found so captivating. The round finished with the radio contestant scoring a measly nine points, with an obligatory moan about how tough the questions had been. The DJ gave a half-hearted platitude in return, having heard every excuse under the sun through his decades of hosting the popular mid-morning show.

'And how many points did you score, Detective Constable?' Becky asked.

'Not much better than that guy. Just twelve today,' he lied, having actually answered all bar two of the questions correctly. 'Listen, can I speak to you in private?'

'I'm afraid this place isn't really designed for privacy. My office is probably best. Well, I say office, but it's really just a desk. Everything's open-plan here. Moira, will you keep an eye on the troops while I speak to this policeman?' she hollered to an assistant.

'Sure, hun,' came the reply from a stout middle-aged woman who was washing up her coffee mug.

Dugdale now had Becky all to himself. If he hadn't been so professional, he would have asked her for a date. But right now, he was following an old-fashioned detective's hunch.

87

Press release
SEPTEMBER 6TH

'I see you sent your publisher the biography, then?' Connor said, calling April on her mobile. He was relieved she had started answering his calls again.

'How the hell did you know that?' she asked incredulously.

'Because I'm staring at a press release with the headline "Harry Hanlon – the lottery dream that turned into a nightmare. In his own words."'

'And they always accuse the press of being sensationalist,' April moaned.

'Oh there's more: "Harry Hanlon's explosive memoirs, which he completed before his brutal murder, shall be released on October 30th."'

'What? I've only sent them the first three chapters. After you visited, I switched on my laptop and emailed the publisher. I then told them to stop sending me threatening letters and I'd get the rest finished as soon as I can.'

'Well, they obviously liked what they read so far.'

'But why send out a press release?' she wondered.

'Two reasons. One, it'll get your arse in gear to finish it; and two, it will get a bidding war going for the serialisation rights.'

'And I thought newspapers were cut-throat. The book world seems worse.'

'That's business. Anyway, got to go – I have to write this press release up as a page lead, and you have a book to finish.'

'Don't I know it.' April groaned.

'Every paper will carry this tomorrow: "Harry Hanlon's words from beyond the grave",' Connor said in a B-horror movie style.

For better or for worse, April was about to become a published author.

88

Generosity
SEPTEMBER 6TH

'Can you tell me what Michael Hanlon's like?' Dugdale asked the day-centre manager, Becky Hardie.

'Of course. He's lovely. And the way he looks after his brother is nothing short of heroic, especially with his own studies. We all cried the day he was accepted into medical school. He's also really generous. He donated three laptops to the centre after his dad's big win. Then, when they all got infected with viruses because someone forgot to renew the McAfee subscription, he cleaned them all up. He's a great help with all our IT issues. He's an amazing kid and so is his brother Billy. They are really fond of each other, which is nice, especially after what happened with his dad.'

'Did you know their dad?'

Becky's smile disappeared. 'I know you shouldn't speak ill of the dead, but he wasn't a nice man. He was so selfish. When he heard Michael had given us the laptops, he tried to charge us for them. Honestly, the nerve of the man. Sometimes it was hard to believe Michael was actually his, because he always thinks about others.'

'The laptops must've cost a fair bit – are you not worried about a break-in?' Dugdale said as he scanned the room.

'We were until Michael donated the CCTV system.'

Dugdale's ears pricked up. 'CCTV?'

'Yes, he was upgrading his system at home so he gave us his old one. He set that up for us too,' she said, pointing in the direction of a digital video recorder sitting on a shelf in the corner, along with a flat-screen monitor split into quarters, showing four simultaneous images from outside the building.

'He's a little genius,' Becky added, beaming that smile of hers.

But this time Dugdale didn't notice her smile. He had his eyes set firmly on the DVR. 'When did he fit it for you?'

'Oh, a little while back now.' Becky started rifling through a drawer to retrieve a red A4-sized folder. 'This is the centre's ledger. Or the Captain's Log, as someone once called it.'

The geek within Dugdale appreciated the *Star Trek* reference.

'I always take note of any new equipment or donations we receive.'

'For insurance purposes?' Dugdale asked.

'Well, partly. But sometimes there have been – how shall I say? – "ownership issues" with some of the things people bring in.'

Dugdale liked Becky's delicate term for stolen goods.

'So I started writing it all down for any such disputes. Here it is: "Michael Hanlon kindly donated and fitted a CCTV system, estimated value £800, on March 16th." I've even added a little smiley face beside it. I was so happy because we'd had half a dozen break-ins until that point. But nothing since, touch wood.'

March 16th was the day after Harry Hanlon was murdered. Michael had taken his brother to the day centre less than twenty-four hours after their father's death. And Dugdale was sure he had taken the DVR system from the Macarena with him.

'That was just after his dad was murdered,' Dugdale pointed out.

'Yes, I remember now. I told him to fit it another time, and he said it was okay as he wanted to do it there and then to keep his mind off events at home. He knew we'd had break-ins and wanted to help. As I said, he was always thinking of others.'

'Can I take a photo of that ledger entry and take a statement from you?'

'Of course,' Becky said with a quizzical expression.

'And I'm afraid I'm also going to have to confiscate the DVR.'

'Why? What for?' she asked.

'I think it may contain crucial evidence related to Harry Hanlon's homicide.'

Read all about it
SEPTEMBER 6TH

DCI Crosbie got the Google Alert that there was a new news story about Harry Hanlon. He clicked on it to find several publications were reporting how a Scottish-based publisher planned to release his autobiography on October 30th. The *Daily Chronicle*'s article was written by Connor Presley. It mentioned that the 'warts and all book' by the award-winning journalist April Lavender contained interviews conducted right up until two days before he died, at the hands of his now-deceased son Robert 'Shifty' Hanlon.

Crosbie had stopped reading the rough draft of April's book once Shifty was murdered and Harry's case was officially closed. But now he thought it would be a good idea to complete the memoir before it was released to the general public. He retrieved the tattered A4 pages from his bottom drawer, found a bookmark three quarters of the way through and started reading where he left off.

Another person had also got the same Google Alert as Crosbie, and they were far from happy about the impending release of Harry Hanlon's biography.

Forensics
SEPTEMBER 6TH

Dugdale arrived at the forensic lab with the digital video recorder he had seized from Ruckhouse day centre wrapped in an evidence bag. He had filled in the label with the date, time and full address of where he had retrieved it.

'I wish all your colleagues were this meticulous,' forensic officer Susan Purdie told him. 'Some have trouble spelling their own name.'

Dugdale gave a non-committal half-smile. He hadn't been in the door long enough to have developed an opinion about anyone except DCI Crosbie.

'I see you've written "Trainee Detective Constable" on the label,' said Purdie. 'I take it DCI Crosbie is mentoring you, since he was handling the Harry Hanlon case?'

'He is, ma'am,' Dugdale replied stiffly.

'I hope he hasn't turned you into a misogynistic pig.'

'No, he hasn't,' Dugdale answered, keeping matters as formal as possible.

'Well, don't be picking up any bad habits from him. Believe me, he has plenty.'

Dugdale changed the subject. 'How long before they can analyse the DVR?'

'How long is a piece of string?'

'The date we're looking at is March 15th, the day of

Harry Hanlon's death. If it had recorded the crime, I suspect it was switched off shortly afterwards.'

'Why didn't they just destroy it?'

'I believe they were spooked and chose to hide it in plain sight rather than risk being caught trying to dispose of it, which would imply guilt. They probably hoped that formatting the disc then continuously recording over it would erase any footage of the attack.'

'They are probably right. But if anyone can retrieve erased data, it'll be our IT guys. Shall I ask them to call you directly or would you rather they speak to your boss?' Susan asked, with her pen poised over her notepad.

'Calling me would be fine,' he said, giving his mobile number.

'I may just do that,' Susan replied, 'if you're available that is?'

Dugdale's face reddened for the third time that day.

'Sorry if I seem forward. In the lab, everything is pretty sterile, including most of our conversations,' she said, only half-apologetically.

'Yes, I'm available,' Dugdale said, 'and I don't mind you calling me sometime.'

'But you'd rather it was the IT team calling with a result first, right?'

'Truthfully? Yes.'

'I understand. Duty calls. Here's another piece of advice: don't let the job take over your life, or you'll end up a nutcase like that boss of yours. There is always another murder case waiting to be investigated, no matter how many you solve.'

Dugdale hadn't actually thought of it like that. After Harry Hanlon's homicide, there would be another one. Then another after that. 'Thanks for the advice' – he saw Susan arch her eyebrows, as if he was being sarcastic – 'No, seriously. I'm new. I'm just learning. But I think I may have stumbled upon something here.'

'I'll personally deliver the DVR and make sure it's their top priority. I'll tell them it's for a friend of mine,' Susan said, escorting Dugdale to the door where she gave him an unexpected brief kiss on the cheek.

He left with thoughts of Susan Purdie and Becky Hardie from the day care centre racing through his mind. Until this week no one had been interested in him and now suddenly there were two. He wondered if this was to do with being a detective. If it was, he rather liked it.

91

End of the pier

SEPTEMBER 7TH

April thanked Connor for the coverage on Harry's book that appeared in the paper today, and on the *Chronicle*'s website yesterday, but really it had just been an excuse to call him about something which had been troubling her.

'Do you think Robert Hanlon really killed his dad? I've just edited Robert's chapter in the book and he didn't come across as a cold-blooded killer to me. Not at all.'

'He has a long history of violence and has probably killed before, so to answer your question, yes, I think he probably did kill Harry,' Connor replied.

'The cops haven't hinted that it may have been someone else?' she asked in hope.

'Are you kidding? They couldn't wait to close that case. Shifty's death wrapped it all up nicely for them.'

'Was there anything actually linking him to his father's murder?'

'Well, their main clue was the large knife left sticking out of Harry Hanlon's back. There was only one man with the power to sink that home in the Macarena and that was Shifty,' Connor stated. 'Look, I've got to go, I'm taking Natasha swimming. Some of us still get the weekends off, remember? But, look, I'm pretty sure Shifty was the killer,' he added before hanging up.

April was far from sure. She thought about what Connor had said about the main clue being the knife in Harry's back. She repeated the word 'clue' softly to herself before she opened the drawer in her office desk and retrieved the manila envelope containing the manuscript Harry had asked for when he had made some minor adjustments to the crossword chapter. She freed the A4 sheets and thumbed through the amended section, finding Harry's cryptic clues, which he had altered with his red bookies pen.

April's heart began to race as she read his clue *Brickwork repairs at the end of the pier, the last face some saw as the end came near.* It was an eleven-letter word, and April finally knew the answer. 'Pierrepoint,' she shouted out loud. 'I'm a crossword genius.'

Albert Pierrepoint had been Britain's most famous hangman, executing over four hundred prisoners at the gallows, including around two hundred from Germany and Austria, who were found guilty of war crimes after the Second World War. In 1950, he also hanged Timothy Evans at London's Pentonville Prison for the murder of his daughter. Evans received a posthumous pardon sixteen years later after it was discovered the perpetrator had actually been his neighbour, John Christie, who was also executed by Pierrepoint. The wrongful execution of Evans is generally acknowledged as a major contributing factor for the suspension of the death penalty in Britain in 1965 before its eventual abolition.

'Aw, crap, it starts with an "E".' April felt utterly deflated. She was sure Pierrepoint had been correct, as everyone of a certain age knew the hangman's name. But she had been wrong when she was so convinced she had been right.

92

Thud

SEPTEMBER 7TH

It was Saturday morning and Dugdale was trailing Michael and Billy back from the shops. The weather was more like a normal Scottish September day: cold but sunny. After the intense heat of the hottest summer on record, the falling temperatures were welcome. Billy and Michael had eaten in the Manhatten before picking up a prescription from the chemist. Now Michael was pushing his brother in his wheelchair, occasionally assisted by Billy's massive hands, which could turn the wheels with ease.

Michael looked tiny compared to Billy's bulk. He could have really done with an electric wheelchair but the occupational health assessors had decided that the exercise would do Billy good in the long run. It wasn't a view shared by Michael. His appeals for a new chair had also been rebuffed by their late father, who was of the firm belief that the state should pay for everything because he had paid into the 'system' decades ago. Instead, it was left to the youngest Hanlon to haul disabled Billy around.

Michael and Billy occasionally stopped to speak to neighbours, exchanging friendly words and a laugh or just a wave. Billy looked happy. He appeared well-known and well-liked. Even the perpetually moody Michael looked happy. Strange that he despised the Ruck so much when the community seemed to respect him so much. And Dugdale could see why they would. Not only was he a caring soul, who looked after his disabled brother, but he was smart enough to train as a doctor. In the eyes of many, that was a greater achievement than his father's lucky windfall.

Finally, they reached the gaudy entrance of the Macarena where the brothers were met by Kendal, who had arrived five minutes earlier and was now leaving in a hurry. She exchanged some words with Michael. Whatever she had said he obviously didn't agree with – he appeared to remonstrate with her before giving a shrug of the shoulders as she roared off in her Mercedes Coupé. Dugdale then saw Michael whisper something to his brother, before they began the cumbersome procedure of trying to get in their front door. Billy hauled himself to his feet using the guide rails that had been bolted to the doorframe and which Harry Hanlon had previously removed when renovating the building, as they ruined the Spanish villa 'look'. Harry only relented when Billy had once got stuck in the front entrance, forcing his dad to return early from the Woodchopper, which he hadn't been happy about. The handrails had been reinstated the following day.

Dugdale kept his distance as he watched Billy steady himself, while Michael bumped the empty wheelchair up the stairs and into the house. Obviously, a ramp had been a compromise too far for their late father. Billy walked the three steps into the house, finally shutting the door behind them.

Dugdale walked briskly past the front gate of the Macarena, taking note that the triplets' Minis were gone, which meant there was a good chance the two brothers were home alone. He turned around the side of the block of buildings, making his way to the rear of the Macarena. He still didn't know what he was planning to do next but he remembered the flats to either side of the property had been vacated because of the Hanlons' extreme anti-social behaviour.

He climbed over the rear railings into the empty courtyard of the abandoned building. The concrete paving slabs were slippy with a layer of green moss, which had grown in the shade of the 10 ft-high wooden panelled fence that surrounded the Hanlon property like a fortress. Dugdale leapt on top of a brick bin shelter to try to peer over the top, but he needed more height. He returned to the concrete slabs to wrestle one of the filthy wheelie bins from the shelter and managed, with considerable difficulty, to manoeuvre it on to the roof and on to its side. Foul-smelling garbage juice poured from the lid all down Dugdale's front. It took great self-restraint not to swear loudly. The trainee detective had just clambered on top of the bin shelter again when he heard the sound of the patio doors squeaking open from the Hanlon property, followed shortly afterwards by the unmistakable sound of a ball being kicked off a wall.

Dugdale stepped on to the side of the wheelie bin, which gave a loud crack as the plastic concaved, but didn't break. Fortunately, the sound was drowned out by the thud, thud, thud from the ball repeatedly hitting the wall. Dugdale was now precariously balanced on the side of the bin, and, at this height, there was a good chance he would do some serious damage if he fell. Using the top of the Hanlons' fence, he pulled himself up to a standing position. The person playing with the football was blissfully unaware as Dugdale fetched his smartphone from his back pocket and took several pictures. He then turned it to video mode to capture the football player in action. Although of high quality, the images would have been unusable had he been a journalist, as the subject was on private property where they had a reasonable expectation of privacy. However, for a criminal case in a court of law, they could be used as evidence.

Dugdale lowered himself back out of sight and listened to the rhythmic thumping of the ball. He was about to send an image to DCI Crosbie and ask for further instructions when his mobile started to vibrate violently. He hit the automatic reply message – *Sorry, I can't talk right now* – as quickly as he could. A moment later, he received another message notifying him that he had voicemail. He dialled 121 to listen to the recording, pressing the phone firmly against his ear to muffle the sound.

'Officer Dugdale, this is Derek Muir from IT forensics. We've managed to retrieve footage from the DVR you submitted for the time stamp March 15th. Before the recording ended, it shows a man approaching the victim in the hot tub. You can't make out the suspect's face but he does appear to be holding a knife. The quality of the retrieved footage is, in my opinion, good enough for trial.'

If there was anyone geekier than a forensics officer then it was an IT forensics officer, Dugdale thought to himself, wishing Derek Muir would get to the point.

'The suspect is a large, heavily built white male. My rough estimate is he's at least 6 ft 5 in. If you have any suspects fitting this description then I would suggest this is your man. He's also wearing blue gloves – to prevent him leaving any DNA traces, I guess. But there's more. A much smaller male is then seen inspecting the victim's body after the attack. He does something to the blade. It's hard to work out exactly what, but I think he swabs it with something. I know this sounds bizarre, but if I was to give an educated guess, it looks like he wipes a used tampon on the handle. Anyway, call me if you need to discuss this further. And good luck with the case, but I'd be careful if I was you. The big fella really does hit the victim with incredible force. It looks like footage of a car crash.'

Dugdale hung up, with Muir's warning words still ringing in his ear. While listening to the voicemail he hadn't noticed that the noise of the ball had stopped. Dugdale turned to see where the footballer had gone when two shovel-sized hands grabbed his arm and yanked him from the top of the shelter to land head first on the concrete slabs. The trainee detective lay unconscious, with blood pouring from his right ear, matting his carefully coiffured quiff.

93

Solved

SEPTEMBER 7TH

April returned to Harry's cryptic crossword. How could she be wrong? *End of the pier* just had to be Albert Pierrepoint. April then remembered Harry once telling her if the clue was too easy, then it probably was, and you then had to search for the second meaning of the clue.

'Okay, it's eleven letters across, starts with an "E", and is definitely something to do with Albert Pierrepoint. Right, what else was he? Hangman.' She wrote the word down on the manuscript then scribbled it out again. 'Seven letters, too short. Gallows? Noose? Come on, April, think. Executioner?' April wrote the word down and added up the letters. It was eleven letters long. 'That's it, eleven letters starting with an "E" – EXECUTIONER. Brilliant, April, you clever little thing,' and she began searching for the pack of biscuits she kept in a drawer by her bed as a reward for her endeavours, only to find they were long gone.

'Okay. On to another clue. *Family background, occupation and date of birth, not of mine.* Seven letters and starts with "L". Occupation? Date of birth? This is bloody hopeless. But Harry always said concentrate on the one part of the clue which does make sense. Family background, starting with "L". It's *LINEAGE*,' she squealed with delight.

'Right, c'mon, I'm on a roll here,' she said, psyching

herself up for the final clue. 'Gateway to the Lakes leaves a minty taste. This seems so familiar.' Not surprisingly, April's mind drifted towards the food part of the sentence. 'What leaves a minty taste? After Eight mints – mmmm, I love them,' April said, recalling the Christmas favourites of wafer-thin mint squares dipped in dark chocolate and presented in their own little individual envelopes.

After Eights always took April back to her childhood Christmases, and the days when the chocolates were truly seen as a once-a-year festive treat, unlike the king-sized tubs of assorted sweets that are now available all year round. She had enjoyed a nice childhood, even though her family were skint: her mum and dad had loved her and done their best to take her away on day trips to the Ayrshire seaside on Scotland's west coast, where they would join the queues for a legendary ice cream from the Italian café, Nardini's. She realised that most of her memories revolved around food, like the time when she was nine and felt sick in the car all the way to the Lake District, where her dad swore that the local mint cake would cure her nausea...

April stopped tapping her pen on the manuscript to write a six-letter word. 'Gateway to the Lakes leaves a minty taste. It's Kendal in the Lake District, with its lovely Kendal mint cake. I can't believe I didn't get this sooner. It's KENDAL. Well done, Harry. From beyond the grave, you've just told me who murdered you!'

April stared down at Harry Hanlon's solved crossword puzzle with the word 'Kendal' overlapping 'executioner' and 'lineage', which Harry's clue had said was 'not of mine'.

Kendal was the executioner, and she wasn't Harry's kith and kin.

'And I'm the only one who knows,' April said.

It was only then she realised the danger she was in.

94

Property of the state
SEPTEMBER 7TH

DCI Crosbie was sitting at his kitchen table poring over the pages of April's draft book when he spotted a sheet with a handwritten note saying *KEEP THIS CHAPTER IN!* Crosbie guessed correctly that the instruction had been written by Harry and began to study the crossword clues.

Brickwork repairs at the end of the pier, the last face some saw as the end came near.

'An eleven-letter word starting with "E". That doesn't make any sense,' Crosbie said. But somehow it also did. His mind drifted back to his days when he was a young trainee detective himself and had been taken to Barlinnie prison and shown the unmarked graves of the prisoners who had been hanged inside the walls of the Victorian jail, and buried there as properties of the state. They had included Peter Manuel, a serial killer believed to have murdered nine people before his date with the hangman's noose on July 11th, 1958. Crosbie recalled how Manuel was one of only two prisoners from Barlinnie to have been hanged by the UK's last state executioner, Harry Allen. Six others had been hanged by Albert Pierrepoint, while two before them were executed by Albert's uncle, Thomas Pierrepoint. He wondered if the uncle had been proud of Albert continuing the family business. The graves of the executed were no longer in Barlinnie, having been exhumed then reinterred elsewhere during renovation works in 1997, but they had left a lasting impression on Crosbie, as they did on most who had seen them. It was a sobering thought to think the condemned were still not free men even after being put to death.

Crosbie's mental wanderings came to an abrupt halt as inspiration struck: 'Of course, "Executioner" – it must be.' He counted the letters. He was correct.

Crosbie looked at another of Harry's cryptic clues: *Family background, occupation and date of birth, not of mine.* 'Well, Harry was looking into his family background and he's saying someone is not his.' Crosbie didn't bother trying to get the answer right as he understood what Harry had meant by his question. He moved on to the third and final crossword clue: *Gateway to the Lakes leaves a minty taste.*

'Fuck this,' Crosbie exclaimed, 'I've not got time for these stupid riddles.' He grabbed his smartphone and entered 'minty taste lakes' into Google. The DCI arched his eyebrows at the first search result that came up.

'Shit,' he said. 'Kendal. It's Kendal. I should have known that. Which means April's in deep shit.'

95

Awake

SEPTEMBER 7TH

Dugdale came to on a white-leather couch inside the Macarena. The pain in his head was almost unbearable and there was a loud ringing in his ears. The last thing he remembered was being hauled from the top of the bin shelter and seeing the ground hurtling towards him. It had happened so quickly he had barely been able to get his hands out in front of him to break his fall. After that he must have blacked out, but he had no idea how long he'd been unconscious.

He gingerly opened his eyes, no more than a slit, and immediately saw the giant figure of Billy Hanlon looming over him, watching intently, almost daring him to move. He wasn't in his wheelchair. He could also hear, somewhere in the background, Michael Hanlon speaking frantically on the phone. It was difficult to make out exactly what was being said above the ringing in his ears, but Dugdale picked up fragments of the conversation.

'Fractured skull ... but survivable – the pulse is strong,' the young medical student was explaining. 'Make it look like an accident ... We've got his phone. Okay, we'll do that ... before he wakes up.'

Dugdale closed his eyes again and remained motionless. He wondered what the Hanlons had planned for him and if those plans would change radically if he woke up. His only hope was that backup was on the way, but he hadn't even told his boss where he was. He heard Michael walk into the room. He would have to take a risk and let them know he was conscious, if only to play for time.

96

Intruder
SEPTEMBER 7TH

April froze when she heard a voice from her hallway. She had been hurriedly packing a bag since deciphering Harry's clue from beyond the grave and planned to check into a hotel. Once safe she would phone her daughter, then Connor, and then tell the police all she knew. But now there was a strange voice in her house. She held her breath to try and hear what was being said when she heard it again. Someone was definitely inside her house.

Suddenly, she was struck by déjà vu: she had been here before, when the satnav had suddenly sprung into life. April thought for a minute. Had she used the infuriating device lately? She consoled herself with the thought that it must just be technology tormenting her again and breathed a huge sigh of relief. She had a lifelong habit of bringing anything of value in from the car, which included the satnav, and placing them on the hall table – which was where the voice had come from.

She continued packing her bag when something brushed against her foot, making her jump. It was her cat, Cheeka, dashing under the bed. She hissed. Cheeka never hissed. Something had spooked her. Then April heard the voice again, closer than last time. It was not the metallic sound of the computerised American twang from the satnav.

'Aaaa-pril,' the voice said in a slow, sing-song manner. It was female. It also had come from right outside her bedroom door.

'Aaaa-pril, I know you're in there.'

The door opened, and April was rooted to the spot with fear.

'We need to talk about the book,' Kendal Hanlon said, holding a gun.

97

Squeezing
SEPTEMBER 8TH

It had just gone midnight when Michael asked, 'Are you awake?' The youngest Hanlon was by Billy's side, peering down at Dugdale. 'So what gave the game away?' the trainee doctor asked the rookie detective.

'You'd have to ask my boss, DCI Crosbie,' Dugdale replied, his voice dry and crackly. Now he was fully conscious he noted a dark red patch of congealed blood had spread over the white-leather couch. It had to be his. He looked at the two brothers, who really were the epitome of brains and brawn, with the younger Hanlon's small skinny frame completely dwarfed by the man-mountain that was Billy. 'But if I was a betting man, I reckon it's his legs,' Dugdale said, pointing at Billy's thighs. 'They're like tree trunks. I've seen people who are wheelchair-bound – their muscles can waste away, leaving matchstick legs. But Billy's look as powerful as a weightlifter's.' Dugdale was simply applying logic from a personal observation.

'Very astute, for a trainee detective.' Michael sneered.

'Not really. It's my boss. I didn't suspect anything until he told me to tail you,' he lied.

'Either way, I'm just surprised there's a policeman with more than one brain cell. Remarkable,' Michael said, his superiority complex coming to the fore.

Dugdale studied the young man and didn't like what he saw. There was a nastiness to him he had never noticed before. He now knew Crosbie had been right about all the Hanlons being dangerous. 'My boss is a pretty smart guy,' he said, trying to keep the conversation going, as he had been taught at police college.

'Amazing how smart people can grow from a cesspit like the Ruck,' Michael remarked, and Dugdale knew Michael was talking about himself now, rather than Crosbie. 'The wheelchair was my father's idea. He wanted the Disability Living Allowance. Would piss it all away at the Woodchopper, of course. He even kept claiming it after he won. He said it had been his idea so it was his money. Can you believe that?'

Dugdale reckoned that sounded like a decent motive for murder. They had then kept up the ruse after his father's death, as it provided a perfect alibi.

The youngest Hanlon seemed to read his thoughts. 'It was hard to stop the pretence once we'd started, of course. But Billy played his part perfectly.' Michael reached up to place his arm around his brother's wide shoulders. 'Shortly before our father's death he eventually relented and allowed us to keep the benefits we were due. Which was sorely needed, let me tell you.'

'Sorely needed?' Dugdale asked.

'For food. As far as he was concerned, he put a roof over our heads and paid the bills. The rest was up to us. It's hard to earn extra when you're studying and caring for your brother at the same time. And all the while our father was sitting on a £100 million fortune.'

'And he gave you nothing at all from it?'

'Are you kidding? If anything, he got worse. He would never tire of telling us it was his money and his money only. He claimed he didn't want to spoil us, but we all knew the truth. He was Dickensian, although even Scrooge changed his ways. Our father never had that moment of enlightenment.'

'I can understand why you wanted him dead.'

Michael laughed before replying, 'Oh, I didn't kill him.'

'But Billy did,' Dugdale replied coolly.

'What court would convict a learning-disabled adult with the brain of a six-year-old?'

'So you're not his carer? You're his handler?'

'If it wasn't for me, he wouldn't have survived. Isn't that right, Billy?'

'That's right,' Billy said robotically.

'You're smart enough to know you can't get away with killing a policeman though,' Dugdale warned.

'Of course not. They'd lock us all up for that. But Billy here is another matter. Billy,' Michael said, now addressing his brother, 'this policeman is going to try and break us up. We don't want that now, do we?'

'No, I want to stay with you,' Billy said.

'We'll have to put the policeman to sleep then.'

Dugdale raised his voice, trying to take on an authoritative edge: 'I really wouldn't do that. Backup is on its way.'

'I doubt it. You've been here for hours now and we haven't heard a peep.' Michael grinned.

'Assault of a police officer is still a lot less serious than murdering one,' Dugdale replied desperately.

'Again, that doesn't apply to Billy,' Michael said with glee in his eyes. 'He won't even stand trial. You're just an intruder and he was protecting his family in the only way he knows how.'

As Billy advanced towards him on the couch, Dugdale pushed himself as far back as the white-leather upholstery would allow. 'You know the difference between good and bad, don't you, Billy?'

'Don't speak to my brother,' Michael snapped.

Billy grabbed Dugdale by the shoulders and hauled him to his feet with consummate ease, the sudden motion sending another sharp jolt of pain shooting through the trainee detective's head. Dugdale was fit and strong, but he felt as defenceless as a child when Billy wrapped his powerful forearm around his neck and began to squeeze the air from his body in a chokehold.

'You don't want to hurt me like you hurt your dad?' Dugdale gasped, as he grabbed Billy's tightening arm, trying to prise it from his airways. 'They made you kill your dad, Billy.'

'Keep squeezing, Billy,' Michael encouraged.

98

In a tight spot
SEPTEMBER 8TH

April knew there was no chance of escape or to call for help. Not only was Kendal Hanlon a fit younger woman, but she was pointing a gun in April's direction. She'd been on the receiving end of fists before, and also miraculously managed to escape unscathed from a lunatic with a knife, but being held at gunpoint was a first.

'Is that thing real?' April asked, trying to mask her terror. 'Because I've only ever seen them on the telly before, so I wouldn't know.'

'Do you want to find out?'

'No, dear, I don't. I really don't.'

'You told me you'd quit writing. That you would never finish my dad's book. That you were retiring. You lied to me,' Kendal said with venom.

'I didn't. I was. I mean, I had no intention of finishing it but the publishers were threatening to sue me. I had no choice,' April pleaded.

'I told you not to go opening that can of worms, but you didn't listen to me. You ignored me, didn't you? How many copies of the book do you have?' Kendal demanded.

'Well, I've got the file on my laptop but the only printed version is this one your dad asked for, which is here,' April said, pushing the manuscript across the table towards her. 'It's expensive to print out, but your dad preferred to read things on paper rather on screen. In fact, I'm not sure he had an iPad or a laptop, did he?'

'Shut up! You don't half rabbit on.'

'I'm just a tad nervous, dear. What with the gun and all.'

'Did you ever email a copy of the book to anyone?'

'Only the first few chapters to the publisher.' April didn't mention that Police Scotland had also taken a copy the day after Harry Hanlon was murdered.

Kendal flicked through the bundles of bound A4 paper. She remained silent for what seemed an age as she turned over page after page with one hand while the other continued to steadily point the gun at April's midriff.

'Did your father really molest you?' April asked.

'Yes, he did,' Kendal replied, her eyes still studying each page.

'It's just I asked him about it and he said you had threatened to blackmail him.'

'Well, he would say that, wouldn't he?'

'He told me you'd say he demanded oral sex, but you told me it was masturbation.'

'A blowie? A handjob? What does it matter?'

'Quite a bit, actually. Not in the eye of the law, but certainly when it comes to corroborating your story. You see, the truth will out.'

'Well, here's another cliché for you: "the chickens have come home to roost". My dad only got what he deserved.'

'No man deserves to have false child abuse allegations made against him, though. No matter his failings.'

'So what if he didn't abuse me? He may as well have. I had to turn tricks because he wouldn't give me and my mum enough money. It was disgusting, pimping out my own body to every grubby little bastard who could afford it – and the teachers, too – only to find my own dad had spent all my money in that dump of a pub.'

That April could believe.

'So he robbed me of my money and robbed me of my childhood and then tried to rob me of my inheritance.'

April felt that Kendal, like her mother, was overcooking

her role. 'So it was blackmail, to make sure your dad paid up? But even if he disinherited you, you could still have fought for a share of his money. I read loads of cases where a will has been overturned before.'

'Doesn't apply if you're not his.'

The truth shall out indeed.

'He DNA-tested us all. Made us swab our mouths then sent it off to some lab. All the others were his biological children, but I wasn't. He planned to gather us all together and reveal the results. But I got there early and he was so happy with himself. Told me he was delighted me and my "whore" mother wouldn't get a penny.'

'So you killed him?'

'Ha, I'm not that stupid, I...' Kendal stopped talking as she came to the chapter on crossword puzzles. 'What changes was he making here?' she demanded.

'Just the clues to his puzzles. You know what he was like with his crosswords, dear.'

'But why were these clues so important?' Kendal said suspiciously, before spinning the manuscript around 180 degrees. 'What do these mean?'

'Don't ask me,' April replied, just a little too quickly. 'I'm hopeless at crosswords. Your dad ... do you mind if I still call him that?' When Kendal didn't respond, she continued, 'Anyway, he was always trying to teach me, but I could never quite get the hang of it.'

'And the cops? Have they seen these clues?' Kendal demanded.

'No, dear. And I don't think Scotland's finest would understand them any better than I do, even if they did have them.'

Kendal knew a lie when she heard one. She raised the barrel of the gun to head height, closed one eye and took aim. 'You gave the cops a copy of this book, didn't you? I've had just about enough of your shit, old yin. Tell me what the fucking clues mean or I will shoot you in the fucking head, and don't think I won't.'

99

The wheelchair
SEPTEMBER 8TH

'We found the DVR,' Dugdale managed to rasp as Billy's grip tightened. 'We have recovered the footage. We know Billy stabbed Harry. We know you swabbed the knife with the triplets' blood from one of their tampons.'

'Shit,' Michael said, 'let him go, Billy.'

The pressure eased and Dugdale coughed and spluttered as he filled his lungs again with precious air. 'No one could figure out how you hid the DVR' – he took another deep breath and coughed some more – 'or how you smuggled it into the day centre right under the noses of the police. But you used Billy's wheelchair, didn't you? His seat is about the same size as the DVR. You took the foam out of the seat cover and put the DVR in there. No police officer would have ordered a disabled man out of his wheelchair. Billy was sitting on it, wasn't he?'

'It was very hard,' Billy said. 'It made me sore.'

'Shut up, Billy,' Michael snapped.

'I bet it was sore, Billy,' Dugdale said. 'You had to sit on it for hours, didn't you, as the policeman went through your house?'

'Yes,' Billy replied.

'But Michael told you to be brave.'

'Yes,' he said again.

'I told you to shut up, Billy,' Michael ordered. 'I need to think.'

'Michael is always telling you what to do, isn't he, Billy? He told you to hurt your dad, didn't he?' Dugdale pressed further.

'They said it was a game.'

'Who's "they", Billy? Who else told you to hurt your dad?'

'Put him to sleep, Billy,' Michael said, urging his brother to attack the trainee detective again.

'My sister. Kendal. She said it was a kid-on knife. It was just to give Dad a fright.'

'But it wasn't kid-on,' Dugdale said. 'It killed your dad.'

'Not another word, Billy,' Michael warned, a slight panic rising in his voice.

'And you covered it up, didn't you, Michael? It was you who swabbed the knife with the triplets' DNA. You knew it would ruin the investigation. That had been your plan all along. How did you know the triplets were monozygotic?'

'It's pretty obvious if you look at them.' Michael scoffed.

'So you were prepared to set up your own sisters?'

'No jury would ever convict them,' he said loftily.

'But all your careful planning was undone,' Dugdale pressed on.

'Kendal should have waited. She made Billy go too soon,' Michael replied.

'He was supposed to wait until the DVR had stopped recording, wasn't he? But Kendal had been angry. She's always been impulsive like that, hasn't she? She's the real head of the family, not Shifty.'

'Put him to sleep, Billy,' Michael barked.

'I didn't mean it,' Billy said as he placed the trainee detective in a chokehold again, with tears in his big, innocent eyes.

'Of course you didn't. They tricked you, Billy,' Dugdale said as he managed to get his feet up on the couch, easing the pressure a little. 'They said your dad would be alright. But they lied. Michael and Kendal lied to you, Billy.'

'They said Dad would be alright. But I hurt Dad.'

'You hurt him bad,' Dugdale agreed.

'Kill him!' Michael shouted. 'Finish him off, Billy.'

'Blood. He had blood on his back. I hurt my dad.' Billy sobbed.

Billy's grip relaxed ever so slightly around Dugdale's neck, and then he let him go. The young detective collapsed back on the couch, clasping at his throat. 'Thank you, Billy. You're a good person. It's Michael and Kendal who are bad.'

'Very bad,' Billy agreed, turning towards his little brother.

100

The end game
SEPTEMBER 8TH

April knew that Kendal would pull the trigger if she had to. She also knew the only way to convincingly tell a lie was for it to have an element of truth.

'Look, I've been trying to work the clue out as well, especially since your dad was mur ... killed. I felt it was important somehow. I've been writing down various answers on my notepad. It's in my office.'

'Show me,' Kendal said, dropping her aim ever so slightly, before adding, 'and you better not try anything.'

'I wouldn't dare. Look at the size of me. I'm not going anywhere fast. And you have a gun.'

'Yes, I do.' Kendal grinned menacingly.

April made her way to the spare downstairs bedroom that she'd had converted to an office years ago when Jayne had moved out. It was where she'd finally written the book she'd always threatened to write – a book that was now likely to kill her. She knew Kendal would shoot the moment she realised April had lied and already worked out Harry's clue. But what else could she do now? April trudged towards her office like the condemned going to meet Albert Pierrepoint's noose. How ironic.

As they entered the room, Kendal fumbled for the light switch by the door, only to feel the snap of cold steel around her wrist. She pulled the gun's trigger, letting off an explosion in April's ears. The gunshot was followed by the ratcheting noise of handcuffs securing Kendal's other wrist behind her back.

'I always say cuffs are the master.' DCI Crosbie grinned as he stooped to pick up the still-smoking gun that lay beside Kendal. He straightened up to see a stunned-looking April Lavender standing by the window, staring at a perfectly round bullet hole in the pane of glass just inches above her head. She looked as white as a sheet.

'That was a close call,' Crosbie said as he called for backup.

All April was able to mutter in reply was, 'Oh my.'

101

Emergency services
SEPTEMBER 8TH

Billy Hanlon had Michael firmly by the throat. His younger brother's toes barely touched the ground as he kicked and writhed, but he could do nothing to free himself from Billy's vice-like grip.

'You made me hurt Dad! You made me hurt Dad!' Billy repeated over and over as Michael's face went from red to puce. Oxygen starvation was kicking in and he soon stopped squirming and fell unconscious.

Dugdale called 999. 'This is trainee officer Dugdale. I need police backup immediately to…' In the heat of the moment, he couldn't remember the exact address of the property, merely shouting, 'It's the Hanlons' place. The Macarena. In Ruckhouse. I need police and an ambulance.'

With the call made, he now tried to save Michael. 'You don't want to hurt your brother, Billy. Why don't you let him go?' Dugdale said as calmly as possible, desperately trying to defuse the situation.

'He made me hurt my dad.'

'I know. And that was very, very bad. But hurting Michael is also bad. You don't want to hurt anyone else, do you, Billy? Why don't you let him go?'

Michael's face now looked puffy and purple. His brother was tightening his grip, his immense strength lifting the teenager's feet completely off the ground. Dugdale knew in a few moments Michael would be dead or severely brain-damaged.

'He made me hurt my dad.'

Dugdale knew the best tactic was to change Billy's focus. 'Didn't Michael always remind you of your manners, Billy? Well, it's impolite to strangle someone, isn't it?'

'Lady says I'm polite.'

'Which lady?' Dugdale asked.

'The fat lady. The one writing Dad's book.'

'Ah yes, April Lavender. She's a nice lady.'

'She's fat.'

'Yes, but she likes people with manners – people like you, Billy. People who wouldn't hurt others. Polite people. A gentle-man, like you.'

Billy turned his head slightly in Dugdale's direction. 'Fat lady is nice to Billy.'

'Yes, and I bet you have always been nice to the fat lady. You are nice to everyone. You're nice to your brother even though he's been bad.'

Billy looked at his brother's bloated, purple face and frowned. He then stared at his fingers buried deep in Michael's neck. Suddenly, Billy let him go, allowing Michael to fall to the floor.

Dugdale dashed to the teenager's aid. He wasn't breath-ing, and the trainee detective could see that the boy's windpipe was misshapen as a result of the blunt force trauma. Dugdale knew the only hope of getting him to breathe again was with a crude tracheotomy – making a hole through the front of his throat. But if he cut into Michael, the shock of seeing blood could lead to Billy attacking him again. In the distance he could now hear the wail of approaching sirens – he would have to leave Michael's care to the professionals.

'Well done, Billy. That was very, very kind of you,' Dugdale said, while slipping the cuffs on Billy's thick wrists. He made no attempt to resist. 'I've put these on you so we can go for a ride in a police car, Billy. You'd like that, wouldn't you?'

'Yes,' Billy said, his eyes lighting up.

'How about I ask them to put on the flashing blue lights and siren for you? Does that sound fun?'

'Yes.' He beamed.

Dugdale would be true to his promise. It was the least he could do before Billy was taken into the care of the state for the rest of his life.

102

Once in a lifetime
OCTOBER 2ND

'Under Scots law a disinherited child still has a claim on their parents' estate,' Paul McFadden explained to April Lavender after he had summoned her to his city-centre office. She had been shown in by young Warren, who she correctly suspected was the solicitor's lover.

McFadden's décor was exactly as she had imagined: almost a lawyer's stereotype with the mahogany desk, oak-panelled walls and green leather chairs. She noticed McFadden's chair had been set higher than hers, so he could literally look down on his visitors. It also enabled him to see over the top of his computer screen, as he was not a tall man.

'So even if Harry wrote in his will that Kendal wasn't to get a penny of his fortune, that wouldn't matter?' April enquired.

'Correct, in Scotland. She could still stake a claim.'

'So she would get an equal share along with all the other children?'

'Absolutely.'

'What's seven into £100 million?'

'Just over £14 million.'

'But if Harry could prove Kendal wasn't his?' April asked.

'A child brought up informally would not qualify for a claim – and Kendal was never formally adopted by Harry.'

'And Harry knew this?'

'Of course. I was his advisor. He asked me what would happen if he hadn't fathered one of his kids, and I told him that child would have no claim on his estate.'

'And he never told you Kendal wasn't his?'

'No. Harry had his suspicions but couldn't be sure until he made them all take a DNA test. From that moment on, they were on edge. He knew he would be in danger. That's why he gave the cryptic clues to you: it was his insurance policy. In the event of his death, his wishes would still be carried out.'

'Kendal needed to delete any mention of her not being Harry's child from my book – so that she could make a claim after his death. What would you have done then?' April asked.

'It'd become tricky as his body was cremated,' McFadden conceded. 'I have a copy of the DNA report, but it only states that sample three wasn't a match to Harry. It didn't contain a name. So any decent counsel acting for Kendal would have demanded a retest. That's why your book was so important. It states, albeit through a cryptic clue, that Harry says she wasn't his.'

'And what about the police? They swabbed them all, didn't they?'

'I only agreed if forensics didn't cross-match with Harry's blood sample. The siblings had insisted on it because obviously one of them wasn't Harry's. Of course, it would have been Kendal who coerced the others, but I wasn't to know that at the time. So I made it a legal requirement that Police Scotland wouldn't cross-match, because at that stage they were still all witnesses and not suspects, so the cops couldn't even demand the samples.'

'I still don't understand why Harry didn't tell you he wasn't Kendal's real dad?' April asked.

'He had to be sure. Apparently, when he got the DNA results he planned to gather the whole family together to tell them Kendal wasn't his. But he never got the chance because that was the night he was murdered.'

'But why leave the clues with me?' April asked.

'Every time he spoke to me he knew the meter was running. He couldn't wait to get off the phone, especially as I would always ask him to pay up his last bill, too. But with you, he obviously felt more relaxed. You were actually paying him. I have a copy of the contract on file … £500 advance and a further five hundred on publication. It obviously came to him that he could give you the information as insurance. Cover his bases. He must have felt very relaxed in your company.'

'Surely you could have settled with Kendal? Given her a token payment to go away?' April pondered.

'It was against Harry's instructions. He was explicit that only his biological offspring were to benefit. And anyway, Kendal doesn't seem like the type who would be bought off for a token amount, does she? She would have wanted every penny of her £14 million, plus a portion of Shifty's share, since he's dead.'

'But why did Harry do it? Why didn't he want her to receive a penny?'

'He was a betrayed man. It must have been eating away at him for years. Then when Kendal and her mum started plotting for a share of his winnings, he was equally determined that they wouldn't get it. Kendal had no choice but to agree to be swabbed and, from the moment the DNA results came back, Kendal knew the game was up. She had to make sure those results never got out. So Harry secured the inheritance for his biological children and at the same time sealed his own fate. That's when she hatched a plan with Michael for Billy to kill Harry.'

McFadden let that thought hang there as he got up from behind his desk, which completely dwarfed him, and walked round to take a seat next to April. The leather upholstery squeaked as he shuffled to make himself comfortable, his tailored heels just making it to the floor and no more.

'They knew Billy would never stand trial even if he was caught, but they wanted to make sure they ruined the whole investigation in the first place by putting the triplets' DNA on the knife handle. Someone as clever as Michael wouldn't need a DNA test to have known the triplets were monozygotic; he could see from looking at them they were all from the same egg. But Kendal shot her bolt – she was probably raging after Harry goaded her about not getting a penny – and she ordered Billy to attack him with a "fake" knife. Michael swabbed the knife handle with one of the triplets' tampons, then managed to smuggle the DVR out of the house in Billy's wheelchair, right under the detectives' noses. After that, the only thing Kendal had to worry about was your book. She thought you had buried it for good but then she read it was to be released, after all. She panicked. She knew her dad would have implicated her as his killer somehow. She just wasn't clever enough to figure it out. But you did Miss Lavender. You solved Harry's cryptic clues.'

'But why would Michael help Kendal?' April asked. 'Why would he put his whole future on the line? Especially if she wasn't really his sister.'

'Harry shat on his youngest son from a great height for years. He left him to raise Billy practically on his own. He refused to give them any money. Then there were the parties, those endless parties when Michael was trying to study for medical school. Have you ever been sleep-deprived, Miss Lavender?'

'Of course I have – I'm a mother,' she said haughtily, wondering when McFadden had last missed out on any beauty sleep.

'Well, you know how sleep deprivation makes you do crazy things. But more than likely Kendal would have told Michael that their dad was trying to freeze one of them out of his will. She may have even told him the truth that she wasn't Harry's biological daughter. Whatever she said, Michael thought life would be better without Harry Hanlon. He also reckoned that with his high IQ he could outsmart the police. Sadly, the jails are full of people who think they're brighter than the police, even if their IQs never quite matched Michael's.'

April felt glum. She shook her head as she thought how the family had been doomed from the moment of Harry's good fortune. '£100 million he won. Imagine that. £100 million and it completely destroyed the Hanlons. Robert was blown to pieces in his own car. Kendal was raised as Harry's own, but then he rejected her as soon as he came into money, and she in turn had him murdered. It's utterly tragic.'

'Indeed,' McFadden remarked.

'And Billy?'

'He's in Carstairs psychiatric hospital and will be detained indefinitely. He's also got Hughes Syndrome, inherited from his father, so his life will be limited anyway. But what he has left of it will be under lock and key.'

'And Michael?' April asked, praying for a glimmer of hope.

'Ah, Michael…' Even the bullish McFadden looked grim. 'The doctors suspect he has some form of locked-in syndrome. They have found extensive brain activity but he's in an almost completely vegetative state.'

'Oh no, that brilliant brain of his. Medical school. It's all gone,' April said, aghast.

'I know. Round-the-clock personal care and his bright mind trapped inside a wrecked body. It's one big Ruckhouse heartache, for sure. There is some good news, though.' McFadden flicked through his smartphone to show April a photograph. 'The triplets have gone off to live in Florida – three very rich young ladies. Looks like they're enjoying themselves, doesn't it? And no wonder: they've inherited the lot. Shifty's dead. Kendal was disinherited and Billy and Michael were involved in Harry's murder, so the girls have been left with over £33 million each.'

April sighed. 'I hope that means they're out of the porn business for good.'

'They're Hanlons – they'll screw up their new beginnings somehow.' McFadden chuckled. 'I'm told they have got in with some investment banker, so we'll see how long it takes him to gets his hands on their money, or whatever else he's after. Hughes Syndrome was also found in the blood sample found on the knife handle, so at least one of them has the inherited condition, too,' McFadden added.

The lawyer let April have a moment to digest everything he had said as he went to retrieve a file. 'But now we come to the purposes of our meeting – your book, Miss Lavender.'

'My book?' April asked. She hadn't worked on it since the night Kendal had tried to kill her. The last three weeks had passed in a haze of police interviews and visits from her worried daughter and granddaughter. Even Connor had started visiting her on almost a daily basis. She didn't have a moment to herself.

'Yes, the book to die for,' McFadden said, 'what are your plans for it?'

'The publisher is desperate for me to finish it. They had planned to release it on October 30th, but obviously they will have to wait until after Kendal's trial now. I wish I had never started the bloody thing. That book has brought nothing but trouble.'

'Oh, I think you actually made a very wise decision writing your book – financially, at least. You see, the estate of Harry Hanlon would like to make you a very generous offer for it.' McFadden grinned.

'What?' April said, struggling to understand what he meant.

'We want to buy your book, Miss Lavender.'

'But why?'

'So we can bury it. Make sure it is never published, or as Harry put it…' McFadden said, while retrieving a pair of reading glasses from his top pocket to read the file in his hand, 'I've to offer the "cracking big bit of stuff" the princely sum of £1 million for the rights to the manuscript.'

April thought McFadden could have ditched the theatrics, it was dramatic enough. 'But why?' was all she could splutter again.

'He didn't like it. Not your writing – not that at all – but the whole story. You told it ever so well, Miss Lavender. Too well. You exposed all of Harry's failings. He didn't like what he had read, but he also took it on board. That's why he told me to make sure all his children were properly looked after. All his biological children.'

'What about the publisher?'

'I've read over the contract Harry gave me. There are a couple of options: I can say you fear further repercussions and threats upon your life if it's published. Or perhaps I can dream up some breach of contract that the publishers might have committed, which would make the agreement null and void. But most likely I will have to make them a settlement offer of around £50,000. I have been instructed to pay whatever it takes to make sure that this book never hits the shelves. But really, it's all down to you, Miss Lavender.' McFadden took his glasses off and leaned back in his chair, placing his hands behind his head. 'You could take your chances, of course, that you have an international bestseller on your hands, if you ever finish it. Or it could be a massive flop that only makes you back the meagre advance ... if you're lucky. On the other hand, you can take the £1 million on offer right now. But it's only on offer for the duration of this meeting. This is a once-in-a-lifetime opportunity. You won't get a second chance.'

April just looked at him, unblinking.

McFadden smiled. 'So what's it to be, Miss Lavender? Fancy making an instant killing?'

103

The offer

OCTOBER 3RD

'Busy, Elvis?' Connor's news editor Big Fergie asked as he entered the broom cupboard office.

'Just annoying the government. They've been on the back foot, auditing everything. They're paranoid about another methadone scam, so the shadow health minister told me. Apparently it hardly fits with their image of being fit to govern a "future, independent Scotland".'

'I just love it when we piss off the government, or the cops, or both. Means we're doing our job,' Fergie said.

'I know, there is nothing like it. I still get a buzz from papers, when it's like this.'

'Talking of which, there's another cull about to begin.'

'I heard. Is it time for my tap on shoulder, Fergie?'

'Well, if the twats in HR had anything to do with it,' he said, brandishing an envelope marked *Private and confidential*. 'I've to formally make you an offer, but you do not have to take it. I mean it. We won't try any funny stuff and try to force you out. I don't want you to go. The pen-pushers only look at the salary, not the person.'

Fergie placed the envelope in front of him. Connor always knew this moment would come. He'd rehearsed it several times during his 'leaving fantasies', when times had been bad and he had dreamed of moving on to a new chapter in his life.

But not when he had come off the back of a groundbreaking story of the methadone scandal, on top of all the drama that came with the Harry and Shifty murders. They had got him fired up, just like the old days.

'Don't you want to know how much it is?' Fergie asked.

'It's £84,000, or it should be. I know exactly how much my twenty-two-year service is worth.'

Big Fergie laughed. He knew that most of the senior staff had calculated what kind of a pay-off they were due from their old newspaper contracts. 'I really hope you say no, Elvis. There is no other reporter like you on the paper. I doubt there will be again. But it's up to you. You could work for another three or four years maybe, before they make you an offer again.'

'Or we could go bust and I get nothing,' Connor mused.

'Yes, there is always that. It's a gamble. Have a think, though. Mull it over before you decide to stick or twist. Let me know in your own time,' Fergie said, before adding, 'as long as it's within five working days. Sorry, Elvis: HR insisted.'

'No problem. I'll get back to you,' Connor replied absent-mindedly.

'Why don't you hit the road? No point you hanging about until six. Go and talk it over at home. We're journalists, you and I, Elvis. Always will be, no matter what we do after this.'

Connor logged off and headed to his girlfriend's restaurant, his redundancy offer in his suit pocket.

104

A counter-offer
OCTOBER 4TH

Connor was in turmoil as he waited for April to arrive at the Peccadillo. He was too preoccupied to even notice Martel's overt rudeness.

'Hello,' April said brightly.

Connor was unsure if he was ready for her relentless cheeriness. 'I got the tap on the shoulder,' he said, handing her the company offer.

'Great,' April said, while indicating her desire for 'the usual' to Martel.

'I thought that's how I'd feel, too, but now I'm not so sure. I've been in papers all my life.'

'What did Anya say?'

'She said I could work for her in the restaurant. I don't mind helping out, but I don't want to work for my girlfriend,' he said gloomily.

'You're right, that's a bad idea. Take your redundancy and come and work for me.'

'As your full-time carer? No, thanks. I'm not ready to wipe arses just yet,' Connor said dismissively.

'No, I'm serious. Come and work for me. Not as an employee, but a partner. But with a salary. I will pay you exactly what you got from the *Daily Chronicle*.'

'I'm on over £60,000,' Connor said incredulously.

'That much?'

'Yes,' he snapped.

'Okay, I didn't know it was that much. How about £50,000 a year, on a two-year contract, plus a 50/50 split of any profits.'

'Have you finally gone round the bend?'

'Nope.' April beamed.

'Have you won the lottery then?'

'Kinda.'

'What?'

'I have been given lottery money.'

Connor stared at April for an age. He actually couldn't think of anything else to ask.

'Look,' April said, passing Connor the letter from the Hanlons' lawyer. 'Paul McFadden bought my book off me. Harry didn't want it published – too close to the bone, apparently. So I took the money instead. £1 million.'

'You're a millionaire,' Connor said in amazement as he read the settlement agreement. 'A fucking millionaire.'

'Yup.' April smiled.

'Then take the money and enjoy it. Travel the world. Take the granddaughter to Disneyland. Live your life. Enjoy.'

'And after I've done all that, I'll be the size of a house. I'll just get fatter and fatter until I can do no more.'

'So?'

'So, I want to keep working. To keep writing.'

'But papers don't have the money to pay freelancers much anymore,' Connor said.

'Then we'll diversify. Write books. Or become private investigators. How exciting would that be?'

'Alright, Jessica bloody Fletcher, let's not get ahead of ourselves.'

'Why not? I've been handed a million pounds. I will never have to worry about money again. But I do worry about my weight. And dying young.'

'Ha … young!' Connor scoffed.

'Okay, youngish. But the main thing is, I want to keep working. I need to have a reason to get up in the morning.'

'And you want to employ me?'

'Yes, we'll see how it goes. If you hate it, we'll go our separate ways. No hard feelings. But it's not as if we haven't worked with each other before. We know each other's quirks.'

'I certainly know yours.'

'And you have plenty of your own, sunshine.'

Connor laughed. 'Are you serious?'

'Yes. The only proviso is we meet at the Peccadillo at the same time every morning.'

'So you can eat to keep the weight off?'

'Exactly.'

'Can't you buy the place and fire Martel?'

'Absolutely not, I love how she makes you squirm. So what say you? Are you up for it?'

'I must be mad, but yeah, fuck it. Let's do this thing.'

April leaned over the table to kiss Connor on the forehead, almost spilling his cup of coffee in the process.

'So what are we going to call ourselves? Presley Publications? ApriCon Services?' Connor joked.

'What about Lavender Investigations? I think there's a certain quality to it,' she replied.

'How about the Lavender Files? We'll be filing copy and private investigation reports. Or Lavender Solutions – the sweet smell of success?' Connor suggested, half in jest.

'Lavender Solutions – the sweet smell of success,' April repeated with closed eyes. She was imagining the name emblazoned on the outside of a building. 'I love it.'

'I have one last score to settle at work first, but then I'm all yours,' Connor said. Then, 'I wonder if we'll be successful?'

'If only you could find Mystic Matt, you could ask him.' April laughed.

But Connor was suddenly serious. 'Shit, I forgot: he told me I was facing a major career change and that Harry Hanlon had been killed by a child. Billy Hanlon has the mental capacity of a six-year-old, doesn't he?'

'Bloody hell,' April replied, the colour draining from her face, 'the psychic fraudster was right all along.'

105

The curious tale of the purple orchid

OCTOBER 5TH

Connor's 'last score' to settle at work had been cleared by the newspaper's duty lawyer and approved by the editor. Only Big Fergie seemed nervous.

'Are you sure you want to do this?' the news editor asked, having only just got over the shock that he was about to lose his best reporter.

'Yes, I'm sure,' Connor replied, although he wasn't really.

'It could cause you a lot of unwanted grief,' Fergie warned.

'This will be my last act as a journalist. I want to go out with a bang.'

'Shifty Hanlon went out with a bang. I don't want the same to happen to you, mate,' Fergie said, placing his hand on Connor's shoulder. He had never called him 'mate' before. It was always 'Elvis', but never 'mate'. It made the moment feel special.

Connor closed the door on the converted broom cupboard office for the last time as he brought an end to his long career in journalism and headed to the pub with Big Fergie. He had a feeling he was going to need a drink as it wouldn't be long before the first editions would be hitting the streets. Connor turned round to look at the newsroom for a final time when he realised that all the remaining staff were on their feet. They were standing for him. He smiled and gave them a wave goodbye before heading for the exit, leaving behind the noise of feet stomping and hands thumping on desks. Connor was being 'banged out' – one of the oldest newspaper traditions. He stepped outside into the cold night air and inhaled deeply.

Elvis really had left the building.

FAREWELL, by Connor Presley

After nearly thirty years in journalism, three press awards and over 6,000 stories filed and published, I am finally moving on to pastures new.

I have met the good, the bad and the downright nasty over the decades, from gangsters to politicians – although sometimes it's easy to mistake the two.

I have reported on miseries and triumphs in equal measures and just occasionally got to actually make a difference, like the recent Daily Chronicle investigation into the large-scale corruption of the government's methadone programme.

But as much as I took personal satisfaction in exposing wrongdoers, thieves and hypocrites, there are always the ones who got away scot-free.

During the course of the methadone investigation, addicts in Glasgow's Ruckhouse district were dropping like flies.

The police paid scant attention to the pleas of their families who insisted someone had fed their loved ones a final fatal dose of heroin.

When urged to DNA-test the envelopes the drugs had been delivered in, one flatfoot even told a grieving mother to her face, 'This isn't CSI, missus.'

Don't get me wrong, this is not a farewell piece designed to give the Old Bill a boot in the bollocks on my way out the door, but more a reflection on society as a whole.

We do not care about drug addicts.

I know why. I would no doubt feel aggrieved if my house had been turned over to feed a junkie's next fix. Or if my gran had been robbed of her handbag by someone high on smack.

But dozens were dying in Scotland's largest city and no one, except their families, gave a damn.

Well, I cared. I cared that someone out there was murdering – and I use that word advisedly – recovering addicts in their own homes by feeding them heroin that was too pure for their weakened systems to handle.

They cynically knew that they could keep sending the packages with abandon, safe in the knowledge that society hates addicts and the general consensus is that the best junkie is a dead one.

So they posted the deadly powder, with jaunty little messages printed inside cards wishing the poor addict all the best, like giving a death row prisoner their last meal, without actually telling them they were heading for the noose.

But this sadistic serial sender could not have achieved this on their own. They had to be fed targets – names, addresses – and with full knowledge that they were on the methadone programme and trying to get clean.

In other words, some of the most vulnerable people in society were deliberately selected for termination while at their lowest ebb.

This information could only have been obtained from a pharmacist's methadone register or from their doctor.

Most of the drug deaths I investigated had links to Saltire Pharmacy in Ruckhouse, along with Ruckhouse Medical Centre.

I can say no more than that because there are two active cases involving personnel from both establishments.

But neither is being investigated over any of the addicts' deaths – that is something I hope this article will change.

For what was going on, in my view, was the equivalent of Nazi Germany, where those not deemed fit for the new world order were put to their deaths.

But while Hitler's Final Solution came from a warped ideology, the addicts of Ruckhouse were being killed for profit. I honestly don't know what's worse.

Again, I cannot say much more, lest I be held in contempt of court, but let me just add that I found out that a dead drug addict, who isn't removed from the methadone register, is also a very profitable one.

And I also discovered who was posting the cards with their final fix.

I stumbled upon this when a former colleague was sent a retirement card from a well-known Glasgow 'businessman'.

It was from one of those apps that allow you to pick a design and write a message.

So this 'businessman' would choose a card, which would then be delivered to his premises, where he would add a small packet of pure heroin and then let the Royal Mail do the rest by delivering the deadly dose directly to the intended victim.

It sounds almost too simple.

Most of the cards sent to the addicts featured a purple orchid. Some had a different design, of course, but I reckon out of force of habit the 'businessman' got used to just clicking the same purple orchid card on his app.

My ex-colleague received the retirement card along with an expensive bottle of gin. She drank the gin but, fortunately, kept the card.

It featured a purple orchid.

So my last act as Chief Investigations Editor of the Daily Chronicle will be to pass to the police the purple orchid card sent by the Glasgow 'businessman', who I am naming here as Colin Harris.

I will also give them all the other purple orchid cards – and the various others – found in the possession of the murdered addicts. I'm pretty sure that if the cops have the cards and packages tested, they will discover traces of pure heroin.

I shall leave Police Scotland's finest to do the rest.

Because, by committing all this to print, the police will finally be forced to act and maybe, just maybe, society will start to care about the drug addicts in our communities.

Even dead ones.

106

The man with no name
NOVEMBER 1ST

DCI Crosbie decided he would walk all the way from his office to his sister's house in Ruckhouse – it would only take him around fifty minutes, at most. Although it was cold, it was dry and he was in the mood for it. It would also give him the privacy he needed to make a call.

Crosbie held an evidence envelope in his hand as he began his journey. It contained the purple orchid greetings cards – the one sent to April Lavender and the others, including the one that found its way into the hands of Gerard Clarke, the recovering drug addict who couldn't resist that final hit. They had all been handed over by Connor Presley, along with a precise list of dates and names and locations where they had been found.

Dugdale had also managed to ascertain from the internet card company that a bulk-buy of purple orchid cards had been delivered to the Portman Bar in Glasgow's Kinning Park district, an establishment not officially owned by Colin Harris, but most certainly part of his business empire.

DCI Crosbie had questioned Harris, who had protested, 'Those cards could have come from anyone.' Their long conversation concluded with a solemn promise from the gangster that he would send no more greeting cards to addicts, leading Crosbie to quip, 'Good, you know how much people hate "junkie mail".' Harris had laughed without conviction.

There was also another vow made, but this involved a percentage of profits for the DCI to turn a blind eye to a different lucrative 'business' plan Harris had in mind after his methadone scam had been stopped in its tracks by Connor's investigation. Harris had warned how he had 'plans for that bastard Elvis', but Crosbie warned against any retribution: 'That's Russian tactics, to bump off journalists. It's not what we do in Scotland. You will only bring more scrutiny on yourself and your business.'

As for April's retirement card and all the others, Crosbie now discarded them in a public bin as he headed towards the old streets he once called home. He took his time, strolling along and marvelling at his change in fortunes: from being in the final throes of his police career, to once again sitting on top of the pile. With a promotion in the pipeline promised by the chief constable, and a new revenue stream in the offing from Colin Harris, the future was looking very rosy indeed for DCI David Crosbie.

Crosbie eventually reached the local shops next to Saltire Pharmacy, where he decided he would buy some sweets for his nephew Damien, but definitely no Irn-Bru. He would also pick up a bouquet of flowers for his sister.

As he left the store with a box of Celebrations chocolates in a bag and a dozen red roses tucked under his arm, Crosbie had possibly never felt happier in his entire life.

The blade struck with extra force due to the rigidity of the orthopaedic metal splint on the attacker's forearm and wrist. The added weight gave the thrust more momentum. Crosbie felt the blade crunch through bone as the knife pierced his ribcage and sliced its way into his right lung. He attempted to lunge forward, away from the weapon, but it was stuck fast, deep inside him. He reckoned it must've been one of those zombie knives that are so favoured in the Ruck, with its jagged serrated edge gripping his innards like shark's teeth.

His attacker let go of the knife, causing Crosbie to fall forward onto the pavement. For a brief moment this gave him hope of escape, but then he could see the white trainers on the feet of the person who stabbed him, already covered in blood. Crosbie's blood. That's when he realised why his attacker had let go of the knife handle which was now protruding from his back. It was job done.

Crosbie turned on his side as far as he could to try and ID the knifeman, but the blade's handle prevented him moving any further as it jarred against the pavement. The blood-spattered trainers did not move. Instead the attacker knelt down, so Crosbie could see him. *White Nike trainers, blue jeans, green T-shirt*, Crosbie noted inwardly, a detective to the last.

His attacker's face came into view, blocking the sun directly behind him, and forcing Crosbie's eyes to adjust.

'Remember me, pig?'

Crosbie thought how things hadn't really moved on since the first time he had been called a 'pig' as a trainee detective. It was funny the thoughts you had at a time like this. The DCI studied the face before him – it didn't ring any bells, but then again it was out of context, as he had never been in this position before, being asked to recognise someone with a knife sticking out of his back. He then studied his attacker's arm with the splint, and something deep within his brain started to stir: *broken arm … Dugdale … 'Cuffs are the master.'*

His attacker could see the recognition in the detective's eyes. 'Aye, remember me now, don't you, pig?' he said before he spat in Crosbie's face.

Crosbie had broken his attacker's arm while showing off to Dugdale on their first day on the Harry Hanlon case. He had expected him to scurry off wounded, telling the people of the Ruck that there was a new detective in town and he wasn't to be messed with.

The DCI would now pay the ultimate price for his exhibitionism.

'I was about to start a job. But I couldn't when you broke my fucking arm. See, when you've nothing to lose, you can do whatever the fuck you want.'

Crosbie had bullied and injured his attacker to make an example and feed his own ego, with no regards for his victim's life, hopes and ambitions. He should have been better than that. He should have also remembered that the people of the

Ruck did not respond well to authority figures abusing their position of power. Poke them and they will bite back. Break an arm and you risked being mortally wounded. He began to laugh, but it didn't last long as blood from his punctured lung erupted from his mouth like a crimson fountain.

'What's so fucking funny, pig?'

'Your name,' Crosbie said, clearing his throat as best he could from the blood spewing up like a well from below.

His attacker moved his face closer to Crosbie, until they were just inches apart. 'What about it?' He snarled.

'I don't even know it,' Crosbie spluttered.

Suddenly, there was a scuffle, with the man in the white trainers now on his front, his hands cuffed behind his back, lying next to Crosbie. The DCI could hear Dugdale shout into his radio 'Code 21, code 21,' meaning that paramedics were required urgently. But Crosbie was far too sleepy to be bothered by all the commotion. He closed his eyes and started to drift off, with Dugdale's frantic voice becoming more and more distant until it was barely audible.

He liked the silence. It allowed him time to think. He now knew it had always been inevitable his past would eventually catch up with him. He had done some terrible, terrible things. He had killed with his bare hands, beaten suspects for fun and coveted his neighbour's wife.

Now he was paying for all his sins. Murdered by a man whose name he would never know. It was almost a relief. There would be no more lying. No more tormented, tortured soul. No more DCI David Crosbie. No more Bing. He smiled as he remembered a phrase from his childhood: 'Don't fuck with folk from the Ruck.'

Crosbie had always been desperate to leave the place where he was born, but felt it fitting he should come home to die.

'Hang on in there, sir,' he could hear Dugdale saying as he pressed down to try to stem the bleeding, but it was too late.

'*Il tuo riporto non nasconde la calvizie, e' solo ridicolo da vedere. Abbraccia la calvizie!*' Crosbie said, the Italian words rattling in quick succession from his bleeding mouth.

'What, sir? What did you say?' Dugdale asked, as he

scrambled to retrieve his smartphone and press the record function, while still kneeling heavily on the back of his mentor's attacker.

'*Abbraccia la calvizie! Abbraccia la calvizie!*' Crosbie repeated in barely more than a whisper, using up the last of his breath in the process.

Perhaps in another life, Crosbie would have lived in Verona, the Italian city he so loved – probably because it was as far removed from Ruckhouse as it was possible to be.

It was a soothing last thought. David Crosbie took his last breath. Finally, he was at peace.

Epilogue

The turnout at Ruckhouse crematorium was huge. There was a large media presence as well, because unlike many other Western countries, a police officer dying in the line of duty was still a relatively rare occurrence in Scotland. There had been around twenty-five deaths in the new millennium, and most of those had been road traffic accidents or heart attacks. The last serving officer to have been murdered in Scotland was back in 1994.

Dugdale deeply disliked funerals, not for the grief and sorrow, but because he found them such impersonal affairs. Paying your final respects seemed to be the last thing on many of the mourners' minds, viewing it more like a day off work and intent on a massive piss-up. He remembered attending his gran's as a teenager, a woman he had loved, and not one of his relatives even mentioned her name as they enjoyed their free buffet and bar in a local hotel afterwards. Dugdale had eventually stormed out in disgust.

Then there were the mind-numbing clichés that were always spouted. How such and such's death had 'put every-thing in perspective'. He often wondered why it took some-one's death to realise your own mortality.

But today he heard another over-used funeral phrase that actually did sum up Crosbie. A fellow officer said, 'They

331

certainly broke the mould when he was born.' This was true. Dugdale had never met anyone like David Crosbie in his life. He had been an incredibly flawed human being. But he had also solved the Hanlon murder, dying in the process. He doubted if there was another detective in the entire country who could have cracked the case. Dugdale concluded that Crosbie had been a genius, albeit one who'd eventually been driven mad by his brilliance.

The young detective listened closely to the instructions from the undertaker on how the coffin should be lifted and carried. He didn't know the other bearers, but they were all serving officers, wearing full uniform like Dugdale. He didn't even know whether Crosbie had any close family – presumably not if they needed six policemen to carry his coffin. Or was this a ceremonial thing? He honestly wasn't sure.

Their slow and awkward march into the crematorium did not last long, and Dugdale could hear the camera shutters clicking like machine-gun fire. Once inside, he scanned the front pews and spotted an elegant blonde woman, in a black hat and veil, dabbing her eyes as she quietly sobbed. Dugdale guessed she had been Crosbie's neighbour, whom he had so often boasted about sleeping with. Beside her was a stony-faced man who looked far from happy to be there, and he stared daggers in the direction of Crosbie's coffin. Even in death, the DCI still had his haters. On the opposite pew sat Chief Constable Eric McNeil and his deputy Mike Bruce, eyes forward, making sure they did not fix on anything or anyone in particular, being as aloof as bosses always seemed to be.

The undertaker gave a brief instruction and the bearers simultaneously laid Crosbie down. They took a step back in unison, and Dugdale decided to take a space beside a woman sitting with a young red-haired boy. She thanked him for carrying 'my brother's coffin' and introduced herself as Linda and her son as Damien. So Crosbie did have family, after all.

Dugdale wasn't the crying type, but he had decided to pay proper tribute to the man he had only briefly known, but would never forget. As the humanist took to the pulpit to conduct the service, Dugdale removed his police hat to reveal a newly shaven head, his quiff and elaborate comb-over gone.

He had recorded Crosbie's last words on his smartphone and eventually played it to a friend of a language professor who was able to translate their meaning:

Il tuo riporto non nasconde la calvizie, e' solo ridicolo da vedere actually meant, 'Your comb-over doesn't hide your bald patch, it just looks ridiculous.'

Crosbie had finished by adding, *Abbraccia la calvizie* – 'Embrace your baldness.'

Dugdale watched as Crosbie's coffin lowered out of sight before the curtain came down, concluding the ceremony. He felt liberated ... liberated from the madness of working beside his mentor, and now from trying to pretend he had a full head of hair.

He not only had embraced his baldness, but was now ready to embrace his career as a fully-fledged detective.

Acknowledgments

My heartfelt thanks to Dave Reynolds and Tom Churchill for their help compiling the crossword riddles, which have always baffled me as much as April. To Pauline McCallum, for the Italian translations, and the serving detective and childhood friend for the detailed explanation on how 'cuffs are the master! They certainly are. Then there's the expert edit once again by Craig Hillsey, which no doubt completes his hat-trick of misery. Special thanks also goes to Victoria Goldman and Graeme Donohoe for their eagle-eyed proofreading, Susan Gay, chief of the apostrophe police, and to my former colleague and long-time friend Yvonne Bolouri, who not only came up with a name for April Lavender, but also many of her actions too, simply by being herself. My mum's late pal Celia was also an invaluable help with the complicated workings between the pharmacists and the government's methadone programme, and will be sorely missed by all. Diana Gabaldon, who in-between writing and producing a global TV show based on her multi-million selling *Outlander* books, actually took the time out to read my little nutty novels. Her kind words even landed me a US publishing deal, although, sadly, I'm yet to replicate her success. Since I'm namedropping, there has also been long-standing support from Lorraine Kelly, who believes April would be an excellent replacement for Taggart in the TV schedules, and ironically from Alex Norton too, who used to help fill those timeslots with Taggart as DCI Matt Burke before his role as Eric in the excellent BBC comedy *Two Doors Down*. Incidentally Alex also wrote one of the most entertaining showbiz autobiographies I've ever read, *There's Been A Life*, so go and get it right now. Then there's Ian and Janette Tough, aka The Krankies, who are two of the nicest – yet most outrageous – human beings I've ever met. I was a childhood fan who one day would be lucky enough to count them both as friends. I then took great delight in seeing my own children howl with laughter at The Krankies, the way I used to as a kid. They are the reason I can call myself an author, having ghostwritten their 2004 autobiography *Fan-Dabi-Dozi*. In turn, I hope I prolonged their careers just that little bit longer, or as Janette once remarked, 'I'd have retired years ago … if it wasn't for you,' which I'm sure was meant as a compliment. Way back at the start of this novel, I dedicated it to my uncle Ian and my aunt Sam, who had been a district nurse for over 40 years and relentlessly encouraged my writing career. She would also give, whenever asked, sound advice to my community nurse wife Amanda, while Sam and Ian would babysit our kids when they were young, which allowed us to keep working. They were a pair of gems and we miss them both terribly.

But it was actually broadcaster and columnist Tam Cowan who started my book-writing career, albeit accidentally. It was on his hugely popular BBC Scotland show *Off The Ball*, which he presents with Stuart Cosgrove, where I heard The Krankies tell a hilarious anecdote about working with the ventriloquist Roger De Courcey, who after facing a particularly hard crowd, had been spotted by Ian and Janette backstage kicking lumps out of his puppet Nookie Bear, while muttering something along the lines of, 'You'd think one of us would have got a fucking laugh…' It got me thinking, *I wonder if they have enough stories to fill a book?* Fortunately they did. Tam also had me on as a guest when my second novel *DM for Murder* found itself on the shortlist for the Bloody Scotland Book of the Year, and hosted the launch event for my third *Wicked Leaks*, where he confessed the last time he'd been inside a book shop was to buy Madonna's nude book! And when I was desperately struggling for a title for this novel, he invited his readers at *The Scottish Sun* to get their thinking caps on, so I have Peter Lowles from Gourock to thank for the excellent title *Rollover and Die*. And lastly, while searching for some way to round off the plot, I heard the renowned lawyer Austin Lafferty on *Off The Ball* as a guest, discussing the intricacies of Scots inheritance law. It was the final piece of the jigsaw I needed for the murderous motivation. So thank you to Tam and the team.

Finally, there's also a small band of hardworking authors out there, including Douglas Skelton, Ed James and Mason Cross, to name but a few, who continue to cajole the likes of myself and others to write the very best they can. Encouragement like that really does go a long way, so if you've enjoyed a book by an author recently then why not post a review online or message them and say so. And if you haven't enjoyed it, just keep your opinions to yourself, because you don't know how bloody hard it is to write a book until you've tried!

Peace and love to you all.

Printed in Great Britain
by Amazon

57987642R00206